MOLLY FALLS TO EARTH

Maria Mutch

Published by Simon & Schuster

New York   London   Toronto   Sydney   New Delhi

SIMON &
SCHUSTER
CANADA

Simon & Schuster Canada
A Division of Simon & Schuster, Inc.
166 King Street East, Suite 300
Toronto, Ontario M5A 1J3

"You that come to birth and bring the mysteries" [4 1.] from
RUMI: THE BOOK OF LOVE: POEMS OF ECSTASY AND LONGING,
TRANSLATIONS & COMMENTARY by COLEMAN BARKS ET AL.
Copyright © 2003 by Coleman Barks. Reprinted by
permission of HarperCollins Publishers.

This Simon & Schuster Canada edition April 2020

SIMON & SCHUSTER CANADA and colophon are trademarks of Simon & Schuster, Inc.

For information about special discounts for bulk purchases, please contact Simon &
Schuster Special Sales at 1-800-268-3216 or CustomerService@simonandschuster.ca.

All photographs by Maria Mutch.

Manufactured in the United States of America

1 3 5 7 9 10 8 6 4 2

Library and Archives Canada Cataloguing in Publication
Title: Molly falls to earth / Maria Mutch.
Names: Mutch, Maria, author.
Description: Simon & Schuster Canada edition.
Identifiers: Canadiana (print) 20190176466 | Canadiana
(ebook) 20190176474 | ISBN 9781501182815
(softcover) | ISBN 9781501182822 (ebook)
Classification: LCC PS8626.U885 M65 2020 | DDC C813/.6—dc23

ISBN 978-1-5011-8281-5
ISBN 978-1-5011-8282-2 (ebook)

to Frozen Sparrow

a.k.a. Hope

Lila

(Sanskrit: "play," "sport," "spontaneity," or "drama")
a term that has several different meanings,
most focusing in one way or another
on the effortless or playful relation
between the Absolute and the contingent world.

—Encyclopædia Britannica

1

AURA

Nine Beginnings

Begin with the found.

You have been lost, haven't you? Searching for someone, or they were searching for you. One thing is certain: people expect you to know.

Whatever happens, you have to remember the way things move, even the way skyscrapers sway in the wind.

"Hey!"

The place is run on the movement of money and cockroaches. The people bundled in their coats, hustling on the avenues. The puddle that shimmers in the breeze.

"Hey!"

Gestures, litter, snowflakes that are forming and falling but aren't here yet. Pipes and cables and roots. Everything is on a search for something, going somewhere. The dogs, pigeons, rats, and squirrels.

And now the people running.

•   •   •

"Did you see that—"
　"Holy shit—"
　"What just—"

A charged current runs the grid of streets and living things, straight into the neural network of people's brains. Even the most disenfranchised have their plots, a territory staked out, what they consider to be their business. At least a few of them would say they belong to this place, and some would say, without irony, that they own it. Others guard the sanctity of their path with an armour of black clothing and set expressions.

"She's down—"
　"I don't get—"
　"What the fuck just happened?"

And whoever is missing, too. Don't forget the absences. A space is a thing that moves.

"Crazy, man."
　"I didn't see whatever—"
　"Hey!"

The thoughts you think and the ones you haven't gotten to yet.
　Stop, start, dart, jump, and fall.

• • •

Hey. But the park right now is more still than usual. The year is new, though it's late in January. No one remembers.

The chess players are gone, the Scrabble players, too. No guitars or opera or tai chi. No open cases or backpacks to collect the coins and bills. No one sits on the benches or on the grass, which are snow-covered. Another storm is coming.

The marble arch stands ornately, hardened in the cold and bright as a tooth. At the beginning of Fifth Avenue, it holds the shape of a magnet. The parks' trees—sycamores, ginkgos, redwoods, cornelian cherry, a famous English elm—reach to the sky with leafless branches and can't hold it back. The cloud cover is the kind that makes people squint.

The park pulls the humans and animals and plants toward the watering eye of its centre. (But the fountain is dry, with a layer of snow over top, filled with foot and pawprints.)

At the edge of the park, however, people and dogs resist the pull, drawn instead by the idea of where they have to be.

"God—"
"Phone's dead! Yours?"
"Where's a cop when you need one?"
"Mother of—"

||

In the apartment in the West Village, the choreographer Molly Volkova stands beside an armchair. She is tall and angular and holds a glass that contains only ice because she has been dipping her fingers in it and playing with the cubes. She makes mental notes about the winter light coming in through the living room windows, about viscosity, and how her fingertips blaze. She plans to put the ideas of light and ice to use later when she returns to the studio to work on a commission that will open in two short months. Her husband, the artist Rafael Massimo, lies on the sofa, fast asleep on his side with the cat, fat as a bun, perched on his shoulder. In his grey curls there is a stroke of gesso, and another on his cheek, because he had been sneaking a cigar. He is drooling on the silk pillow, which will bear the mark from this point onward, tucked under his head. He has been painting since 8:30 a.m. and it is now 1:00 p.m.

Their children, Stella and Augustin, born on the same day nine years and two months ago, lie on their stomachs on the floor with markers and pens, working on a get-well poster for their fourth-grade teacher. The teacher, Ms. Gomez, was hit by a car while carrying a bouquet of flowers across the street, the flowers having been intended for her friend who was in the hospital after a tumble down a flight of stairs. Ms. Gomez and her friend ended up on the same floor. Stella and Augustin don't know why their teacher carried a bouquet so large that it obstructed her view. The flowers had been bundled with both elastics and twine, and topped with a taped-up paper cone, well enough for carrying but not, apparently, for absorbing the impact of a car that had been racing the light. Roses, Peruvian lilies, and asters sprayed impressively into the air on impact, creating an array of colourful arrows around the horizontal body of Ms. Gomez and the stopped cars and some onlookers. The design of the accident was seen from the third-floor apartment window of a woman in her nineties. The old woman declared to God, in whom she did not exactly believe, that she would give her own life if the woman on the pavement lived. Ms. Gomez was taken away in an ambulance with only a broken ankle and a few tweaked ribs, and the old woman in the third-floor apartment died in her sleep that very night.

Stella and Augustin don't know about any of this, but they do know about the appearance of synchronicity and randomness because they experience both, but especially the first, on a regular basis. They were simultaneous water creatures, after all, and were born only one squelchy moment apart. They don't merely finish each other's sentences, they finish each other's thoughts, even though they are not supposed to be any more alike than other siblings. They love to hone this ability—which began as a kind of toddler lark but turned uncanny through sheer practice—mostly because its effect on adults is fascinating. They have noted in their journals marvelous gaping and spooked expressions and actual incidents where an adult has backed up, or even left the room. They haven't noticed this same response in other children, who usually just carry on as before. It is the adults alone who seem unequipped to grasp certain alignments and come apart such that they have to go hide themselves. The twins discuss in their heads what to make of this, and try to come up with the possible scenarios that might occur between their *now* and the adults' *then*. The cataclysms, shifts in consciousness, the black holes.

They lift their heads at the same moment to look at their mother, because she seems to be in thought or entirely absent, which happens sometimes. They are especially attuned to her movements. Though they are the children of two people who make things out of their thoughts, they are the most interested in Molly, because she makes people do the impossible. Her work also tends to involve more people than their father's, requiring dancers, often stage set and lighting designers, usually musicians, and at least one person with a clipboard, who seems tense and will possibly shout or hiss, to manage it all. Sometimes her work has meant journalists in this very living room and bouquets of flowers much bigger than their teacher could carry. And because she can be controversial, it has even, on rare occasions, meant death threats. This last thing they know about because they have the stealth of snakes and cats, and because they have listened with a glass pressed to the wall, siphoning words. Their mother is a person of secrets, it seems to them, and strange gestures, like right now. She will stop in midsentence on occasion and seem to go away, even if her body is right there in front of them. She makes no mention of this, however, and so it is another aspect of the adult world that is a puzzle.

The twins know something, too, about this day, that their mother is changing before their eyes, and that therefore they are changing, too. Rafael will likewise be different, but they will always have their mother's voice in their heads, telling them not to be seduced by the surface of things. Whatever energy had occupied her brain a few moments ago has moved along, and she has come to stand beside them where they are working. The day is January 23, but she is wearing open, flat sandals with cork soles and gold straps wrapping up her ankles like an Athenian, like a goddess. They can see the state of her toes, which are clusters of bunions and malformations, with bright peach polish on the remaining toe nails. She is a column of muscles and jutting bones, and she has wrinkles around her eyes when she grins. Stella loves the wrinkles so much that years from now she will remember them and the look on the face that smiled down at her and Augustin. She doesn't understand the words, however, that her mother is saying to them, because they sound like *My name is Lila.* Which isn't right at all; though the face looking down on her, the place where the words originate, is not the least disturbed and, in fact, seems to be enjoying a riddle.

Their father has opened his eyes and glanced over as if he, too, finds it quizzical and wonders if perhaps everything he is watching is part of the dream he was having. Life with Molly is often like this, involving a conflation of other realities and the elision of this one. He watches her as she stands, smiling, declaring who she is, a name he doesn't know, this Lila. But it makes no difference in the end because she is always a shifting, mercurial being, and so he simply makes a note to remember this vision and continues on with his nap.

––––––––––––

Seven minutes, that's all that this seizure will take. All we have. In seven minutes you can boil an egg, read a poem, produce an orgasm, or listen to Glenn Gould playing Bach's Fantasia and Fugue in C Minor. We're always counting, but clocks don't allow for the incongruities. The warp. You can hold decades in your body, if you wish, or only the present moment. Set your watch, let it count down. Prove to me that your seven minutes are different from mine.

It is only a shift in person, or tense, or maybe both. Don't be rattled.

It is only play. None of this is as serious as we think.

III

No. Begin with Stella yelling, "Mama, wear your hat!"

I wore a scarf and jacket because she complained yesterday that I don't dress warmly enough. I couldn't be bothered to change the sandals for boots. I was hurrying. No hat and my body, then, through the apartment and out the door. The elevator with its tenuous grip, its nervous cables. You can find death in any moment, or a piece of it: something breaks or bursts or flattens. Natural locomotion meets disaster. But then disaster doesn't happen, and we forget.

Through the lobby and down stone steps to the street where the day was more than half over, and the air cold and salt-flecked. Dieseled and full of honking. I held ideas and messages in my head. Too many, apparently. I've wondered how the idea of a storm begins, what mind contains it. No doctor has ever agreed with my theory, however, that the beginnings of my seizures move along in winds and currents, the thought process of a wave. The idea takes time to reach me, but then it does. It finds me.

Sometimes the possession is more subtle, a prolonged déjà vu, more real than reality, or sometimes it leaks out as a smacking of lips or a checking of pockets, as if I'm only going through the motions and I'm not really there. And then there is this: the sidewalk. I can say that I'm more fully here, more real than ever, but how would you know? I give you my heart, which races. I'll sweat. I'll urinate, or my bowels will let go, the things people fear most. Sometimes the world that opens up is an ecstatic one, another thing to fear.

IV

Begin with a boy who can't see his mother. He has lost her, but ahead of him a group of people seem to be looking at something on the sidewalk.

He lives several blocks from here. His shoes have pressed along this particular path almost every day of his life when his mother has walked with him, or trailed along behind him, first to his preschool, then to his elementary. There is a spot where a piece of concrete isn't flush with the one beside it—he has learned to bring his foot up and over it—and the bricks around the base of a nearby tree lift at various angles where the roots have pushed up from below. To him, that is the evidence of an underworld swelling in places, one separate from and more mysterious than the subway system, and at odds with the grid of streets laid over top. He stops to look at this slow-motion battle of the tree and the bricks and wait for his mother to catch up, but then he is captivated by the people who stand, bend, or kneel. Their heads appear to stick out abnormally from their mufflered necks and thick hoods, their bodies a collection of blacks and greys, with a single neon pink toque. They pose like the soldiers in bronze statues or the people in Renaissance paintings that his aunt has taken him to see.

Something will happen, he thinks, and whether it's good or bad, he can't tell. But as he approaches he can see that someone is right there on the sidewalk, partly obscured by the people. The bits that he can see, part of a torso and legs, jolt and stop repeatedly. He's reminded of the pigeon he once watched in the park, one with a broken wing that tried to take off but remained stuck there against the ground. The idea of flying wasn't enough to leave the ground. He worried about the fate of the bird, as he worries now for the person on the ground, and wonders what the crowd is doing. A helpless tension binds the group, and their postures say they are transfixed by something terrible. He wonders if also beautiful.

Eight, now nine, people stand around me, or kneel.

Three men in sweats. University students. The Musketeers.

Two old women who were, only moments before, sipping green tea down the block. I will call them the Crones, which I mean respectfully. They have noble, wrinkled expressions.

A teenage girl with a blue-tinged face and a heart condition who is unsure of whether to go or stay. She feels a turmoil that constricts her breathing even more than the cold air. Maybe the storm suffocates her, too, even though it has been and gone. She takes in a breath, roots herself to the sidewalk, with her hands jammed into her pockets. A spectacle is a spectacle no matter who you are. *Better you than me*, Blue Girl thinks, putting her hand to her mouth.

A dancer approaches who thinks she recognizes me. Who auditioned years before for the company I led at the time, and who wasn't accepted on account of the wrong lines, the wrong presence. I wanted to see someone animal, full of blood and secrets and shadows. Someone with teeth. "What would you sacrifice?" I'd said. But she didn't know, and now her sneakered feet are a mere eighteen inches away from my hip bone. Her name will be Revenge.

To the left is a middle-aged man, the Lover, on his way to the affair he's having, which shows the power of what I've done, shaking and lying on the concrete, that he would stop to gape. Revulsion swims off him in slick waves. He wears a navy suit with a grey topcoat, and I feel some satisfaction that his white shirt is marred by a tiny brown splash of sauce. Even better: in a mere two years an inch of steak will clog his throat like a marvelous shit in a toilet pipe.

Their words and thoughts jostle with their movements as they trade positions, bend or stand, approach to see me better, turn away in panic, return. The edges of their jackets and coats get caught in the wind when it surges, a man on the periphery clutches his hat.

"My god."

"What's happening?"

"She's having a fit. Some lady's having a fit."

V

The boy is lost and hasn't seen his mother in several minutes. I understand something of this space, having lost my own mother, and my father, when I was twelve—though I lost them permanently. He doesn't seem to mind his status. His body is still, but his energy hovers, hummingbird-like. His socks, which show below his too-short pants, are melon coloured. I want to talk to him, convey something of what I'm seeing. He understands shadows and animals and secrets, he is full of them. His fingers are as fine as those of a much younger child. His eyes have minky lashes that make his lids appear to be in slow motion when he blinks. He understands time. He makes me think of Augustin, but Augustin is robust and always hollering or running. Stella is much the same, though she is attuned to the outside environment in a way that this boy would comprehend. She has, at times, the same fluttery heart, and a lightness, until she is angry. At which point she is volcanic and a tiny bit monstrous, a tiny bit like her mother.

I would like to shut out my children. Make them vanish, just for an instant. But they are everywhere in this atmosphere, this part of the city, this sidewalk, where we've walked so many times. They gather with the people around me as if they are ghosts or vibrations. They have never in their nine years seen me exactly this way. They've only witnessed the lesser angels and absences that flicker through. I'm an expert at covering up the moment when consciousness returns or alters, and can smooth over almost any conversation that has been temporarily lost. But they are glossy-eyed and watchful, always picking up the slightest ripples in the energy around me. They understand things, I think, that I haven't understood myself.

But I've seen the boy before. People are more connected in the city than you might imagine. I know his face. His name tastes like graham crackers, and something silver, and I feel grit, too, though I think that it was shoved in my mouth when I fell. The falling involves twists and slams that I often don't recall, scraping the mouth as if to eat the ground and take in a surprising amount of dirt and sand grains. No one will have seen it happen. What they see is the toppling, shaking body and a mouth holding grit of a mysterious origin. How did it get there? they say, to the person already on the ground. *I feel in some strange place.*

Come back. Someone followed me, and was familiar and not. At first just an energy in the city that gradually emerged, developed a colour, and rose up, as if out of a sea. The shape followed me along streets, through crowds, through little parks, under awnings and the bare branches of lindens and silver maples. Maybe it floated over the heads of the people striding or moved through them, even beneath them. Over the blocks, I kept the same pace, and never looked back.

I think of the uncanniness in certain relationships, the ones to do with sex, what some might call love, how connection is sometimes there even when the love is no longer practiced and absence has come to stay instead. Prescience doesn't leave, the ability to know the unknowable, the sense of the other person in the hordes and traffic, or the perpetually lighted ether. I knew he was there without looking back.

VI

This was the late nineties, before cell phones were everywhere. The towers still stood, blinking sleepily at the sky. I called him from an oily pay phone whose plexiglass was printed with the fingers of countless others. Desperadoes who had stood in this same spot, watching the falafel truck unfold itself.

I said, "Don't make me beg," into the receiver, and then I said it for real when the line was connected and he was at the other end. It was a form of begging I had never envisioned. I would have said I simply wasn't capable of forming the words, I didn't possess the DNA, the molecules, the chemistry, until suddenly I did. I almost started to laugh, so startled was I by the sound of it. No, I did start to laugh, which made him hang up.

I sank another quarter into the phone's slit of an eye and spoke into its mouth. "It seems to me that we've left kindness at the curb."

"It's a packed curb, then, because we've put some other shit there as well."

"Start again."

He sighed.

I sighed. "Unwind the film to before the dysfunction."

"Doesn't work."

"No, you're right. It doesn't." Neither of us said anything for several moments, so the city filled in with its huffs and sirens and honks. The distant murmur of a jackhammer. Something clanged. Two neurons, ones that have been tickled or exploded or inverted by him. My body was suddenly tired. Perhaps it was changing its mind.

"I want to hear you say it," he said.

"This is a negotiation."

"This is a fucking negotiation, Molly."

"You want to hear it," I said.

"I want you to work for this."

I watched an Italian widow dressed in black amble along the sidewalk with a plastic bag of library books. Her thick ankles protruded over the top edge of her shoes, which were heavy-heeled and also black, and I loved her deeply. Everything about her. I could have put the phone down and walked up to her and wrapped my arms around her. The whole prospect was wildly tempting.

He whistled a show tune while he waited. Something from *Phantom of the Opera*. I started to laugh. And then I started to cry.

"Close enough," he said.

———————

He had come to track me down on my way to my doctor. A pursuit set to the tune of Thelonious Monk. He followed me along streets and streets, and I lost him in elevators and brilliant corners.

The previous night he had held me close while we lay in bed, and I begged my brain to quiet its campaign, to let me sleep under a roof that didn't shake and rattle. *Be still*, I thought. And he understood that I was in some nameless distress, and he held me with his whole body, with a completeness that made me ache, while he stroked my hair.

I heard him rise and go to his desk. I heard him in the kitchen and ice tumble in the glass, because it was summer again and hot and I knew he longed for cold and something to numb his mind. He sweated for both of us, drank for both of us.

In the morning, I found him on the floor beside me, because it was cooler there, he said.

"Is there something wrong with you? Is there something you want to talk about? You can tell me," he said. "Absolutely anything. Please trust me. Always trust me."

"We're like fireflies," I said. "We pulse off and on."

"You can still trust me."

"I'm still fine."

"Are you?"

"I'm a simple woman," I said.

VII

Sabine made trips into the city less and less, and only to see her brother. Mostly Seth had come to her. The last time he visited, he was heading north and decided to snowshoe her mountain on his way. She had watched him load his car with the gear that he kept at her house and felt a prescient sense of loss that was strangely enervating, almost sleep-inducing. She knew somehow that he would fall or lose his way.

"People are always getting lost on those trails," she said to him, standing there on the cold front step in her bedroom slippers and robe. "Or swallowed up the mountain, and you know what? Some of them don't come down." The mountain did things to skiers and hikers. It broke legs and threw bodies, or hid them in caves. She supposed it wasn't the mountain's fault but its nature, much as the city had a similar tendency to devour. He had various devices for being found, but she thought the beacons would fail, the signals through the air would be too thin, the batteries could leak their charges, or people wouldn't listen.

"I'm not listening," he said, and smiled. He kissed her cheek and hugged her. It was one of the last times, and the one that stayed with her. His face had had a diffuse, underlying hunger that suggested he might be using again. She replayed this in her mind, again and again, the warmth of him, how solid and real he had been, and how thin and ghostlike he was now.

She herself had been drinking too much lately, and so she supposed it was cyclical. One became absorbed in the problems, and then, later, one didn't. But he had returned, exactly on time, and grinning and exhilarated, and that worried her, too.

"I'm alive!" he'd said, arms up. Excessive, maybe, for this place, and a sign somehow. He would, in fact, disappear soon afterward, November 25, 2009, and absurdly. Even though she had predicted it, she couldn't deny the question, once it had happened, of how someone could go missing. All the eyes and cameras and signals and trackers and beeps and lights. The planet was overwhelmed with witnesses. People were always scanning the heavens for word from other life-forms—what about their own? He had become something distinctly mysterious and other. Seven weeks ago, and no word since. No information, no trails to follow, no messages or signs. Only a curious and impossible space in the pattern of her life where he was supposed to stand or send up a flare. The void became sickeningly wider, like a gap in ozone. As the options for his disappearance grew, so did the void. His last known sighting had been in the city, when his landlord came to fix a broken window in his apartment, but he was always taking trips, could never be still for long. His phone had been left behind, but his car was missing, and possibly some of his gear, though she couldn't be sure what exactly was gone.

She left behind Ellena, again, and the dogs, including the lame one they had just adopted, and the house they lived in. She could have done the drive from her house to Seth's apartment in one straight shot, without having to stay the night in a hotel, but the stop was what a stop was meant to be: a barrier between her and the city. No one, apart from the desk clerk, could say who she was, and no one could say what she did and why she was there. The lobby had small trees in large containers, vines and palms that pointed to a place far from here. Possibly all the leaves were plastic, and some of the sun-bleached ones were turning blue.

She couldn't have recalled this place, and yet the precise alignment of the sleek lounge chairs seemed familiar. She had seen it only two weeks before. Three clerks stood behind the desk, two of them helping other people. On a table, there was a towering arrangement of flowers that Ellena would have called a "derangement." She listened to the clicking of luggage hooves on the dark tiles as people regarded each other and saw their own displacement. The hotel tried to protect the traveller from too much otherness by being recognizable at the same time as anticipating a want. She didn't care, however, if the hotel had the usual spike of indifference through its corporate heart. She only wanted to throw her long black and tattered coat onto a chair and heave herself onto a bed where she would be comatose until morning. She didn't mind if the bed had not been properly made up since the last people, or hair still lurked on the pillows or the bathroom floor and spittle remained on the water glasses. She did not need the erasure of others, any more than she needed a hotel genie to unbottle.

"Thank you, Ms. Stein," said the clerk, pushing the key cards in their small envelope across the counter. "Anything else I can do for you?" The clerk's face was pasty and too pale from all the conciliations, Sabine felt, and yet she suddenly wanted to bang a fist on the black marble and make a demand or a declaration or lodge a complaint.

Instead, she laughed a little wildly. "Can you find my brother?"

The clerk appeared alarmed. "I'm sorry? Is he registered here, ma'am?"

She touched her fingers to her lips before she answered. "Don't worry. I can find my own brother. He'll turn up." *Make him appear*, she thought. *Produce the motherfucker*. She would give anything for his deep laugh, his talk of the treks that took him up mountains or along rivers or through deserts. Even if he couldn't, as she had, wrest himself for good from the city where they were born. Make him appear. Bring him back. If the hotel could do that, she would give it her soul.

VIII

The soul being a slippery entity.

A woman who stops to watch me is pregnant with twins. Her winter coat is slung wide, black clothes underneath. She has a shining ring through her septum (she is, perhaps, the Bull) and one hand on her stomach. She pleats her brow and shuts her mouth tight when she becomes aware that it was open. She takes my voltage personally. I'm here on the ground, a thing she doesn't have room for. She feels that spaces have been smaller lately, tightening, and two children in one uterus is a particular burden. They seem to want to push each other out. Her lover told her about the sand tiger sharks who eat their siblings while still growing inside their mother, and this information haunts her. She regards animals more highly than people, so where does this leave the creatures she's carrying? They have taken her over. When she really considers it, she knows that she is the one they are trying to shove out, with their powerful brains and dividing cells. They become bigger, and she becomes smaller, even if she doesn't appear that way.

She watches my body and feels pity, a separation despite the short distance between us, now just a few feet. Her hand brushes the delicate boy who is also there, the one with a lion in him. She notices that he seems to belong to no one. She is taken up once more with the feet and heads right under her heart. I make the sound that causes her to see me again, and she thinks it is ungodly. She wonders if the two creatures hear this, the folding together of worlds: one collapsing, one being born. But the twins are taken up with her beats, the slosh of her breath and the burritos she had for lunch, their own plans. She doesn't know what to do with this scene, the grey tones, the city park and the arch nearby. She is getting smaller, she feels, so small, and there are feet and elbows and skulls that roll within her with a force she can't explain.

I can explain it, though she won't hear me. The body is a vessel for what happens.

IX

Even though people are missing,
    hearts have been broken,
    and tucked away in buildings,
    and right there in the parks and on the streets,
    sex and death happen . . .

Seven minutes, that's all that this seizure will take. All we have. In seven minutes you can boil an egg, read a poem, produce an orgasm, or listen to Glenn Gould playing Bach's Fantasia and Fugue in C Minor. We're always counting, but the clocks don't allow for the incongruities. The warp. You can hold decades in your body, if you wish, or only the present moment. Set your watch, let it count down. Prove to me that your seven minutes are different from mine.

Playful, remember? None of this is serious.

Yes.
    No.

2

Sabine

"No, what I want is a smoke," she said aloud, but she couldn't have one unless she found the hotel's rooftop patio as she did the last time, where dirty water pooled reassuringly. She had looked out at the sprawl of wide streets and strip malls, trees that appeared to be exactly fifteen years old. The light poles straining against the open blue sky had felt malevolent to her. The elegantly dipping electrical wires, too, and the flat, garish colours of the signs. She thought she felt a finely wafting, invisible exhaust, and imagined every crevice jammed with a grit that had travelled from the distant city or even the other side of the world.

But that was during a freak wave of heat that had come through the area, melting the snow and ice for just a few days before retreating. The air was cold again. January. The month of the dead and the new. She dared to believe he was dead, though she felt ashamed to think it. And nothing was new.

She decided on the lounge instead, which was dim and had a fish tank with dark, silvery inhabitants. She took a seat at the bar, and turned to see that many of the tables were occupied. In her experience, hotel bars, the truly liminal ones, were strangely cool and deserted places, but this one contained bridal parties, people from a conference, or a guided tour. Silver-haired men and women regarded a map—the paper kind—in one corner, and someone from another group intermittently shrieked with laughter.

The bartender gave her a glass of wine, and it was a heart in her fist.

"One of my favourites," he said. He had an enormous beard and mustache so thick his lips were undetectable. His eyes crinkled up so she could tell that he was smiling. He said something absurd about the wine; amenable notes of black raspberry and bacon fat. Tiny metal spikes shot from the arc of his ear. Deep in the thicket around his mouth, the glint of a piercing or maybe a capped tooth. He waited patiently as she sipped.

She nodded. "The lust of a woman. That's all I get. But it's good." She could see the gold tooth in full.

"Here on business?" he said, and she wondered if this was a bit sarcastic. Whatever it meant to be someone on business, she did not resemble it.

"I'm looking for someone," she said, and felt immediate regret. She had a notion to never confess her plans to strangers, which was not so much for personal safety but for something existential that rattled about in her chest and needed shielding. But the words were out, so she shrugged.

"I'm looking for an old friend of mine. Not here. In New York. Just stopping for the night." All of which was true. She wasn't only looking for Seth, whom she didn't, deep in her heart, expect to find. She was also making this particular trip in order to find Molly, who at one time had known them both. Loved them both, hadn't she? If she could not find the first, she could find the second. Molly was alive and well, and finding her should have been easy, considering. Yet the old numbers and contacts hadn't worked. She had sent an email to the last address she had but had gotten no response.

"Anyone I might know?" There was the gold tooth again.

"That depends. Know any dancers?"

"Depends on the kind of dancing."

She raised her glass to him. Then drained it. She left her money on the bar and stopped momentarily to watch the tank. The large television behind the bar was reflected in its glass. Headlines rolled by underneath the fish, calamities of displacement, versions of being missing. Lost things. Wars and countries and children.

A Neuron Containing Sabine

I can't approach it. It's like looking at the sun. I don't mind the hyperbolic. What has to be remembered is that I had never met another Orphan, capital O. I had been in that circle, that empty pool, alone.

We lay on our sides in bed, facing the same direction. The mind had had an idea, and the body had gone along with it. I moved her long hair out of the way and drew a map over her back, her shoulder blades, and tried to locate myself.

"You are here," Sabine said, and breathed deeply.

"Am I?" I said. Perhaps I was already backing out. Whatever the computations and calculations, an error had been made. It was, perhaps, too early for judgment, for the fun and games of coming apart. I held the metaphorical seam ripper and began my work, but a shiver in the postcoital haze made me pause. The spine, in the end, seems so vulnerable, a thread that believes itself protected and ends in that tumult called the brain. She murmured in her half sleep, and I rested my hand on her hip. I stroked, slowly, her lower back, her ass.

"You must wake up," I whispered.

"Why? Let me sleep." She reached behind her, took my hand, and moved my arm so that I clasped her stomach. When she was breathing deeply again, I extracted my arm and lay on my back. The ceiling of her bedroom was translucent and then transparent, I felt, and I could see upward into the apartment above and the ones above that, all the way to the top of the building. And if I looked over the edge of the bed, I could peer down into the lower apartments in exactly the same way, people on top of people on top of people, in their beds and chairs and making their toast and pouring their coffee, arguing over the television station or the sour milk of the blinkering refrigerator. The season wasn't summer but the dead of winter, and when we put our clothes on, we would be dressed for arctic conditions.

"Wake up," I said.

"Wake up, Molly," she murmured, and I sighed, and it is possible that I went to sleep.

Sabine

She rode the elevator back up to her room on the fifth floor. She had the sense of being followed, but when she turned the hallway was empty. Nothing except the one tray on the floor outside a room. It held a steel carafe and white napkins that hid a mound of things. Jam packets peeled back and partially eaten. The nude crust of a pale toast suggesting teeth and tongue and the habit of leaving something behind. Proof of life. She picked up one of the jam packets and sniffed it, then ate the contents. She considered the crust, and ate the buttery end of it. She could not have explained herself, except to say that the conditions for eating the remnants of a stranger's breakfast had been right. She wondered if her brother, wherever he was, was hungry. If there was something he wanted, if there was an empty space he needed to fill.

She slid her key card into the lock and waited for the light to turn green. She dawdled. She wanted to be followed, to be searched for and found, which she didn't think was sinister. She realized that she was still wearing her coat, that her big boots clomped when she walked. Her hair was dark, long, and loose. A mess, in fact. She supposed that she was the one who might seem sinister, what her mother or her father would have called "a fright" when she was a child. She stood looking at the door's peephole. An alive portal, brass trimmed and lustrous as a fish eye. But there was nothing to see, so she opened the door at last and went in.

• • •

She lay on the bed and turned on the television. She checked her phone and found three voicemails, two from Ellena:

"You there yet, luv? Miss you already. Beezely and Mr. Man miss you, too. Don't you? Yes, you do! I know you do! Ha ha—lots of wagging. Okay, talk to you later."

And "Hey, baby, do you know where the fucking corkscrew is? Why do we only have one of those? Note to self: pick up corkscrew. Let me know, yeah? Not that I'm drinking without you. Ha ha— okay, love you! Talk soon."

The other was from someone who said they didn't have Molly's number or address. She made a note of it in her journal, as if she were an organized person, but she was not. The process, whatever it was, slipped through her fingers. She was not someone of contacts and answers. Her trips to Seth's apartment had so far been aimless, aside from the simple desire to be among his things. Other people with missing relatives were focused and driven. They were on ceaseless hunts; they formed task forces; they sought witnesses. Moreover, they seemed to possess an unflagging belief in the person's aliveness. She had no particular fidelity to a theory, though it seemed to her more likely that, if she could not phrase it another way, he no longer *was*. And yet she felt him, maybe more so than ever, as if a part of him had grown while his material presence had shrunk. She kept a file of the related paperwork, the bureaucracy of being gone, but she could barely stand to look at it. Her brother had been reduced to some am- biguous notes, copies of forms that featured his name, and reminders to herself to pay some of his bills. She wondered what Molly would say, and she wondered, too, if Molly would care. Ten years had passed.

• • •

She called Ellena, who didn't pick up, so she left a message. "At the hotel. Love you, El. Uh, don't bother calling back. Gonna sleep." She texted her: *Corkscrew in bathroom closet. On account of wine in tub. Sorry.*

She flipped through the channels on the television, looking for something that would tell her how to proceed. She had become interested in documentaries about missing people. Ellena had said two days ago, "I mean, I get it. I do. He's your goddamn brother, after all. So, not criticizing, right? I just wonder if it's, you know, good for you. To watch so many of them . . ."

True enough. Only the night before, still at home with the dogs at her feet, she had found one about people who had gone missing on federal lands. All those national parks, it turned out, swallowed the occasional person. Often they were never found, no body to send home and bury. Sometimes a rescue happened, or sometimes the victim found their own way. They emerged from the trees, from the caves, from the fog, now a ragged creature with a feral look in their eye, permanently astonished. She tried to imagine which of these circumstances belonged to Seth, whether he was the never-found, the body brought home, or the astounded.

The documentary she found contained the story of a boy who went missing on a family camping trip. When his parents were occupied, he drifted up a steep embankment not far from them and disappeared into the waiting forest. A frantic search was conducted, eventually involving the police and many of the locals, which turned up nothing. A few days afterward, the boy emerged from the trees, naked and carrying his own clothes. In the documentary, the boy was now a man. He showed his clothing to the camera, unfolding from a neat stack the exact striped T-shirt and pair of shorts he had worn on that day, and a little pair of shoes. He regarded the camera with a placid expression, unable to illuminate the mystery. He remembered nothing, he said, about his time in the woods. Nothing about the essential character of being missing, who or what he saw or what he did. The boy he'd been was also missing for him. The boy with his name had emerged from the forest and approached a speechless member of the search party. He still had the clothing, which he held tenderly, evidence that he had once been that boy. But the tiny clothes that he could hold in his hands seemed to suggest that he should know.

She turned off the television. The problem with it was the lack of static, the way that the stations were continually on, never stopping. She missed the snowy static of childhood, which took over at night after the stations had signed off. The sound was waves or traffic or wind or breathing, and conveyed that it had travelled a long way to deliver its message. Even if the knowledge wouldn't stay, she had once regarded it, and it had regarded her.

She decided on the clock radio, which was small and black with its cord threaded through a small hole in the bedside table. The time on it incorrectly said 2:54 a.m., but she didn't mind. She scanned until she could hear the aliveness of static. She pulled on the clock radio so that its cord stretched out and she laid down on the bed with it, placing it on her chest. Still wearing her coat, she fell asleep this way.

The Documentary

A man has been looking for his missing brother every day over the course of a year, rushing from his small apartment when he gets word about a sighting. His apartment is dim, and he has lined two walls with maps, the fliers he has created over the last months, notes about possible sightings, and photos of his brother. The coffee table is home to a photocopier, cracker boxes, and soda cans; mugs with his brother's face on them; and the results of tarot card readings. He regularly consults his computer, which is set up in a central position near a window with the shade pulled down, and scans for evidence.

He occasionally receives emails from strangers with attached photos that arrive grainy or shadowy, of a figure half-formed or half-glimpsed. The messages sometimes contain footage from a store's video camera, with a similar result: the figure in question walks among other figures, joltingly and blurred. He often can't discern gender or race or age, let alone know if the person is his brother. The only fact is that the figures are human. Though he has begun to question even this—who knows the true material substance of some moving pixels and grains and the colour grey?

On occasion a stranger will write him with a remembered detail, how they saw someone matching his brother's description, they're sure of it, but when he contacts them they often back away from their assertions. Maybe they know something, maybe they don't. He lives in this unstable territory, one that is just becoming or gaining clarity, or is actively trying to disappear. Whichever it is, the territory contains shadows and doubt and the mood of objects whose usefulness has been depleted. Dead things. Then someone calls and he is out the door, and feeling the rush of energy that could be mistaken for progress. He has done this many times before, leapt into his compact car with his phone glowing beside him, telling him the way.

With his hands gripping the steering wheel, he says to the person in the car with him, the one filming, "When I'm driving around, I look at everyone. So I do a lot of driving. And hoping. I can't stop myself."

The world he once barely noticed has become so noticeable that he can't keep up. The effect is not unlike seeing the blurred photos and videos. His brain works to test the remembered image of his brother against the people walking along the sidewalks, the hordes of them. Does he see one who looks particularly lonely, or hunched, or moves his large frame slowly, as if he is lost / not lost? When the man gives out fliers, he tells people, gesturing with his hands, drawing a shape in the air, that his brother is *big, bigger than me*, *a bit hefty—tall*. *You can't miss him*.

You can't miss him.

The Sidewalk

Oh, it's brilliant. Begin there, not with the sun, which is missing, and not this piece of sidewalk with its glinting bits of ice and salt, and not the strange faces peering over her, but with the snow crystal two storeys up. That small bit of electricity, which shines. But people are looking down because of her, and they don't look up.

They have already made assumptions about her, and one is that her mind isn't here, she is insensate and doesn't see them crowding around her, blocking her view. They don't know that she watches, anyway, beyond their heavy coats and hatted heads, the single drifting snowflake that is two storeys up. The building behind it is the colour of the seamless cloud-filled sky, so there are layers of absence. A storm is coming, and it will heap four feet of snow on a city famous for its ability to absorb terrible things. But for now the sky, a glowing grey wash behind the angles of rooftops, has vanished.

Even if the people can't believe their eyes, this is not new to her. She prefers the old term *grand mal*, more than the rhyme-y *tonic-clonic*, as she likes the aptness—the big bad—and its literal grandness. She is, after all, experiencing a head-to-toe relinquishment, something almost lavish, if unwanted. She has another, more subtle mode in her repertoire, originating in her temporal lobe, called the *absence* seizure, pronounced the French way. Conversation stops, she seems to drift away, makes a gesture maybe, and then returns. A moment of absence, but she knows the absence is contained more in the witness. If anyone asked her where she goes during her abductions, they wouldn't get a satisfactory answer.

She has a theory that turbulence in the atmosphere causes head-aches to swell to the top of her skull and her balance—normally so well-tuned—to falter. She starts to sweat easily. Her doctor has said to her that she is imagining it, that it is an anxiety attack and that is why she feels those things, but she has concluded otherwise. They have long disagreed about her symptoms and what she considers to be her triggers. He can't know everything about her brain. She knows that electricity comes for her from the cloud formations roiling over the sea, that her seizures begin in the middle of the Atlantic Ocean, right in its steel-coloured mind. Neurons organize themselves in great surges of communication, forces of an unseen world. It is a felt thing, a shimmer in the viscera that builds, grows spikes and speed. The beginnings of falling down.

This bit of sidewalk is now a territory that belongs to her, and a bet-ter spot than, say, a subway platform, with its oiliness that is part machine, part sebum, a distillation of millions of people and their metal counterparts. You can scrub for days and still feel it mining the skin. Better, too, than stairs, and the tension in those angles, the way they calibrate gravity and measure it. They declare *the only way is down*. Boom. A body can be flung. Transformed. Another dimen-sion ruptured. There is the patient long ago who said to the English neurologist John Hughlings Jackson, "I feel in some strange place." The landing comes, a bursting through to a new territory, familiar and not.

———————

The boy is there, at the edge of this portal. He has never encountered a woman whose body appears to be opening and closing. Her face has a grimace that reminds him of the faces he has recently seen, photographs of mummified humans emerging from ice floes with their ancient, constricted grins. She seems tall, even though she's on the ground, with a shock of white-blond hair, short and wild. The connotation of lightning.

I am lightning. I have lightning. I hold it here in my head. As if the words are right there in his own mind. Her hair fascinates him as much as her condition, because the strands have been spiked with paste and teased up, a detonation from her scalp. He wonders who the shaking woman is, what her name could be.

———————

It's Molly. But they could not have gotten her more wrong, she wishes to say. The trouble seems to reside in that *-ly* and which she thinks is not quite the right fit. *Fit*. See there, she can't escape the connections; they spin out to eternity. He smiles at her, he enjoys this game. But he glimpses something that later on he won't like to remember, a space or a colour that makes him frown and draw back through the crowd. His mother, if she were here, would catch his arm, feeling sorry that he has seen this, the fallen woman, and pull him to the side so they could bypass the scene on the ground. He hasn't spoken since the age of five, but he tilts his head back to look at something no one else can see and says the single word *location*.

———————

Location, they say, is everything. The proximity of thing to thing, person to person. But see also the impossibility of locating. A person can disappear in the city with ease. She is more indelible than ever, but she had been looking for someone, hadn't she? The last few days are themselves hard to locate—the thoughts she had been absorbed in, who she had been with, had dinner with. She had been working on a performance.

The city knows who you are, however. It assumes people at every corner, and wakefulness and continuity and never sleeping. It knows you're there, emitting your carbon dioxide and hot breath. You can't hide from the city, but it can perform the neat trick of hiding you, if you so desire. It can drink you down, provide a cloak, make you entirely ungraspable, almost as if you had never been here in the first place.

The irony of the most dramatic episodes occurring in public isn't lost on her, and occasionally it has happened, though not for some years and not on a downtown street; not on a sidewalk. She had her first one at age thirteen, a year after her parents and the house. She once seized in a library, in the section of narwhals and porpoises, and opened her eyes to silent rows of blue spines. Two years later she was overcome waiting for a subway during rush hour. The congestion of people appeared to collapse over her in waves—the faces and hands and iterations of boots. It becomes easy, then, to appreciate the invisible, the efficacy of a secret.

Sabine

Sabine drove the rest of the way with focus, sometimes speeding. There was the matter of what to do with the car, the difficulty of parking. She had the feeling that if she took Seth's spot at the building's lot, it would somehow, inexplicably, prevent him from coming back. She decided to leave the car at a railway station on the outskirts and take the train the rest of the way in. By late morning the city had grown up around her, frigid and steaming and pulsing with people. She proceeded then to bypass the subways and taxis and instead walk with her bag the entire twenty-two blocks to his building along streets that were icy in places and wet in others. She wanted to dislike the smells, the urine puddles, the padded people, the rushing, but in truth she felt perhaps more at home here than anywhere. She had been surrounded by this place for the better part of her life. Before she left and said she wouldn't come back.

She liked living near mountains in a town of only two thousand in the off-season, but she didn't dress or speak or act like someone who was comfortable in trees and dirt. When she hiked, which she did just to stare out at the local lakes and ponds, she wore her big boots, regardless of weather. She was not prepared for anything except finding her way back to her car. She was not the chopper and keeper of wood for the stove—she left that to Ellena. She did once climb the ladder leaned up against the house so she could pull fistfuls of wet leaves from the gutters, but she had done so wearing her long black coat. She ripped the lining of it on the way down but never bothered to fix it, so a frayed bit of dark silk was still visible. She did not possess power generators and puffer jackets and skis and kayaks. There was no roof rack on her car, which was small and tended to slip and grind uselessly in snow. She was unadaptable to seasons, and disinclined to acknowledge transitional rhythms as they are known in rural areas. The locals looked at her with curiosity, maybe contempt. Yet she was unbothered by this, as it was the others who saw her as resistant and a misfit. She herself was simply along for the ride of things, wherever she was. To her way of thinking, the whole world, just about, was interesting. She would have said that the viewpoint of the outsider was the key to comprehension generally.

She had to confess, however, that she did not always comprehend her brother. His apartment, too, was mysterious. Years ago he had embarked on a sudden passion for the outdoors, for forests distant from the city, mountains, deserts, and oceans, and any reason at all to be in them. His apartment had turned into a container of the gear that went with his pursuits, all the devices and gizmos that were bright yellow, red, orange, collapsed into themselves or folded in ingenious ways, an origami of tents, camping chairs, even a kayak that when not in use was a small cube in the bottom of a closet. He cultivated lightness in travel and carefully weighed his backpack, extracting items until what remained had transformative qualities or nested perfectly inside something else. He had organized some of his gear—ropes and carabiners and tools—carefully on pegs on his living room wall. Another wall held maps with pins of the places he had been and still wanted to explore. Otherwise, he was not prone to neatness, left the dirt on his boots, his clothes in a heap, and his hair wild. Molly had, many years ago, called the look in his eyes *chaos*. Sabine knew well the aspect she meant—the unsettled, shifting one was ever present. The one he assuaged with expeditions and alcohol, sometimes drugs, sometimes sex. He was always in the process of leaving the city, would return to it only to get out again, but he could not seem to make the move permanently. She herself had no problem with abandoning the city. The place seemed to be synonymous with self-loathing, unsettledness, eclipses of reason and sanity. She had left it, good riddance.

Yet, here she was.

———————

And here *she* is.

"Ma'am? Ma'am? Jesus."

"I think you're supposed to check her mouth or something."

"Her belt—and her shirt—are they tight?"

"No belt. Ma'am?"

"I think she's wet."

"Wet? Really? It's cold to be wet."

"Well, she is!"

"Her face."

"She needs—"

"Here—put it under her head. She needs something under her head."

"Are they coming?"

"Was she with somebody?"

"Wouldn't they be here if she was?"

"I dunno! I've never done this before. Why you asking me?"

"Be fucking quiet, you know?"

". . ."

"Jesus."

Sabine

Sabine sat on one of the armchairs in the living room of her brother's apartment. The cup of coffee with cream from her last stay was still on the little table between the chairs. A spectacular mould floated on the surface with a deceased cockroach on top. She imagined the roach to have ended in a fungal bliss, but she made a vow to take better care. A stack of notebooks sat beside the cup. Most of them were hers, but on the bottom of the pile was one that belonged to Seth. She had scoured it already for information, or insight, or signs of life, but all he had written in the first pages were a few lists of supplies. The remaining pages were blank, and their emptiness, the naked and pale blue lines with no words between them, seemed especially delicate and cruel. She thought he should have left signposts and signals. Things that *said*. She almost took it personally, his lack of consideration in leaving behind so little to go on. And so little about his mental state. She did not understand the lists, which seemed to be cryptically abbreviated. She had shown the notebook to a police officer, who expressed exactly zero interest in it and waved his hand at her as if she had interrupted his flow of thought. He had stood in the doorway to the apartment before turning on his heel. Then thought, perhaps, he'd been too abrupt and turned back to smile at her.

"Sometimes people do it on purpose," he had said. "Especially men. Especially grown ones."

"It?"

"Leave. It's a thing," he said.

Or perhaps she was making that up. She had been in the way, it

seemed, and the officer hadn't liked the look of her. He had asked
for her name three different times, though she had been to the station already, and on the phone, and everyone knew who she was, and
he himself had already written it down. Tight block letters on his
pad. Smiled. Gone, too. Perhaps he had memory issues, or perhaps
he had been expecting someone else. Perhaps she was really asleep
in bed with Ellena beside her, with the dogs wedged in between, and
the officer was merely a smoke of neurons. He was a composite, an
inexplicably glistening face, a slight smell. He stirred the dream air
when he left. Poof.

She wanted to smoke, so she opened the sliding door to the little balcony and stepped outside. She put a cigarette to her lips and felt inside
her coat pocket for her lighter, finding instead the stone that Seth had
pulled from a mountain stream and given to her. She didn't know
the type of stone and didn't look it up. She preferred the simple idea
of it, something that pointed to the volcanic and prehistoric. But the
stone was really a placeholder or pin. On her last visit, she had found
an open tourist map in a nearby deli and took out her pen to mark
a black dot in the approximate location of his apartment. Point last
seen.

She found her lighter in the other pocket and was relieved to
smoke where the air was already compromised; in the bracing atmosphere of the mountains, she felt the violations of her habit. The
railing, decorated with guano, was losing its paint. Beyond the railing, there was the icy freefall of space between the buildings, the windows and naked rooftops across the street, the miniatures of people
on the sidewalks below. She watched the buildings, what she felt was
their rigid masculinity. The lines and grids were placed on the back

of what had been a keenly feminine wilderness. She was held in a trick of bricks and steel, the layers containing people, animals, the ten thousand things, but only the echo of her brother. He was a kind of erasure, but still tangible, and together they floated aboveground, stacked up, seemingly alone.

Rafael

Rafael considered his painting, the indigo lines on a white background, one of forty-four similar iterations. The exact shade of white had been painstakingly obtained and the exact shade of indigo, too, to say nothing of the precision in the grid. Everything deeply contemplated, meditated on, reapproached. He worked most often in acrylic, but some of the smaller pieces were in oil. His studio was a mess in places, in spite of shelving systems and tables, and jars and boxes in which to house everything from the brushes to finishing nails.

Almost the entire locus of order was held in this particular series of paintings and stood in contrast to his usual mode of work, which had tended to the flamboyant, the big and wild gesture. The disarray of his canvases led somehow to an innate sense of order in chaos. It was his particular talent, the thing he was known for. A mysterious energy was at work between his mind and the chance organization of paint laid down in mad, vigorous rushes. He was celebrated.

But the turn of late in his work toward a leaner presentation flummoxed some, including himself. He knew only that it was a tack he had to follow. He had the windows flung open to expel the smell of the paint and because he had a tendency to run hot. He had another studio in a warehouse in Queens where he could deploy his more massive works. His home studio was originally the apartment beside the one he and Molly lived in. They had bought it when the twins were toddlers and torn down the walls to create his space and an office for Molly, though she tended to be elsewhere.

The problem of this day was that his attention was drifting to the scarf, carefully folded and rolled as small as possible, that he had placed in his leather knapsack. Claire had left it behind when she was last in his studio and Molly had not been home. It was the sort of forgetful gesture—though his own actions were rife with exactly this same insouciance—that he abhorred in others, particularly younger women. Particularly younger women in whom he had placed his faith, his attention, his sexual curiosity. The code was one that did not allow for the accidental—or purposeful—dispersal of items of jewelry or clothing, tangible expressions of affection, such as photographs, or even a long strand of hair that could not possibly have come from the head of Molly or the twins. In other words, nothing that would tell. That Claire had forgotten the scarf, and possibly shed it with something else in mind, rattled him. He did not love her, not in the particular egoic sense of passionate affairs, though he loved, he supposed, her humanity, that she lived and breathed. He simply was less interested in her, much less, than he once was, which had seemed to result in her sudden appearance of forgetfulness. She had been an excellent, and quiet, co-conspirator, a mutedly buzzing secret, until she started texting him at the wrong times and shedding pieces of herself as if she were leaving bread crumbs.

He frowned at the canvas in front of him. She wanted, it occurred to him, for them to be found out. He had not explained to her Molly's particular feelings in this regard—that she would likely be undisturbed by this development. He could have enlightened Claire, told her that if Molly had found the scarf, she might have picked it up between her index finger and thumb as if it were a dead mouse, or a hair clog from a drain. Or, conversely, being a lover of scarves, maybe she would have admired it, slung it around her own neck, and sat down on the sofa to read the Sunday *Times*, waiting for him to walk in and see what he would surely recognize as belonging to his lover. And that she would be smiling. Possibly demonically, but smiling, and it would be at least partially meant. But there was something deflating in the thought of telling Claire this. The fun was supposed to reside, dear Claire, in secrecy, an abundance of it, a duplicity sanctioned by the heft of its obscurity.

"You are nothing," he said out loud, and involuntarily. He was surprised at the uncharacteristic darkness of his thought, its annihilation. He stood with his hands on his hips, regarding the floor.

"Oh, I don't think so," Molly said, and he turned around abruptly. She laughed. "So sorry! Didn't mean to scare you."

She almost never entered his studio without knocking. He knew, however, that she wouldn't say another word about overhearing him. She grinned, and he was disarmed.

"My love, I have a question. I need advice."

He rubbed his hands in mock recognition that he loved to give advice and she, never needing it, rarely took it. "Indeed. Have at it."

She was holding a small white paper bag and went to sit on the worn-out sofa that he had for thinking naps. "I have treats, by the way. Ill-gotten gains. Entirely bad for you, but then it's no secret that I'm trying to kill you."

He shrugged. "I've never wanted to be too old."

She curled her legs beneath her. "You kind of are." She laughed. On the floor there was a Kashan rug, mostly devoid of paint, with a pattern of hand-knotted predators and prey. "The lions look a little human, don't they? And a little sad." Possibly sorry for the teeth and claws that weren't depicted but implied. She handed him the croissant and kept the scone for herself. He took a bottle of whiskey from his table, poured two glasses, handed one to her knowing she would drink very little of it. They clinked glasses and he stood, leaning against the table, waiting.

"My brain," she said. She picked a corner off the scone and ate it. He smiled. "Okay. I'll bite. What's it telling you? New piece?"

He loved the energy in the apartment when they were both produc-
ing, though he sometimes felt competitive, even ferociously, which
was a feeling he felt no need to reject. Competition was a facet of
aliveness, of vibrancy, of sex, and made people awake. It made them
want to fuck and eat and produce things. It made the world spin.

She took a drink of the whiskey. Then another, then drained
it. He raised his eyebrows. She rarely drank, exactly on account of
her brain. He watched her as she sat, staring into the empty glass.
She wore a black T-shirt without a bra and a pair of track pants that
she managed to make elegant, simply through the articulation of her
body.

She noticed his look, and her expression darkened. "I need to talk
to you. Seriously."

He said nothing.

She rubbed her face. "I'm sorry," she said. "It's happening again.
They're back. And I don't want to take the medication. Not yet. And
I want you to know that. I want a clear mind, such as it is. I want to
make some new work. This piece, especially. I've been waiting for it."

He nodded. "You don't need my permission. You're a free agent.
We do what we like." He said this pointedly and was ashamed. He
cleared his throat. "Do you remember the first time I saw one of your
seizures? One of the little ones?"

She smiled whenever he referred to one of her complex partial
seizures as "little." "Maybe. Dinner, I think . . . Spanish restaurant.
You had the mussels *and* scallops *and* clams. I remember thinking,
Here is a man who loves the sea."

"You had been telling me a story about your grandfather, and
then you just stopped. Midsentence. You were looking at me, but then
you were looking somewhere else. . . . You unmoored and floated off.
You moved your hand, like you were releasing a bubble or a bird."
At the time he felt it was eerie or primordial or mythological, or even

beyond language. "I loved you right then, that you could do such a thing."

He sat down beside her on the sofa and picked up her hand, kissed her fingers while watching her face. "I know you hate them," he said. "It won't help you to stress about it. Create your piece."

"I don't hate them. Not always," she said, and shrugged. "Other people do."

He kissed her face, her mouth. She touched his face, then stood up, putting the remainder of her scone in the paper bag, and left the studio. He watched her go before eating his croissant in three bites. Then he went back to stand in front of his painting with his whiskey. He rubbed his chin and contemplated the forgetfulness of Claire.

Sabine

She did not avoid the puddles as she walked. She couldn't storm along as she used to, when she owned the place. She had forgotten how to enter and exit a confluence of people. She preferred to be unaware of her body when possible, slightly removed from it. She preferred to be cloaked. As she walked ineptly along the sidewalk, she was pushed into a derided shape, hissed at. This particular January was less cold than usual, and damp. The sky was grey behind grey buildings. But at street level there was the tumult of desire and rejection, the things to eat, the things for sale, the things discarded. An unceasing, living capriciousness with just enough forethought to seem on purpose. She didn't notice what she once thought was beautiful and vital.

In her coat pocket, along with the stone, was a piece of paper with Molly's address scratched onto it, almost illegibly, as if in code. She didn't know why she wrote it that way, only that she did, but she had the location committed to memory anyway. She had finally called someone who used to work with Molly and was willing to help. *Oh for sure I'll give you her address lemme look just a sec.* But what she found on writing it down was a kind of disappointment, how the search was ostensibly over. She felt a curious sensation, the urgency detached and gone. Taken away on a current, now a speck.

She was only a block and a half from Molly's apartment building. A person got into a cab, leaving a glove behind in an icy puddle. A cyclist covered half his face with a scarf and also departed. The street was the kind that, despite its restaurants and markets, briefly emptied before filling again. She regarded the pause as eerie, and stood on the sidewalk, willing the gap to fill again with people. A kind of knowledge developed within her on a mossy, visceral level; however unlikely it was, she would see Molly before Molly saw her.

Only moments later, as cars materialized again and doors opened and closed, she saw Molly take shape across the street. Sabine watched her enter a café, two children trailing behind, a boy and a girl. Unmistakably her. A swatch of white-blond, an elegant scarf, a T-shirt as if the month were May. The children, bundled, were perhaps eight years old, or maybe they were ten, or even twelve. Which couldn't be true, they couldn't be ten or twelve, as she last saw Molly a decade ago—unless the children didn't belong to her, which was certainly possible, or they were adopted. Anything could be true. Sabine stood under the awning of a pizza place and felt a large drip fall to her scalp and slide icily down the side of her head. Yet she remained perfectly still and people walked around her as the café door swung open. Molly and the children waited for customers to exit before they went in. Once they were inside, Sabine walked down the block to cross at the lights. She walked slowly, and no one jostled her.

She knew the propensity of the city to obscure, how it stirred its contents ceaselessly. A person could hide in plain sight, and she thought, as she stood at a vegetable market two doors down from the café, that if her brother was in fact alive he could be doing something similar. He could be counting on doorways and crowds and traffic to blur him into the background. His face could appear in the window of a cab, or stare out from a cocktail bar; his form, stock-still, could be overshadowed by oaks in a corner of a park. A blink, then gone. Would he do that? she wondered. Would he shed one life for the illusion of another? As if the mind could be changed by giving itself another name.

As if his troubles, whatever they were, resided in a sound formed by the mouth. Exhaled like smoke.

She lit a cigarette, because she was cold, and watched the café door.

"They boiled."

Sabine turned toward the voice, which had come from a woman standing behind her. The woman seemed to be wearing numerous sweaters and jackets. She was perhaps not that much older than Sabine, but she looked old. Sabine didn't say anything. She just smoked and looked at her.

"They boiled. The whales. They were in a tank, it's where they lived, and they boiled." The woman looked at Sabine's boots, nodded, then stared into her face. "Down there, you know. Probably twenty blocks. Not like you can see it anymore. Doesn't exist. Where the fire was."

Sabine turned from the woman and watched the café again. The door opened, but it was some students who emerged.

"It was the Barnum Museum, 1865. You know it?"

"I know the one you mean. Haven't been there personally. Have you?" She looked hard at the woman. "Have you been there?"

The woman burst out laughing, continued laughing so hard she bent double. Then straightened. "Maybe I have. Maybe I was the one who started it. Burned everything up. All that foolishness. The conjoined twins, the mermaid skeleton. They tried to rescue the wax figures, can you believe that? But the whales. What could they do about the whales? Not a fucking thing."

Sabine had nothing to say.

"There was a giant named Anna Swan. Ever heard of her? Came from Nova Scotia. They got her out. Swung her out on ropes and put her in a giant carriage and she rode away. Isn't that something?"

Sabine watched the café.

"They were belugas, the whales. One was twenty-three-feet long, and the other was eighteen. There were lions, too, you know. They fought and growled while the place burned. The snakes blistered up. The monkeys broke out of their pens and ran into the city. Imagine that. The mayhem of that. Monkeys in Lower Manhattan. Imagine the ladies with their long skirts." She smiled slyly. "They could hide the monkeys."

"Sure."

The woman stopped talking, and Sabine hoped she would wander away. But then the woman said, "I know what you think."

Sabine looked at her.

"You think I'm a cliché."

"You don't know what I think."

"You suppose I'm not drawn right." The woman smiled, and she had perfect, gleaming teeth.

"I don't even know what that means."

"You think I have no consequence. I came out of nowhere saying random things."

"Just smoking, you know that? Just smoking." Sabine turned to watch the traffic.

"Find comfort in the random, I figure," she said, nodding. "You just have to look more."

Sabine sighed, glancing sideways at the woman. "Been looking. Believe me."

"I want you to have something." The woman dug into one pocket, then three others, parting one layer to reveal another, until she pulled out a folded paper and held it out for Sabine to take. "I want you to have it. It's important information."

Sabine took it and opened it. It was a smudged photocopy of an article from the *Times*—1865, the corners battered.

"It's beautiful." The woman rapped the paper with her bent

finger. "The reporter wrote about what was in the museum. He did a line about an electric eel and an alligator. I have it memorized. He wrote, 'An electric eel, six feet long, divided the attention of the juveniles with an alligator, who ate ducks and yearned for babies.' See that? It's right there." She rapped the paper again, and Sabine could see that the sentence had been underlined. "'Who ate ducks and yearned for babies.' Yearned for babies!" She laughed again and jabbed her finger toward Sabine. "The alligator wanted to eat babies, you know, the human ones. The ones it could see outside its pen. People would come to see the alligators, holding babies in their arms. But it's a good riff—yearning for babies, which is what I bet that reporter thought women do. So it's conflated. Eating babies and wanting to give birth to them. What an asshole." Her face turned sullen. "They don't write like that anymore."

Sabine took a drag of her cigarette and blew the smoke out in the direction of the street. "No."

"They surely don't," said the woman. "The brain loves to figure out a pattern, you know, whether it's there or not. It's what this city is made of, how it functions. The random. You keep that somewhere safe. It's the absurd. An investigation of absurdity. Excess. Captivity. The way we gawk. It tells you what you need to know."

"What I need to know . . . ?"

"Everybody needs to know something. Everybody's got one."

"One?"

"A conundrum! Am I right?"

"At least one, I would think." Sabine let the cigarette fall unfinished to the ground and stepped on it with her boot. She folded the paper and put it in the breast pocket of her coat. "Thanks."

"You're welcome. You're welcome. You're welcome." The woman started to walk away, then turned back. "It's good if you say it three times. That's how it works."

Sabine watched her walk slowly up the street, the woman's pant legs dragging on the ground, unfurling pale threads. The frayed hems were a disintegration, but also an energy spreading out, in search of something. She realized she had not been paying attention to the café door. She stepped farther out to the sidewalk to see if she could see Molly and the children. Suddenly the café door opened, and there they were, the three of them clutching small paper bags and walking in the opposite direction from where Sabine stood. They didn't see her. She watched their receding backs for a few moments. She decided to be pulled along the block to the apartment building, the children weaving behind Molly.

The Twins

Augustin laughed. "Not sure what it is *exactly*," he said, "but it's awesome, right?"

Stella smiled and nodded, trying to concentrate. They were seated at the kitchen island, working at a collage assignment for school, *My Family*. Exactly the sort of thing with which she had little patience, though Augustin had been diligently cutting out shapes from magazines. Nothing to do with the project at hand, but he had found, among the large stack of images that Molly and Raf had given them, and which included theatre posters and art catalogues, numerous faces and limbs and animals and objects that were wonderfully weird.

"Well, it's a cat, see, with a monkey's head, pooping out blue cars and a tiny donkey skeleton." When he finished laughing, he followed it with a large face made of breasts, penises, and open mouths that had come from an art catalogue.

Molly said, "Interesting," when she walked by with a cup of tea. "*Not* taking that to school."

"I'm calling it *My Mother*!" he shrieked, and almost fell off the stool, he was laughing so hard. Then he stopped, took a breath, and solemnly said, "Why do we have to do this collage, anyway? What's it have to do with anything?"

She ran her fingers through his hair. "Hm. That's awfully close to a whine. If you're questioning relevance already, this is going to be a long haul." She kissed Stella's head. She took a spoon from a drawer, put it in her teacup, and walked away with it. They understood she was working on something. Stella pretended to be concentrating on cutting out some words, but she kept her gaze on Molly.

"Gussie," Stella whispered. She was the only person who could call him that, except, occasionally, his mother. "Gussie!"

"What?!" He made his eyes bulge while smirking at her.

She swatted his chest. "Be serious. Listen to me." She made her voice as casual as possible. "Did you see that, when we were outside?"

"Uh, nope? I guess not. Was the guy there again with the ukulele? He sucks so bad. He shouldn't play that thing—"

She put up her hand, palm out. She waited several seconds. "I. think. we. were. followed."

Augustin thought for a moment. "Like the time that people walked out of Mom's show and there was the guy who wanted to, I don't know, whatever he wanted to do. Like him?"

"Dunno," Stella said, and shrugged. She went back to cutting out the words.

"That's it? Who was it?"

"How would I know who? If I knew who, I would have said who. Somebody."

"Somebody we know?"

Stella felt the knowledge fall into shadows. She pictured herself, her mother, and her brother walking along the street to their building. She was too young to have the words for the effect, the way the city behind you was sometimes swallowed by what lay in front of you. When you turned to look where you had just been, the sheer number of possessions, and the dispossessed, and the physicality of sound, tumbled together to make a space as blank and undeciphered as an old pool. It was similar to being in a deep forest, but she had only been inside a forest, on a trail with her family, once or twice; a version of her roamed a prehistoric, wordless understory, and could not be adequately expressed. She looked at him and shrugged again.

Augustin understood, however. He had merely tried to conceal what he felt in this one case to be an uncomfortable attunement. He had felt it, too, the arrival of something. It came filtered through the city flotsam, through his sister—because she was always the better conduit it seemed—and then into him.

"Okay," he said, though he didn't mean it. He took a penis and testicles that he had snipped out and put them on the face where the nose should be and burst out laughing.

Sabine

Sabine had watched them disappear into their five-storey apartment building, the glass door with matte black trim closing heavily behind them. On the pale stone facade between two of the windows a carved female figure she assumed to be Greek played a lyre with a distant, serene expression. Air conditioners poked out from some of the windows, and she could see potted plants on the sills, someone's coffee cup on the second floor, the stripes of what she felt had to be a cat. The glass in the upper floors reflected a late-afternoon sea that was somewhere in the future. She wondered which windows belonged to Molly.

What to do now wasn't evident to her. Suddenly the building seemed impenetrable and guarded. She went through the door uneasily and stood in the small foyer, staring at the list of names and buzzers. *V & M*, which she knew referred to *Volkova & Massimo*. While she had not known about the existence of the children, she had known about the husband. She had seen the paintings. She had even managed once to slip into the invited crowd at one of his openings. She had eaten several hors d'oeuvres before she decided, with the crumbs on her lips, that she was incapable of blending in and had to leave. Now, she peered into the inner lobby of the building. The stairs across the short expanse of stone tile went invitingly up, though not for her perhaps. She realized she was already too warm, that the building seemed to radiate. It was possible that carrying an absence rendered her persona non grata, that she had arrived blackened and plague-infected. Fevered. Whatever she had wanted to convey was a retreating thing. She stepped back out to the street, where the wind had picked up and the cold comforted her.

She bought steaming french fries from a food truck parked down the block by a small triangular park and a couple of benches. She didn't want to sit, so she stood and ate, watching the iridescence of several pigeons that bobbed a few feet away. Beyond them, a man pissed boozily against a postal box while singing softly. *She had electric boobs, a juicy fruit, you know I read it in a latrine, oh, oh.* He looked at her while zipping up, then walked on.

She ate another fry. She supposed that she and Molly had not ended on the best of terms. She had watched Molly resume her relationship with her brother, picking up, yet again, one of their numerous dangling threads, and understood that she herself had been, simply put, an investigation. Molly was what Ellena would have disdainfully termed a dabbler. Molly had loved—if she loved at all—not her, but her brother. It was the only time brother and sister had ever quarreled, but whatever argument was there disappeared when Seth and Molly had their final, abrupt split. After which Molly was never mentioned. But Sabine had secretly sat in the audience for no fewer than eight performances of Molly's choreography before finally deciding she could no longer afford to lurk, even if stopping was like the cessation of morphine. She dragged out her remaining time in the city for another two years, before leaving, at last.

The pigeons scattered suddenly when a group of kids ran past. Someone's knit hat landed on a shrub and was plucked by a man walking by in a suit, who stuck it on his own head without missing a step. She looked into the empty french fry box, then crumpled it slowly in her fist. She tossed it into a garbage bin as she turned around and headed back to the apartment building. Once inside, she pressed the buzzer, *V & M*, before she could feel her courage dissipate. She waited and pressed it again. When she heard the crackle, that fizz of static, she exalted. Molly's *Hello?* travelled from another galaxy.

She cleared her throat. "It's Sabine. Lemme up."

She jammed her hands into her pockets even though they had begun to sweat. A pause formed in which ten years spun in a vortex of several seconds. Nothing more from Molly, except the brief renewal of static, followed by the hum of the lobby door and a loud clack as it unlocked. Sabine stepped through.

She felt the strangeness of being in the living room of people she had followed. To follow someone was to objectify them; to stand before them in a shifty black coat, putting country dirt on their floor, returning their gaze, was to wallow in the confrontation of their humanity, and her own. Or some such. Stella and Augustin had come to sit on the sofa, unable to keep away from seeing the body attached to the intercom voice, the clomping down the hallway to their front door. Under other circumstances, they would have sat in the way that unnerved people, sewn close together, with a prim arrangement of hands and feet, and straight backs, something from a horror film. But they sat normally, instead, and took in the presence that didn't seem to want to sit, even though their mother had suggested it several times already. Raf had also wandered out from his studio, so that Sabine was faced with the entire coterie.

She could not help looking at Molly, however, who stood electrically pale and thin in the centre of the room, smiling warmly. But the words they exchanged came out like awkward and sporadic bats darting for the windows. None could be caught until finally Molly suggested they go to her office. Sabine gratefully followed her across the living room and down a hallway. She detected, faintly, the smell of paint. She looked back to see Raf, Stella, and Augustin watching them go with curiosity.

She refused to sit here, also, in the armchairs that were so absurdly compact she doubted she could have wedged herself in. The room was sparely arranged, a tidy desk, an enormous whiteboard with numerous images and notations, an open area beside a partially mirrored wall with a video camera trained on it. She examined, while Molly watched her, the black-and-white photographs along the north wall, trying to avoid catching her reflection in the mirror. Some of the images were stills from performances, the human in tumult or rapture or broken to bits. Others showed dancers in practice clothes grouped together, smiling.

Masks, too, hung on the walls, three large ones and two small, which Molly, breaking the silence, told her came from New Guinea, northern Canada, Japan. They peered at Sabine with their grimaces, smirks, and howling mouths, their consternation and protruding tongues. They seemed to breathe on her. The sound, she felt, would be that of static.

"So." She exhaled.

"Good to see you," Molly said. "You look well."

Sabine snorted.

"You're still in Maine?"

"Yup."

"The pine air agrees with you."

"Doesn't stop me from smoking, though." She was hot and removed her coat, at last. Molly took it from her, folding it over her arm and briefly stroking it before she placed it on one of the chairs. Sabine momentarily shut her eyes against the gesture. She herself lay folded carefully on the chair.

"I emailed you," she said. "I don't know if you got it."

"I did. I did get it. Yes." Molly brought her hands together. "I'm sorry I didn't answer it straightaway. Are you okay? What brings you here?"

Sabine watched her, something welling up inside. "So, how do I say this?" She gestured with one hand. "This might sound weird, but no one has seen Seth. He's missing."

"Missing."

"Gone. Missing."

"Since when?"

"Day before Thanksgiving. No word since. I've been coming to his apartment, off and on. Nothing. The police don't know anything. Nobody knows anything." Her shoulders sank.

Molly was silent, watching Sabine. Finally, she said, "That's terrible. I'm so sorry." She brought her hands to her face. "You must be so worried."

"I wanted you to know. I figure, even with all these years, it still matters."

Molly said nothing for a moment. "Naturally. Of course it matters." She turned away slightly.

"Yeah, it's been a long six weeks. No, seven." The weeks were air-filled, desiccated structures now.

Molly nodded and appeared to be thinking.

As Sabine watched her and the change in her face, how her stance seemed to calcify, she realized that something had been unwittingly but satisfyingly transferred. In saying that Seth was gone, she had somehow passed to Molly the weight of the body, or a limb of it, or the unwieldy skull at least. In its place was the paradoxical aliveness in the giving of bad news, a black delight. Seeing Molly's stricken face, she realized it was that exact expression that she had wanted to witness. Why she had come. She smiled for the first time in days.

She noticed suddenly that the paper from the breast pocket of her coat was now on the floor beside the chair. Molly saw it also, and picked it up.

"That's for you," Sabine said. Molly looked at her questioningly.

Sabine smiled again. Then she laughed, almost explosively, brokenly. She coughed and covered her mouth. She took a small handkerchief from her pants pocket, embroidered with an *E* for *Ellena*, and wiped her face with it. "Sorry," she said. She gestured at the folded paper that Molly held lightly in her hand. "You keep that. It's yours."

The Documentary

In the documentary, volunteers sit in a cramped office with bulletin boards covered in papers. The volunteers have pledged their spare time to recover the unwanted, and the particular woman being discussed has been gone for seven years. She was last seen wandering barefoot along the embankments underneath a bridge, close to the water, her hair matted, her arms and ankles pricked with scars. Her words, though, possessed a clarity that the few people who came forward each remarked on, so that the volunteer named Angela says to the interviewer:

"At least three people said they heard her reciting poetry. All three mentioned an older man, who claimed to be her father, coming up to her and saying he was taking her home. But we learned down the line that her father was already dead. Nobody cares, though. She wasn't in a penthouse or beautiful, and her skin wasn't the right colour. Not only was she a prostitute, she was a crackhead, and bingo: Who gives a fuck? She mattered as much as the garbage.

"The reliability of the witnesses, you know . . . questioned. Nobody wants to spend the time on somebody who don't matter. People say there aren't resources, or real evidence that anything untoward"—Angela says *untoward* with emphasis and almost smiles, takes a drag of her cigarette—"happened. That some people don't want to be found and maybe it's just as well, they say. She fell in the river, oblivious, high as fuck, or she put herself in there on purpose, you know?"

The phone rings in the background and she stops talking to look at the man who picks it up, then starts to talk again. "The thing is, she started out like everybody does, right? A baby. Precious for a minute, and then . . . she believed the worst voice she heard.

"Who knows, right? Downward spiral from there. We could analyze this to fucking death. A person goes missing in Texas or Alberta or Timbuktu, and we have search parties—like hundreds of people and dogs and choppers even—lots of coverage, the media goes apeshit, and then somebody else goes off the end of the earth and you can hear the proverbial pin drop. You want to know what the difference is between those two people?"

Angela leans back in her chair, takes a long haul of her cigarette, blows out the smoke, and says, "If you find out, please let me know. Here's the fucking number."

Luna

People don't seem to see her. She stands in the park and feels the gazes that pass over her, as if she is a gap, in some way undetectable. If people look at her, they do so reluctantly. She has read that, somewhere out in the world, scientists have made a material so black that the brain can't see it. Partly, she thinks, she is unseen because she wears so many layers of clothing. She appreciates the self-sufficiency in the clothing on one's back.

Also, she keeps papers under there, tucked between a man's denim jacket and a mustard-colour woolly sweater, pages from the *Times*, 2001, when ash and people fell from the sky. The paper reminds her, not just with the images, but the substance of them, of the fleeting nature of all things, most especially the newsprint itself. But tucked between her clothes the papers have lasted years, even if crumpled and separated in spots and glued down in others because of moisture (the time she woke in a puddle; the time a man doused her with his hose as she walked by on what he considered to be the sidewalk belonging to his store, therefore to him).

So the paper has turned to pulp in places, then hardened and has weathered, as she has, the fullness of the changing seasons, borne witness to her time, even though the articles are stamped with dates and headlines. The paper has evolved in this way along with her. The names are typed out with the faces of those long gone. The fallen. The falling. She herself had been nowhere near the nucleus but had entered those rolling clouds of ash godlike and straight on. It was important, she felt, to attend the process. Dissipating humans had to be witnessed. She hoped that someone would do the same for her when it was her time.

She loves her shoes the most. The sturdiest boots she has ever owned, a deep red-brown like a third-day scab. They came straight from the people who hand out sandwiches or blankets. She keeps a matchbook tucked into the top of one, and chewing gum in the other, though they get exposed to weather in that location. Still, she doesn't want to mess with a system that says how things are, and speaks a kind of truth, that objects and people go unprotected. We wait to become, she says, when we already are.

She drinks a root beer that she purchased at 11:07. Her enormous watch swings on her wrist if she pushes her numerous sleeves up, and is a part of her survival. The numbers have meaning, tell her when to cross a street, head uptown, eat the half sandwich she has hidden in an alley or a park, find the remedy for a certain ill or ache. Take three sips of brandy at 3:11 or 5:56 exactly or not at all. The brandy is good, too, not cheap. She doesn't keep the bottle on her person but rather tucked in a secret location. Too secret to tell. It is always there, silent and waiting, until she finishes the one and finds its replacement. She likes the right balance of numbers and doing and fate.

Her process is a reckoning of accounts, a result of endless tallying—another use for her watch, which keeps track of the souls. Always so many. And the seconds keep going by.

She scoops a beautiful rumple of blue paper from the trash bin and moves to a bench to sit with it, smooth it out in her lap. But the lettering is unreadable, and the paper was better when it was bunched up, so she balls it and places it in the loose outer pocket of the outermost jacket. Clothing in this way is a psalm of the galaxy; there are layers and rings and regions, planetary orbits in the pendants that hang from her neck. She feels, as ever, the movement, the entropy, of all things. The atrocious urge to expand and keep going.

She herself has a small space in which to live on certain nights, to be confined, though she is never sure of how she gets there. She simply arrives. Always she finds the same configuration of bland terrors—the nefarious others—alongside the offerings of food and water. They give her something for the cough, which they note and discuss among themselves. One or two of them tell her she is stubborn if she refuses. She takes the paper mask with elastic ear-bands and wears it like a hat while her face remains stoic, and always it fools them. She dissolves into the city night. She tells them before leaving that she is a construction of ashes.

3

Cells

Where do you locate loss in the city? Or in the brain. The neurosurgeon Dr. Wilder Penfield poked around a live brain with electrodes and the patient heard a piece of music, long forgotten, and actually sang along. Another neuron is touched and another scene opens, a park bench, a street sign, the taste of an apple. Inside the cells the molecular imprint of what we have devoured or what has been forced on us, brought back to life by that electrode. Molly locates the neuron that contains her mother's hands, another for her bracelets, another for her saying the word *vase*, another for her face backlit by the sun.

Molly could hide Seth, too, in this space, this city of doors and alleys and nooks. She could leave the ideas of him, here and there, until he was so dispersed that she didn't have to worry about coming upon him anymore. The problem of other people was that they sometimes resembled him. Not the hair, exactly, but the shape of the head, or not that, but the rolling walk or the guttural laugh. Enough like him to make her stop and stare. The first time they met it was at a party, years ago, and she noticed, along with the slight stain over his right cheek, the ghost of something, though he smiled.

She holds a small scar of him there in her left hand. A thin wishbone shape in hard gristle along the Mount of Venus. It is a kind of knowledge, ever present, though it edges an absence.

———————

See the Japanese man, for instance, who after losing his wife in a tsunami learned to scuba dive to try to locate her remains in the ocean. He dove again and again, imagining perhaps that she was still the same. Still whole, still her, still locatable. An older woman went to the shore and placed lunches in the water daily for her daughter who likewise did not survive, an offering that attempted to stave off forgetting, how details themselves become lost. As a result of not being found, the missing person becomes an inhabitant of that larger, more nebulous space. They reside in a sea.

———————

People forget the foundation, she thinks, now that she has the time and this particular upward view, that all cities are essentially the same, in spite of cultural assertions and type of buildings and linguistic quirks, which religions and races are grouped where and why. The ego is in love with its lines and borders, and wants to render the separations as absolute; it's always bawling about how individual it is. But the dirt on the subway platform is hybrid, polyglot, even galactic. She wishes to point out that the human body is stuffed with the Milky Way, that's how foreign it is. How far people have travelled, first as particles shot from the rage of dying stars, reassembled here as bones, skin, muscle. Teeth. Permanently alien and yet unequivocally like each other. She loves this place, even this sidewalk with its faint smell of urine, human or canine. Her affection doesn't discount, however, the city's avaricious side. The edges and forbidding creases, the manias that erupt at frequent intervals (and is she afflicted with one of these, she wonders), the din. The city also has a preference for newcomers who are eager and robust, attracting them with its garbage-strewn sequins, because it requires a large pool on which to feed. The city, she wishes to say, eats its young.

Molly

"Ma'am, you gotta breathe!"

A Musketeer grabs at my shirt, before he retracts in surprise. We are all undone by our motions. None of us are who we used to be, who we say we are. That snowflake two stories up has been replaced by another one, equally delicate and astonishing. A crystal palace within the width of a human hair.

One of the Crones strokes, momentarily, the Musketeer's black puffer jacket. Revenge turns to see who might be coming, if the source of the sirens is visible. Blue Girl has been unconsciously holding her breath. Suddenly, in concert, she and I take in the salty, chilled air, bring into our lungs those ashy, harbour-tinged, construction-razed, galaxy-sourced atoms.

"Like she heard you, man—"
   "That was a big one."
   "Fuck me, I can't—"
   "Where's the ambulance, man, when you goddamn need one?"

Blanks

I'm trying to find home, but there isn't one.

Nothing to return to. The house is missing. The parents. The dog. The furniture and the boxes, the stockpiles—vanished. The polished banister and the ancient refrigerator. All of it, lifted off in a blink. Turned to an ash so fragile it could be entirely wiped away. Nothing left but the ground and its scar, now covered and therefore also absent.

Tinder

No, no. Begin with the house, the one that burned. It was in a town in northern Ontario where deer and black bear occasionally wandered onto lawns and porches, and moose came to the edge of the forests to lick the winter salt from the highway. The population was only 1,207 when Molly lived there but swelled to more than five thousand in summer when people turned up at their cottages and the tourists came through to buy ice cream and pastries named for beaver tails or wolf scat. The roads and numerous lakes were lined with huge slabs of pink granite, the flesh of giants left to decompose. The woods that she ran through were filled with the black branches of hemlocks, sugar maples, and cedars, and tamaracks that blazed yellow in autumn. She was feral much of the time, and stood on the hill as the sun was going down to watch her house until her mother stood in the doorway and squinted into the gathering dark. The house was big and old, partly constructed from bricks made from local clay, with a white wooden addition. Its delicate constitution after seventy-three winters caused it to howl when the wind did and allow rain or snow into unseen, papery corners. In the summers, she was sure she felt the house swell with humidity and warmth. There were faint stains around the ceiling lights, which held the shadows of wasps and spiders inside their frosted glass bowls.

She was even more sure, however, that the old walls were shored up by the hoarding practices of her parents and the supplies they kept for a nameless destination in hundreds of boxes that were stacked, numbered, and labelled. Black ink, midnight blue. A repository that waited for something fiery in the distance. They stuffed the house like packing a musket, expressing the fear of a loss they couldn't or wouldn't articulate to her. Her parents' desires did not belong to her. The boxes and stacks, the letter and number system, were meaningless except for being the physical manifestation of a nebulous, psychic darkness. She felt shame whenever a stranger came to the house and the face, eyes wide, registered the size of the collection that sprawled from room to room, around the larger pieces of furniture, and obscured the home's interior structure. Most of the rooms, and much of the basement, were reduced to being a series of narrow walkways, such that the boxes themselves, multiplied so many times, became something of a single entity, one that waited. No doubt the visitors, if they didn't know better, wondered if the family had just moved in or were about to leave, but the organized cartons were labyrinthian, neatly aligned and had none of the unstuffed chaos of a transition. This was an entrenchment so refined that most people, gobsmacked, made no comment about it at all. Her parents' friends, likewise, accepted the cardboard arrangement as if it weren't really there, except that the boxes were useful for resting a glass of beer or an ashtray.

The boxes revealed another aspect of themselves when she was eight and the family had arrived back home from a rare road trip to visit her grandfather in New York. She returned with the imprint of the city, its puzzle of lines and forms and light, and she saw the boxes differently. On the ones stacked up in the room just off the kitchen—what might have served as the dining room for a different family—she drew windows with people sketched in going about their various intimacies above other windows and store signs and the block-lettered names of theatres. She used light strands to stand in for neon signs and light poles and the lit awnings. The following year she added the forms of bankers and construction workers, dancers going to class, artists and addicts, the bumbling tourists, and finally a subway system in the basement using part of her father's train set in the one space left and included some graffiti. She added a cellist with an open case to collect the coins, and the actual mice of the basement she considered to be outsized, zombified rats, true rulers of the underground and the city above.

Molly

Held in the breath. Just a few weeks before the fire, I ran to see the commotion in the backyard but stopped short of the doorway to watch from the shadow of the house. My mother and father hovered drunkenly over a crate of oysters. They wore T-shirts and jeans even though it was freezing out. They didn't know I was home from my dance lesson, dropped off by my friend's mother, and I said nothing.

I didn't know what the oysters had to do with anything, why there was a box of them, or why they were arguing. My mother's long hair splayed in the wind as though she were underwater. There was a plunge in the barometer, or vodka sloshed in their veins. My father was yelling, poking the air with the shucker. He was rarely angry, and for a few moments his rage made him exquisite until it made him clumsy. He jabbed the air, then the oyster he was holding, scooping out the pulse of his hand when he missed. I might have made a sound but they didn't hear me.

The two of them wobbled speechlessly while he bled. Silence so consuming it came for me as well and, for what felt like several minutes, I stayed where I was. Behind me was a kitchen full of crusted pots and dishes, an elderly Saint Bernard who hadn't been brushed in years, a telephone buried in a shale of newspapers. The boxes. I was intensely aware of my body and yet couldn't seem to move. I wanted badly to sleep, and yet red, pendulous drops fell from my father's hand. More and more of them, as they pooled on his shoes, the ground. Finally, my skin rippled and I was released from the spell. I ran to get towels as though I were burning.

At the hospital, after his hand had been stitched, my mother ran her ringed fingers through his hair. He kissed her chest. I was born when they were only eighteen, which means they had just turned thirty. I went to sit in a plastic chair against the mint-green wall. There was a window away from the machines and wires beyond which enormous snowflakes had begun to fall. A nurse came to stand beside me. I thought she would say something about the snow, as grown-ups always seemed to do, how finally it was here or it was too bad or how long it might last, but instead she touched my shoulder and said, "Look after those two."

Supplies

My parents kept their belongings boxed and labelled and organized. I didn't understand there was a word for what they did until much later. I never, strangely, heard anyone refer to them as hoarders, or as hoarding. Their process, to package up and keep time in this way, like trying to collect air in jars, was nameless and belonged to the world of only partly seen things. They couldn't take the boxes with them, or their bodies, all of it transformed to ash. Their desperation, blandly described in their labels, turned delicate and grey also, went up with the smoke to find another home, another physical body to inhabit.

This Is How I Arrange It

When the house burned, it was engulfed so thoroughly that one of the neighbours said the sky inhaled it. There was a series of booms as the flames ran room to room, and then the moaning of the little upright piano from its tight corner in the living room. Boxes of playing cards and cod-liver-oil pills had been lined up under the keyboard so that when the flames reached it, the laminated wood, after a pause, went up in a rush and folded in on itself, though no one was in the room to see it.

The sofas and chaises were gobbled easily. The garage was a bonanza of oily rags, cardboard boxes, and eleven gas canisters, an unused hydroponic system, ten years of seed catalogues arranged alphabetically, and an enormous wooden worktable that would vanish beneath the tools whose blades were found intact the following day. The house, and everything and everyone in it, collapsed and was licked up into the air. My parents, unaware of the dog corralling its last moments in frenzied circles, felt nothing but a suffocation so abrupt it remained in their dreams.

This is how I arrange it. That they felt nothing. I wasn't there.

I wasn't there. I was sleeping at a friend's house.

I was sleeping at a friend's house, disrupting the narrative. Escaping it.

The Neuron Containing My Grandfather

"I can see your heart beating. You're like a rabbit," her grandfather said.

"I know," she said, but it bothered her that he could see it.

She had lost the fundamentals. She stood on the sidewalk with him about to climb the stairs to his apartment, in a three-storey walk-up, what would be her apartment also, the new home. She felt the stony hum of the city under her feet. The sounds of traffic and people hadn't dissolved for her, and they never would entirely. The city was already absorbing her, piece by piece.

"I'm trying not to say something trite, like 'You'll love it here,'" he said, shrugging.

Even though she was twelve, she held his smooth-skinned hand. She looked at the ground. He had lost his wife many years before and been called widower. She called him Daniel. There isn't a word for someone who loses a child. Whatever he considered himself to be now he kept to himself. She was already aware of the O in *orphan*, its shocked mouth, its eternal, unbroken body. She moved like an orphan and breathed like one. Despite years, already, of attention to the body, and the most essential thing, its breath—how deep, how to fill the lower abdomen, use the diaphragm, fill the chest last and reverse this process in exhalation—the creature she had become no longer remembered the fundamentals. Her breath was quick and shallow, or she seemed to not breathe at all. She was holding her breath as if afraid to give it out again, as if hoarding.

He was a retired mathematics professor. His plan had been to read the books he hadn't gotten to, haunt some museums, play bocce. Also make up for the decades he had spent in the guise of a straight man. Raising another child had not been in the plan, and yet he never let on what a burden she must have been, what a terrible surprise. Her mother had adored him, but the physical distance, another country, and her growing obsession with the boxes and the things of the world created another kind of distance, so that in the last few years, they had hardly seen him at all.

"You will love it here," Daniel said.

Her fingers around the suitcase handle. He watched her, waiting. She was filthy. She had been refusing to bathe, even though much of her practice had begun to incorporate floor work. The ground had changed everything—the floorboards or the tiles or whatever she was dancing on, no matter how recently cleaned, was never really clean. She had learned the secret knowledge that something is always raining down, unseen, onto the world's surface. She felt the energy of the ground, the rootedness of it. Flight from it was even more pronounced after she had taken the pulse of it with her whole body, laid down on it. Before her parents died, before she had to leave that house and that yard, she would lie in the grass, do somersaults and cartwheels. The numerous bare patches showed the tight drum of earth, and that tawny nothing colour that no one noticed.

Molly

Stella and Augustin gaped at Sabine, wondering who she was and what had brought her to our living room. She looked like she could have been one of my dancers from long ago. Her coat was enormous and loose on her, like an animal skin over the shoulders of someone emerging from a forest. She stood next to an armchair but didn't sit. When someone has been looking for you and then they find you, there is an interesting adjustment, almost a resistance. Even if they badly wanted to find you, they are sorry deep down that the finding is over.

Raf was holding a section of the *Times*, even though he hadn't been reading it. "Raf," he said, absurdly, hand extended. "Raf." It was almost funny. Often during an episode I feel the sense of stopping, and of physical detachment, as if I could mosey around the people in the scene, make adjustments. Tie Stella's shoe. Wipe Augustin's nose. Apart from Sabine and me, no one in the room had heard of Seth. No one knew who he was. Stella and Augustin knew in the way of their marrow, their breath, they carried a psychic imprint of him that they couldn't yet put language to.

Being found suggests being lost, a wandering off the path. Or being found suggests another person and their particular need. "I have something to tell you. There is something you need to know."

And once found, then what? Only the waiting again, slightly altered. You make a note to hide better next time. And time, that progressive, inexhaustible tick. Chronograph of the heart. The hand touches your arm, or the doorbell rings, or your inbox flickers, or your phone blows up, and you are found.

Begin with being found.

———————

But the boy is lost. Even I wonder where his mother is—I can't detect her in the crowd. He has stopped looking at me and looks down at his shoes instead, which are brown leather. They have brown laces and resemble shoes that might have been worn by boys many years ago. They look as if he's kicked at cans and curbs many times, or keeps them in the bottom of a pile. His jacket is open, and he's only wearing a T-shirt underneath. His socks show because his pants, navy corduroy, only come to his ankles, and the melon socks are pill-y. I can feel the clarity of his breathing, the crystalline intake of air and his exhales, until suddenly he is moving away. He was close to my body, but he's turning, looking back down the block, and he moves through the people gathered and begins to walk along the sidewalk, back in the direction he originally came from, and stops. He is unsure which way is which.

The fact of his dislocation doesn't bother him; not yet. He plays in his mind with the sentences that occupy him. His aunt has been reading to him a Rumi poem.

You that come to birth and bring the mysteries,
your voice-thunder makes us very happy.

Roar, lion of the heart,
and tear me open!

The last two lines affect him most, the idea of being torn open by
sound, by ferocity, or an actual animal—a huge cat—big enough to
eat him. Your voice thunder. He wonders what it means to be eaten,
how fundamental it seems, and he can imagine it. Or if the lion is inside him, comes out of the heart, and if it did, then would he finally be
able to speak? The sound would be like the darkest sky, and maybe
this is what his aunt is trying to tell him. They want him to talk badly
enough that they'll bring a lion to eat him—or they will pull one out
of his heart. Which says that one lives inside there. He puts his fingers
on his chest as he watches the traffic and tries to imagine a cat beneath
his sternum. He wonders if he'll see his mother, where she could be, if
she has a lion in the heart also.

I Have to Talk to You

"Sometimes I'm not sure what you want," Jon said. This was one week before this sidewalk and its watchers, when I was at the studio. "You want a fall. I give you a fall. Right?"

"Right," I said. He was one of twelve dancers trying to understand the move.

"But then you say I'm not doing it. I could swear I'm doing it. I feel like I break my head otherwise."

"I know. I promise you won't. Trust the move. Trust the idea," I said. "Okay, let's go again."

I had asked, demanded, that they fall to the ground, not as if they were pretending to fall, but actually letting go. When the body falls, it has to have complete faith that a different consciousness will carry it down. Some of them have been working with me for years and even they didn't believe in what I had shown them. How to fall, how to forget entirely what it means to resist. But they resisted so much that I was beginning to doubt myself.

And then I saw them do it: remove the structure, unmask themselves. Meet the ground as if their spines were gone. They risk everything to do a move like that, to make themselves entirely vulnerable, including their heads and faces.

They started unfolding, and popping back up, shocked themselves at whatever had allowed the known rules to bend. They laughed and howled afterward, high-fiving. Elizabeth, Sergei, and Trent threw their arms around me. This is the kind of joy that creative breakthroughs render. What I've lived for, those shrieks and eurekas and shocked faces. They get it, at least for a while.

But Sergei stared at me, then squinted. He caught the shadow inside me, and I knew. I can't hide how the pupils narrow to a point so empty and black that it's possible to recognize an infinite space.

* * *

After everyone left, I gathered up my coat, my notes, my video camera, my bag, and turned off the studio lights. My plan was to go to the apartment before Raf and the twins came home and watch some of the footage, see again how that transformation had unfolded, set it on rewind, freeze the frame, allow those falling bodies to stay in the air. Suzi has the best face, if not the strongest body of the group. As I watched them rehearsing, I focused on her expression. She has the kind of face that audiences respond to, sometimes without knowing exactly why. The aliveness is tangible. Ming is a close second— something rushed through her and she made, despite so many years of training, an involuntary sound, which would be there on the video, along with all the other metamorphoses and transits that I wanted to see again.

When I walked into the apartment, I found the stillness that signalled no one was home. I went into my office and checked my email, despite thinking that I should hold off, despite feeling the presence, already, of her words there.

i know it's been how many years?
couldn't find a number for you anywhere, not directly.
i have to talk to you.

The email sat in my inbox, and I decided that if I allowed it to remain unanswered, it would cease to exist. Then she was in the building, the voice of the intercom, a physical presence in my apartment. There were witnesses, and the impossibility now of turning her into a phantom. She delivered her message, and that folded-up paper, too, telling me it was mine to keep.

The Paper

Which was compressed and battered. Dirt embedded in the fibres along the edges created borders within borders and made it beautiful. After Sabine was gone, I sat down with the paper in my office, placing it, still folded, on my desk and stared at it. I waited for it to tell me what it wanted. I envisioned a performance where the paper could surprise the audience by being unfolded to a size much larger than would be anticipated. It might even be funny. The paper could itself become a performer and be transformed, folded into various shapes: a boat, a swan, an airplane. It could become human. Perhaps it would even enjoy its mutability, offering surprise.

I sat there with the folded paper for maybe half an hour before I put it away, unopened, in a desk drawer. Then I changed my mind and decided I would put it in my coat pocket, carry it the way that she did, in the place of the heart. As a heart.

Did I feel something like hatred for her?

Clarity

I think it's possible that I did.

The following day, I sat in the living room, trying to unthink both of them. The brother and sister I wanted to leave unacknowledged, somewhere on the margins of whatever territory I considered to be mine.

But the time was four o'clock, and the light was doing something strange. I became captivated by Rafael's phone, that it was on the coffee table in front of me. It was unusual for it to be out of his reach. Just as I was wondering about the meaning of its placement, if it was conscious or unconscious, a text came through from someone named Claire.

why

No capital or question mark. Just there and gone. After a few moments, during which I waited and watched, the text washed to the surface again, silently, because he had muted the sound.

why

Intimate, and yet. And also clumsy in a way that Raf himself would not normally allow—his rule was *leave no trace*. Nothing so unimaginative as a remnant earring or lipstick mark, no misspoken names, no witnesses. Only the unmarred surface of a scintillate quiet, something that could approach innocence.

•   •   •

The *why* searched with the open arms of its first letter. We don't tend to say *why* to strangers. We implore the gods or the cosmos, or someone close to us, as the mind tries to arrange its causes and effects. We want to understand and want a particular person to respond. She might have been asking, *Why did you say that*, or *Why do we exist*; it didn't matter. For hours afterward, in the dark lake of my mind, the *why* would bob up, sudden as a body part.

I decided then to go to a café a few blocks from home to sketch out some ideas. I brought the *why* and its monstrous simplicity with me. I could sit for a few hours at a corner table and think. I walked in the cold, without my jacket, arriving at the café just as the sun was going down. I settled at my favourite table, one with circular stains like planets embedded in the varnish. I brushed off the crumbs and opened a notebook. The owner, Amina, came over to say hello and bring me biscuits that were still warm and a pot of tea. She returned to helping other customers, but I could feel her gaze. Apart from the businessmen seated by the window, and a few students in line, it was oddly quiet. When the door opened, I could hear something scratching outside on the sidewalk. I lifted out the sounds of people and taxis and heard only footsteps. Only that.

After a while, Amina came to the table again and asked if I was all right. She had the kind of face where the soul appears at the surface. Two deep scars ran the length of her arm, though they were partially covered by her sleeve. The scars were the remnants of an attack she had endured years before, not in the country where she was born, but in this one. The skin was arranged in pleats and it was possible to see that she had been sewn together. She smiled at me and the smile was enormous, somehow unburdened. Before she came back to the table, I had seen a peripheral form, smudgy and grey, that disappeared when I turned to look. Nothing was there. It diminished in the scope of her presence. Her expression turned quizzical, and she touched my arm.

After I had convinced her all was well, I put my notebook back in my bag and left the café. I was trailed by something, a cross between ink stain and dream world, as if another form of incoming message. Near the corner of Washington and Greene, I heard the sounds first, a woman's voice, and turned to see where she was, but there were only the usual fast walkers and students. My brain had either prevented me from seeing her or caused her to take shape, I didn't know which. She was about fifteen feet ahead of me, with a face I recognized but couldn't place. She spoke, pointing to the ten-storey building that rose from the corner in shades of beige and grey, but no one listened to her.

"They fell," she said. "From right up there. The eighth floor. And the ninth. Right up there." She turned to look at me, and her face and voice, which had seemed for a moment like my mother's, weren't that way at all. The face was heart-shaped and lined, and she wore layers of frayed clothing, some strands of beads.

"I know," I said.

"They landed right here. 1911. Right here, on the sidewalk."

"Yes," I said. Her face, which had appeared adamant and concerned, began to change. The more I looked at her, the more elusive she was.

I said, "No, don't go. Don't," and I'm not sure why I said it, when I knew the proclivities of my brain. No one paid any attention to me, either, no one glanced over as if to wonder who I spoke to. I couldn't trust what I was seeing, where I was, even if the concrete under my feet was solid and my hands, which I shoved in my pockets, were cold.

"Name is Luna, by the way," she said.

"It isn't," I answered and turned to leave. "Go away."

"Go away," she said, and I walked as fast as I could back to the apartment.

It seems inevitable to me now that I would end up on the ground a few days later, banging against it.

Luna

I wasn't born here, no. Where I come from doesn't really matter, or not in the way people think.

See that building over there? The one with the stone cornices that line up with the windows. Everyone knows what a cornice is. This is a sawtooth one and has what looks to be teeth. If you take the time to look—not many do—you can see floral etchings in the stone above the windows. They paid attention in those days. At one time the house was a brothel, but before that it was somebody's mansion, and the rich person—the family came from Yugoslavia, I think—killed his wife but did so in a methodical manner. Very clever, taking her on a ship across the ocean to Europe for an extended vacation, *extended* being the operative. Dispensed of her body along the way, and this happened long ago, so her family wasn't expecting to hear from her for months.

Dropped her bit by bit into the water. *Plop. Plop.* Or maybe he pushed her whole body over in one go. Big splash, and then she was just a small shape, something unknown, a gull, maybe, sitting on a crest, washing away from the boat. Then gone. So anyway, it was a brothel after that, a good one, and then a place where the people held dog-fights in the basement. Imagine the festival of alarm and the stench. If you're a dog and survive, you get to do it all over again. So that is that building, and now there's a vintage clothing store, and on the second floor there's a facialist. I went up, because I wanted to see for myself, but they were disturbed by my presence, how I knocked over a scented candle, and they argued for twenty minutes about how that might have happened.

When people think of this place, they imagine crowds everywhere, but it's not really true. You can see space if you look, between people and other people, and between buildings and streets and cars. Sometimes space on the subway platform.

Before I got here, I pictured people everywhere. People per square inch. Like those photos of Japanese trains during rush hour where the passengers get packed in tight by people whose job that is. As many as can possibly fit. The whole city like that.

But you can stand in Times Square at five in the morning, especially when it's cold, and see space. The lights and neon signs are going for nobody in particular, because they don't know how to stop, but maybe you see a person across the street. They're walking along, maybe wondering what you're doing by the statue of Father Duffy, which they don't really notice, or they don't know who Duffy was—he was the chaplain for the Fighting 69th and very brave apparently—and why there's a statue of him. But it's five in the morning and the lights and signs are performing for this tiny audience. The person sees you for a blink before they no longer see you. And that's how you disappear.

•　　•　　•

The people born and raised here—it comes down to one thing, in my humble opinion. Doesn't matter where their forebears came from, what ship they washed up in, or if they can say their ancestors were here on this island with the bears and the trees before the Dutch and their ideas ever got here. Forget religion, sexual partner, or what they put on their bagel. The folks who were raised here, they are all one thing, which is practical. I don't mean to generalize in so particular a way, but there it is. And I couldn't understand it, you know, for the longest time after I got here, because I don't have the particle myself. Also, they are forthcoming—maybe too much so. Just my opinion.

You know how you can tell the tourists and the new arrivals? It's not the athletic wear or the red or yellow windbreakers, or that they're standing in groups looking up at the buildings. You can see they're full of romance and big ideas, unfeasibility being a thing they don't register. It's like a dog whistle, and the ones who were born here can hear it. So that's how the city folk are practical: absence of romance, and ability to detect the high-pitched squeal of the unviable.

You know Martin Heidegger? He talked about the uncanny and said that anxiety could happen anytime, that you don't need the dark to feel worried. I try to stick where the pigeons are, myself, because I don't think they have much anxiety. I'm not sure they even really mind it when they get taken off by a raptor. They're very moment to moment, far as I can tell.

The place where I grew up was full of anxieties. I once had a woman serve me lemonade on her porch and inform me I was the devil.

I said I wondered that she served me lemonade then, and she just smiled at me, which made me question the state of the lemonade. But I didn't want to turn away a drink offered to me by a neighbour. It turns out it was bitter, and that's all it was. The man who became my husband was from the same place, but the other end. Different anxieties, but anxieties all the same. He was so tall and thin, it almost made me laugh when I first saw him. I was working in a restaurant when he came in the door. He had a dog tied up outside, and the dog howled the whole time he was in the restaurant, eating his meal, not especially slowly but not fast, either, which should have told me something. In those days there was one thing I wanted, which was obligations. When you're young you want to belong to something. He was a reader, and it ended up getting into me, and I started to read all the time, too, just so we'd have discussions. But we didn't really. Had three children, though, soon enough, and you know what having three children does? Puts a dent in your reading.

Molly

Consider the designation: *orphan*. Almost a title, and royal. A little like *organ*, an essential one. I figured he knew things that other people couldn't possibly. I kept my seizures from him but knew he had an understanding of this other, perhaps more fundamental, presence—or absence—inside me. We had both lost our parents at a young age, both carried molecular gaps and blanks in our cells, and this was the foundation. Therefore we were twins of a sort, with our own heart gibberish. Like Stella and Augustin, we were at one time similarly wired. The communication was such that we didn't need to speak. Or that was how I interpreted the silences.

"If you want me again look for me under your boot soles," Whitman said. People are unimaginative where they look. The surface is not as solid as it seems. I don't know why we haunt each other. Tucked into the city, or maybe far beyond it, he could be anywhere, or everywhere.

Once, I parted a rack of sweaters in a clothing store to find him in the space on the other side. I had been thinking of him so hard that he materialized in a Park Slope boutique. But it was a stranger who grinned at me, and I left. I hustled along the street with my coat shut tight around my chest and my head down. Then he was in front of me: Seth, the real one, with his hands on my arms, pushing back. His face like a lion's. We didn't say anything, because there was nothing to say. And the dance began again.

I crossed town in a cab one night, pinning down in a notebook open on my lap some ideas for a new piece. The movement toward him, the stop and start. The driver had an urgency that didn't belong to me yet. His long fingers smacked the steering wheel every block, and outside the car night had come. It was as serene as it ever gets. He honked at cars and people, even traffic lights. The cars and people and lights kept on; they were held in a pressure of their own. A cyclist went by on the left, the driver honked, and the cyclist was gone, vapourized. More stopping and starting, and puffs of steam and exhaust. I pictured Seth in his apartment, only one or two lamps on because he liked it dim unless he was sorting his climbing gear. He drank coffee regardless of the hour. I had seen him grind beans at 1:00 a.m., and he often served me a cup on nights like this, so I pictured him in the darkened kitchen working by candlelight, rooting for clean mugs. He would open the door to find me inches away. A wordless, primitive impact.

The cab moved toward him with me in it, and my voice sounded like a stranger's when I hissed at the driver, "Just get us the fuck there."

Plastic Dolls

I sat at the bar with a glass of sparkling water and Seth stood behind it, arms stretched out and hands resting on the edge so that he leaned a little forward. The place was called Hammerhead, where punk and alt-rock bands came to play, but on this Monday night, it was quiet and dark with strings of lit red plastic chilis where the bottles were lined up. Someone had nailed naked plastic dolls down a post that went through the bar top, the bottom one of which would pee into a dish marked *FIDO* if you gave it a bottle. There were a few bowls of nuts and pretzels that Seth had already suggested I avoid. As I sat on the stool, I felt the sort of energy that makes sense of senseless things and forms the spine of bad decisions, rash moves, benders, and obsessions. I had quietly left the apartment of the person I was seeing to plant myself in front of Seth, who had taken me to dinner two nights before. The logic was held and nurtured entirely by the body, and the hope of consuming and being consumed. He filled my glass and had been listening to me talk about the company I was hoping to form.

"Undoubtedly you should do it. You were made for it."

"Don't know yet," I said. But I did know. I was still protecting the idea. I was aware of a chill in my spine, excitement and dread. The bar underneath my elbows was inert and solid, then unstable. I felt the formation of those endless binaries: trust or not trust. I watched his hands as if I'd never seen fingertips and veins before, the ends of the nails. Inexplicable, raging lust.

A man at the bar asked, "What's the meaning of life?" to which Seth said, "Why do you ask?"

The man said, "Aren't you supposed to know?"

"Ask her," Seth said, pointing at me. "She looks like she knows, doesn't she?"

The man turned to me. He was dressed head to toe in navy, as if he would deliver something or fix it. He was thin and his face heavily lined. "Well? What sayest thou?"

"Make things," I said.

He waved his hand. "That's the purpose. What's the meaning?"

"Fine. The meaning," I said. "There's a structure in the inner ear called the cochlea."

"So?"

"It's shaped like a snail."

"Yeah?"

"That's the meaning."

The man looked into his scotch, blinking. This went on for some time. Finally, he said, "Whoa."

"Exactly," I said.

Seth poured somebody a beer. "I think I've just been enlightened, but I'm not sure how."

"You'll get over it," I said. I had the thought, *By the time we're through with each other, we'll question our very existence*, but this didn't seem incompatible with anything, or even much of a warning. The body had made its decision and sat on the barstool with rapt attention. There was nothing to be done.

Eventually the man was gone. Seth polished a glass repeatedly. "Why didn't we sleep together the other night?" he said.

"Not everyone has sex on the first go." I smoothed my hands in my lap primly.

He smiled. "Oh, c'mon. Neither of us is sexually reticent . . ."

I laughed. "Sexually reticent. I haven't heard that phrase before. Okay, sure." I shrugged. "You're right about that, I guess. Or I'll speak for myself and say that's generally true."

"So why?"

"I can ask you the same."

He put the glass down and leaned into the bar. "All right. Fair enough."

"This is a negotiation," I said.

"It does seem that way."

"Are you intimidated?"

"I don't get intimidated," he said.

"Liar."

He smiled. "No, it's true. You don't intimidate me. You intrigue me. I like you. I like your mind. I've seen your work, remember, which is a bit like walking around inside your head. Your fantastically weird head."

"The term *weird* has no place in seduction, you should know."

"Noted. Fantastically inventive mind. Brilliant, in fact. And I'm not just saying that to get into your pants. But if it will help things along, I'll repeat it."

I had been taking a swallow of water and almost choked on it. "Cad. That's forward. Doesn't begin to answer the question, though."

He didn't say anything for a moment. "Here's the problem. Whatever I say, however I approach this, I feel kind of like an idiot."

"How so?"

"I'm not sentimental."

I scoffed. "Oh god, me either."

"I don't wax poetic."

"We can work on that."

"So if this sounds stupid . . ."

"Shoot."

He took a breath. "I want to savour you," he said. He looked down and wiped his hand over his face. "God, that's fucking—"

"No, no." I patted my cheeks. "Wow, I'm blushing. I don't blush. Generally speaking."

"I'm sorry, I—"

"No. It's perfect," I said. "I can say the same. That's the reason, right there."

He watched me for a moment. "Say it."

"Say what?"

"What I said. I want to hear it."

I laughed. "Pardon?"

"Yeah. I want to hear that. I just put myself out there . . ."

I rolled my eyes. "I want to savour you."

"This time with feeling." He smiled.

"Give me your hand." I had a mocking expression on my face, but when he placed his hand in mine, I felt suddenly stricken. "Are the babies watching us?"

He glanced at the pole. "Yes. Yes, they are. Make this good."

I sighed. "Except that I have to ask you about something first."

He appeared disappointed.

"The other night, Sabine at the party." I tried to find some coherence. "She was drunk—really drunk, actually. I don't know how it started or why she said it. But she said that your parents died a long time ago." I veered into arid and dangerous territory, one entirely unconducive to foreplay. I couldn't resist the pull of that place, however. "I don't mean to be heavy . . . No. That's not right. I mean to be heavy. I'm asking because I lost my parents when I was twelve."

A change began to happen in his face.

"Are your parents alive?" I said.

A long silence followed in which he appeared to be making a decision. "No." He shook his head. "No, they're not."

"How old were you?"

"Eighteen."

I allowed that to sink in. Eighteen was close enough. And it meant that Sabine was roughly thirteen or so when the accident happened. I had never come across other tribe members, never stumbled across another who had lost both parents during childhood in all the people I had met in thirty years. But I had found him, and his sister, and we were at the beginning of something, or the edge of it. "How?"

"Private airplane." His expression was the same as at the party. "Mountain." He moved my glass out of the way and held both my hands. "You?"

"Fire. I was at a friend's house." And there it was. A monstrous shadow passing over, as eerie as an eclipse, and all the people turned to ghosts. My heart pounded, and my brain hurt with the incompatible arrangement of commiseration and desire with an implacable grief. But the orphans couldn't kill the libidinous nature of the transaction, and not ten minutes later, he had arranged for someone else to fill his shift. We left the bar to go to his apartment, arm in arm, unable to prevent the force of our collision. I said, as we were walking along and I didn't have to face him, and even if I thought the phrasing insipid, "I want to savour you." He seemed pleased enough.

Thighs

It is possible to hold someone between your thighs who nevertheless inspires some distrust, or disdain, or distance. I straddled Seth's back and traced letters, perhaps maps, on the skin and its tattoos. We had been seeing each other for six months.

It is possible to smell bourbon from the very skin of another person, emanating from the cells, from the human between your thighs.

It is possible to wish for love to remain unspoken, unknown. Quiet in its corner.

It is possible to know someone, the one between your thighs, and not know them. It is also possible that they will not know you but believe they do. It is possible to hear the words *I know you better than you know yourself*.

Bollocks.

He said, "I love you," into the pillow, as if ingesting, as if eating it. A fritz in my brain, a short circuit. Language came to me as roots and branches, but broken ones, and storm sodden. I couldn't locate myself on the map of his back where I had been tracing whatever plans I had, or thoughts, or something unsayable. I felt the man between my thighs, saying the words I didn't want to hear, the ones I couldn't abide. *Fuck you*, I thought. *Do not disturb.*

I felt the muscles of his back harden in response to my silence. The nonresponse of my response. He was transforming into another sort of animal, one with a shell. I knew he itched for a drink, but I stayed where I was, my thighs clenching him in a paroxysm of hate, in a fit of *Who dares to look at the queen?* Affronted. Pinning him to the bed with a rage that made me giant. The bourbon he wanted was on the desk several feet away, and he wanted it more than he wanted the colossus straddling his back, the one who didn't return his love.

Except that I did. *Love!* screamed the betrayer in the temporal lobe, steeped in its feelings and perspectives, while that primitive amygdala, clearly threatened, took out a machete and with one swipe cut the word to ribbons. What I said was:

"I can't stay." Or some such.

"Okay," he said.

"I have a class to teach," I said. I no longer taught classes.

"Okay."

"You shouldn't talk of love," I said.

"Agreed."

"Why did you, then?"

"I'm a simple man."

I could not abide the lie. "You know what a simple man doesn't say?"

"What?"

"A simple man doesn't say that he's simple." I wanted him to buck with rage, I wanted to ride a bull so intent on jettisoning its human that in order to fix my place I would have to nearly choke him. I wanted something that frothed at the mouth. He wanted, I knew, that bourbon. He waited for me to leave. "You are the least simple person there is," I murmured.

I disembarked as if I wore robes. As I gathered up my pants and shirt I didn't recognize my own heart breaking, and neither did the man who was about to say that I didn't have a heart to break. *You'll be back*, I thought. *And so will I*, and both of these things were true.

Oh, but the utter sweetness of leaving.

Beckon

Maybe two months passed before I felt his shadow. And I wanted to feel it, I wanted him to haunt me. In my prayers I asked for it. I said, *Come and get me.* The body, having made its decisions, wouldn't have anyone else. No other seemed to fit, not the way he did, or the way I imagined he did. If someone—man or woman—tried to pull at my hair or pin me down, it did worse than enrage me. It left me stone-cold. I killed people with my withdrawals and silence. How I wouldn't allow. I became a phantom, a ghost, who coasted away from various lovers in those eight weeks, having stuck them between practices and creative sessions and performances. I couldn't abide whatever creature they seemed to be. They didn't do it right, they had everything to prove, and I was monstrous, relishing my exits. It was a form of murder, I think, drowning the sods in that well of disdain that ran over and filled the city.

Come and get me, I whispered to his shadow, *this can't go on much longer.*

We found each other on a subway platform, the Chambers Street station with its extravagant decomposition, as dilapidated and frail as the skin of a shedding snake. Puddles formed at our feet, the lights barred down. It was like an abandoned place, except that it wasn't. It was unbelievably beautiful. The M train came and the wind with it, and we stayed on the platform, letting it go on without us. We stared at each other, and I saw in his face that he had been treating people as I had. Anguish is a thing you carry, though sometimes it belongs to someone else.

"And," he said.

"And," I said.

We were hot and sweating, because it was mid-July, and he had been running to catch the train perhaps, and I was coming from practice. We were filthy, in other words, dilapidated creatures, smudged and torn, ridiculous orphans with a newfound capacity for cruelty and for love. I looked at him and shook my head, but he understood.

"I think it is problematic," he said piously.

"Things often are."

"You were wrong about the meaning of life being the cochlea."

"That's disappointing," I said.

"You just had the wrong snail."

"Oh? How could that be?"

"There's one that makes its shell out of iron. It's even magnetic."

"Magnetic."

"Yes."

"Whoa," I said.

"Exactly." He raked his damp hair with his hand, looked down at the ground. I had, unconsciously or not, inched closer to him. Our fingers brushed. "Take me home," he whispered into my hair.

"No," I said. But I was lying. *I want you to weep*, I thought. And he did.

Kickbox

Perhaps nine months later, a gestational period in which disdain could once again grow, but in the opposite direction, he became taciturn and morbid. And I wanted to fight. Physically. An inexplicable urge that I would place over and over into my work, causing dancers to box each other and rip and tear at the unseen membranes between them. The practice sessions were a mess while these sorts of moves were honed. But they fascinated me, and the faces fascinated me, too. I could peel away the costume of the monster and place it upon someone else.

He came to the studio and watched, standing near the doorway with his hands in his jean pockets, his hair in its studied disarray, his sinewy body. He would have made a good dancer, I had often thought. A heated, glowering look, but no, it had changed and become something else. I squinted from my spot in the middle of the room where I had been showing the dancers how to really unravel. I squinted to see him better and what the expression meant, and the posture, but I knew already. I called for a break and strolled over.

He said nothing, but turned and walked out. He was sober.

Wait

You get used to the weight of the city over your head, you learn not to feel it, or the crowds, in the same way that you can ignore the millions of particles absorbing the urine and rain and spilled coffee on the sidewalks and platforms. The subway stairs go up and down forgettably. You can even unsee the rats, and their spectacular tails, both stiff and slithery, and those magnificent, weird little hands.

Otherwise, the city is a sledgehammer at the mind. The concrete becomes a blank, some folds for steps, the person and the rat next to you a smudge. The train a blur.

I try to resist this, the flattening of everything into nothing, because I'm afraid of missing a detail that could be born again in choreography. The slinky movement of a stranger along the platform, up the stairs. Someone running to squeeze between the doors before they shut, the scream of whistles, and a toddler excoriating the passengers. The people shuffle en masse, like figures in a Pina Bausch piece.

Ecstasy has happened, too, during seizure. I would say crystalline or brightness or joy, but an emptiness falls open when I do. So I don't mention it, or that I sometimes feel the storms out at sea days before they stumble into the coast. Sergei at the studio had asked me if I was feeling all right. *What do you mean*, I said, and his response, *You look . . . your eyes . . .*

And I simply waved him off, thinking that if I did he would forget what he saw. The ghosting in the irises, the storm in my brain.

A Teenage History

My grandmother gazed out, poised and handsome, from a photograph in the living room. Her smile was gentle and ungraspable. She was a warning to us all about a certain capriciousness, as she had died of a stroke when she was barely in her fifties. Daniel had placed her image on the windowsill beside a potted calathea that blocked the view of her from much of the room. Beside the plant, there were tall bookshelves, the fireplace I would never allow him to light, and across the room, his one piece of taxidermy, a failed and deranged-looking fox. I never learned where the fox came from, but it sat like an aberration, its expression faintly amused, human. I worried that if I touched it, it might burst.

We took in a cat from a nearby alley, after I had wept about him. It was the first and only time Daniel ever saw me cry. He simply hadn't the will to argue with me, his granddaughter who no longer had a mother and a father. We called the cat Lucifer and bought haddock for him, cut the fur balls from his gnarled coat, and let him have the run of the place. He was tameless, prone to inexplicable growling in the dead of night, and he slept on my feet, which I didn't dare move. Eventually he located the fox and mauled it open, his ears pinned back in a fit of black-eyed delight. I didn't stop him. Daniel carried the fox remains down the hall and dumped it unceremoniously down the garbage chute.

· · ·

I told him that death was everywhere. My legs were folded under me as I sat at the dining table and picked at my dinner. He had enrolled me that day in dance classes with a teacher who would toss out my shoes and expose me to Merce Cunningham and Trisha Brown and Pina Bausch. Whatever elation I felt didn't hold for long. I sat brooding with a nearly raw steak in front of me, because that was the only thing I claimed to want. I was all bones and thigh muscles, and my feet had scabs and sulphurous old bruises, and a soiled bandage unraveled from a baby toe. I even had dirt on my face.

"So is life," he said. "Life is everywhere, Molly." He marveled that I sat before him, so like my mother, except filthy, and entirely alive. I was proof of the miracle of timing in which previously he had had little faith. But I had been mostly silent since he had brought me to the city and at last I had said my view of things. He had something to respond to. What he couldn't see, however, was a rage so capacious that furniture seemed to rumble in my presence.

The first seizure happened at the new school, during assembly. It was a charge down the rabbit hole in front of the entire student body. Later on, the energy would manifest as a blip in consciousness as though tuning out, or sometimes a sideways gesture like checking my pockets, but the first one came as a detonation. I crashed against folding chairs, tore my chin on the metal edge of a table, smacked against the gymnasium floor, and rattled there as blood streaked my face.

When I opened my eyes I saw the ankles and calves that lined an empty arc around me, a space into which the students and teachers appeared to lean, held back by an invisible railing. The phys ed teacher burst through and asked me something. Her words weren't words at all, but a substance like silt, and nothing I could answer to. I had become concrete, then fluid, over and over, outside of my own consciousness and with legions of teenage witnesses. I had relinquished myself to a force so large it could collapse me to the ground, but was so specific that it would avoid hundreds of other people and come only for me. I hadn't yet entered private school, where all the shoes were the same, and so I stared at an array of winter-denying footwear: running shoes, stilettos and pumps, leatherette ankle boots and beach thongs. A fine grit was against my cheek as someone dabbed at my chin. How was I, then, now that I understood the question.

I slept for days, burrowed into my bedcovers. I thought I could feel the creep of my nails growing, and my hair, too. My body renewed and expanded and stretched out of itself, like molting. Then here, instantaneously, the tuft of new pubic hair which had been late to arrive, as had my period. I balled the soiled sheets and hid them from Daniel, twirled myself back into the quilt cocoon where I planned to sleep until my brain and body behaved. Blood, too. Always it leaked from me, and yet I felt a fondness for it. How had I lived?

Daniel brought me a soup filled with barley and promised, when I begged him, to keep the secret of my seizure, even as its appearance could not have been more public or dramatic. What he referred to as the sordid eloquence of my brain. Deep down, I think he was unsurprised, both by my seizure and my plea for concealment. He saw me, in spite of whatever optimism kept him going, as a broken and patched-together creature. He read to me from Dostoyevsky's *The Idiot*, the parts where Prince Myshkin has complex seizures with ecstatic preludes. Myshkin even has one seizure, perfectly timed, that prevents his own stabbing.

"See that," Daniel said, with the book open on his lap. "Useful, don't you think?"

I could tell that he had immediate regret.

I spoke through the down fill that surrounded my head. The world was merely a plate of light if I happened to tilt my head up to see it. "There was nothing ecstatic about it," I said. "I flopped around. That's what they told me. But I'll give him one thing."

Daniel waited.

"The part about time."

He turned to the pages he had marked and read out loud. "'At that moment the extraordinary saying that *there shall be time no longer* becomes, somehow, comprehensible to me.'"

Time was intrinsically connected to my body. Time as I had known it had simply closed up shop, vanished. While my peers guffawed at what they called my fish routine, I could say that I had, in some sense, contained many years in that position.

I heard the dry pepperiness of Daniel's breathing as he waited for me to say something. I thought, Death will come for us anyway. "Yes," I said, "that's it."

Daniel was not one to let me have the last word. "Life is long," he said, "and the heart is big."

Emmitt, another professor—a specialist in religious iconography— became Daniel's partner. He was active in politics, and took Daniel to a pride rally one year, but Daniel preferred the subtle. He dealt in secrets and close hands and codes, which is perhaps where I get it from. Their acquaintances would begin to die, one by one, three in one year, but whatever pain Daniel experienced, he seemed to me more contented than I remembered him being when I was very small. He had lost his wife to cancer, his daughter to a house fire, and friends to a plague, and yet a peacefulness had settled around him because he was giving expression, at last, to a reality that had been present all along. Emmitt was the one who pointed out to me that my secretiveness about my seizures was analogous to being closeted. It didn't change my mind, however. Peacefulness, I felt, was not a logical outcome of exposure.

Chloe Comes to Stay

I was not, for instance, allowed to leave the apartment in the middle of the night and wander the city, no matter that I had done the equivalent up north, before the fire. I was expected to go to school *daily*, and, finally, to bathe. These were not so much Daniel's rules—he would have been content to see me range where I liked (he was, after all, my mother's father)—but came from the murmurings of his friends and the school. They were, they said, merely stating the obvious. Between Daniel and I, however, the arrangement was one of compatible roommates. If I'd blown pot smoke out the window while holding a snifter of brandy and a Twinkie, he wouldn't have said much, except that I might want to sweep up the crumbs before the mice got them. In fact, he worried about the intensity of my practice, the creative singlemindedness that settled in by age fifteen, and wondered aloud about the state of my feet, my bloody toes, that my hips ached and was I perhaps too thin?

Emmitt was an attentive cook, and on the days that he stayed with us, he would walk in clutching groceries for feasts inspired by his visits to Italy and France. But I campaigned, always, for the bloodiest cuts of meat and picked at the vegetables. Once, I had a full seizure shortly after dinner—I remember gnocchi and the licorice scent of fresh basil—and opened my eyes to see their faces above me, Daniel's hair utterly white and Emmitt's utterly gone, his entire head shiny and unwrinkled, almost one hundred and thirty years between them. I felt Daniel's hands as he gently tucked a cushion under my head. I'm alleged to have said from my position on the floor, "I would like to film you."

I did film them, as well as the dancers at the studio, and whatever friends I could cajole. I began recording voices and ambient sounds, leaving small microphones and tape recorders out in the open because I discovered that people didn't notice them or forgot about them if they did. All of this with the idea that the small choreography I had begun to develop would incorporate voices as a kind of music. The visuals I could project onto the walls and furniture, even the figures themselves. I could generate atmospheric conditions in which to place the body or bodies. I could create a context in which the tendencies of my brain, the flicks and morphs and time lapses, could be played with as a kind of public secret. Right under their noses.

My favourite dancer was not a dancer at all, but Chloe from my algebra class. She had a massive head of hair, the chaos of which was interesting to me in light of the pulled-back hair required at the studio, and unusual flexibility for someone who didn't work at it. Also a willingness to do what I asked. She didn't tire of my demands, or even question the process as we worked through sequences in the apartment when Daniel wasn't there. The confines of the space simply created a challenge, one that caused me to see the possibilities in a small gesture, or a violent one, in a chair or a table. How they contain or confine.

We worked together this way for months, until her mother found out that Chloe had begun to wear nothing but a pair of white cotton underwear during our sessions. It was important to see the lines, the shapes, to get a sense of her body, someone who wasn't me, I told Daniel and Emmitt. They looked at each other over the tops of their reading glasses, then looked at me, then each other again. It was the end of filming Chloe, but we covertly continued to see each other. I worked out choreography on her that didn't require specific expertise, utilizing instead her natural insouciance. I exaggerated her slouches, lunges, the lazy drape of her posture, hand gestures, pouts, how she could fold herself. Had she been practicing from the age of six or seven, she would have had real skill, but what she did possess was something raw and nervy.

Others could see it, too. I saw her unexpectedly at the deli down the block. I watched her from a window seat as she walked in with her mother. While her mother ordered, Chloe stripped the outer chocolate layer from a candy bar with her teeth. A paunchy man beside me, midforties maybe, made his eyes small and regarded her with an intensity that rivalled mine, and about which, she later told me, she was entirely aware. She wore our school uniform, rolled at the waist to make the skirt shorter, the white blouse, mostly untucked, with wrinkles and a vague stain on the back. Her necktie loosened to midchest. Knee-highs and forbidden black combat boots. The man simmered in the no-escape of his personal lobster pot. I wanted my video camera badly, but the scene broke apart, as every scene does. Chloe winked when she spotted me as she and her mother were leaving. The simmering man took the wink to be for him. I watched for the next fifteen minutes as he sat, slit-eyed, in the inertia of a supine shark, paralyzed by it all.

Three Pounds

For a time, medications helped and then they didn't. They were the source, depending, of agitation or heaviness that interfered with my body. Through my reading I became a connoisseur of the ancient methods and approved of their lushness and violence: crocodile feces, seal genitals, the blood of a gladiator who has just been stabbed. I came up with a tamer voodoo of my own, which involved sleeping as much as possible or, as I got older, avoiding alcohol, but the quiet periods never last, as quiet periods never do.

In my twenties I visited Daniel on the weekends and drew the brain in my college notebooks; I shaded the amygdala in mauve, the primitive pons in orange, the corpus callosum in blue, all of which had a tendency to flatten and simplify the territories. The brain is all about the curvature and the fold—its complications.

"The brain feels like jelly," the neurologist told me as I sat in his office. He was a broad man, six and a half feet tall, and yet he had an airiness, a dryness, as if he were a stuffed creature, full of old straw or cotton. Something that could catch fire. I imagined brain tissue sagging between his large absorbent fingertips. I wondered how he could operate with those hands. He told me the incisions were often small, but I pictured him opening the skulls of his patients as he kept them conscious, making them lidless. There was no greater discrepancy, I thought, between the territory and the map than the brain and its diagrams, the pastel regions never revealing the mutinous nature of neurons. The drawings of Santiago Ramón y Cajal were the exception, however, and I had sometimes wept over their beauty, the intricacies and stains and branching networks. They reflected what I knew to be true but could not observe myself when I went to museums to see preserved brains in large jars. The secretly roiling selves were not there at all.

"Eighty-six billion neurons," he said, "and yet it weighs just three pounds. Three pounds that take twenty percent of your blood supply." He turned a plastic, unjellylike brain in his hand as a tiny snot swung in his cavernous nostril. I ground one of my thumbs into my thigh to short-circuit the anxiety in my chest. I watched the enormous curve of his left ear. He wanted, I felt, to beguile me with facts so that I wouldn't cry in his office about the rogue brain I had somehow ended up with. But I hadn't cried in many years and wasn't about to start, so I concentrated on the oscillating mucus.

"I don't think anyone knows much at all about the brain," I said. He allowed the moment to pass unacknowledged. I think he knew by the folded arms that I would refuse his treatments. I went home and drew another brain on a fresh page of my notebook, a diagram that did not have the ferocious delicacy of a Cajal drawing but did have regions of neon pink and yellow. I could make it glow as if irradiated.

I went to meetings in a church basement where I could hold a paper cup of warm lemonade in the presence of my secret tribe. I was there only to please Daniel, however, because he felt I needed something like comrades. The truth was that I didn't feel the meetings or the lemonade got to the crux of the issue. On the other hand, a man I liked stood with his hands jammed down his front pockets, leaning against one of the pillars. Three rows of chairs separated us. His hair was sparse on top, though we were both twenty-five, and this interested me, the merging of young and old. Eventually he met my gaze and smiled. He moved closer to me, casually touching the chair backs one by one in a way that was suggestively tactile. When he got within a few inches of me, he cleared his throat. "Temporal lobe, huh?" It was as simple as that.

• • •

His bed had crumbs and some lint so blue that I thought of keeping it. None of my previous lovers had had seizures or rounded bellies; they tended to be dancers, smooth along the arms and legs, gristly along the spine, and self-conscious, which is not to say shy but, rather, inclined to performance. He lolled naked and soft and half asleep on the covers. My left nipple ached because he had clumsily bitten it while grazing my skin, and I examined it, compared the deepening pink to my toes, which were furious from an all-day practice before the meeting. I left speckles of blood on his sheets.

I wondered what it would be like if two people had seizures at the same moment, if another dimension would open, or two. But he had never had the tonic-clonic experience. His began with an auditory cue that was renowned in the support group for its strangeness and had been plucked from his childhood when his mother had yelled at him for running along the sidewalk. Somehow his mother's words, her exact voice, had set up housekeeping in his temporal lobe. Each and every one of his seizures began with, "Jimmy, slow down or you'll bust your face open," before he would stare and smack his lips.

He began to snore, and the curtains ruffled and someone hollered for Diane out on East Fourth Street. I studied his face, watching him without affection, wanting only to be drawn into his brain and dispersed into the network of pulsations, clean and electrical. My skin tingled as I leaned toward his head, close enough that my hair fell onto his pillow. I whispered, "Jimmy, slow down or you'll bust your face open."

His face was a cow's face and gave away nothing. His eyelids continued their tiny beats, and his lips seemed a bit helpless as he snored, nothing else.

By the time we were eating cornflakes in his kitchenette the next morning, I was oppressed by guilt. The walls and cabinets were a dull green, even the chairs and tabletop. Forest on khaki on shamrock on sea green. Somehow I had failed to notice it when we had walked in. Milk dropped from his chin, and he snorted as he told me the old joke about the two cannibals eating a clown: "Does this taste funny to you?"

I heard myself say in a raspy voice how much I liked him, perhaps too much, etc. How could I put it? Yes, too much. His face looked just as it did when I had whispered to him, and it was my first introduction to this particular facet of my expectations, that I could look at a face in twilight and then in the morning, hoping to find transformation, see that the face was the same, and that I was the one who was different.

4

Sabine Said

"Did he ever tell you the story? The one about Josefina? She looked after us. She had a psych degree. She liked dreams a lot, the meaning of them. She would ask us about our dreams, and how many people do that?

"Nobody wants to hear what you dreamed last night. And, you know—that sucks, man. We enter this fucking bizarre state, and we think it's real. I mean, we fly or whatever and it's real, or someone is trying to kill us and that's real. But nobody is interested, they just glaze over. But Josefina did care, and then she'd say what the symbolism was. Some of it she got from reading Freud and Jung, and some I think she just invented, but she said some pretty good shit.

"I was maybe eight and had this little purse—I wasn't a girly-girl, and no pink, but I had a purse—I think she must have given it to me, actually, because she was tired of carrying my shit around—and it was purple with an appliqué flower on it, and I loved it. I had a series of dreams that I lost the purse, though, and after the third or fourth one, she stopped saying that it was an anxiety dream and she started talking about consciousness and identity. She said maybe I was willing to see past things and into beingness. I was eight, so I had no fucking idea what she was on about. I'm still not entirely sure. I think she ended up becoming a Buddhist.

"She made up for a lot, you know? Mom and Dad were always in absentia, flying somewhere, working, whatever. They took us on vacations a bunch of times—Bermuda, Barbados, Mexico—but otherwise they were out in the ether somewhere. Mom was a teeny bit batshit crazy at that point—she would wash her hands until they bled. But she was an expert at looking like she didn't have a care. Or mind what Dad was up to. I don't know if he had affairs then or not, but he once got a full set of capped teeth when he was on a trip to Paris. No joke. He left one day with a missing tooth that he said happened because he fell and chipped it—which, who knows?—and came home with this bizarre white smile. You could've read by it. He wore Hermès cologne every day of his life. At least the ones I was there to witness. He called Mom *Bets*—I don't know why; not her name—but they loved each other a lot, which is saying something. That's what everyone says, anyway. How in love they were. Somewhat indifferent to us, right, but they really dug each other.

"Anyway, Josefina. Best mother in the world, even if she wasn't really ours. She had breasts like a cliff. She was short, too, so she was all boobs. She sang songs all the time. She'd crank the radio in her room. We'd be crammed in there with her, listening to her little plastic turquoise radio. It was the best room in the house.

"Did he ever tell you about the stroller incident? When he was a baby, she'd stroll him around Lenox Hill every day, regardless, in this big-ass pram. It was family legend. I've seen pictures of it. He was five before I came along. It was like a navy-blue metal boat, except that it had huge white-trimmed wheels. So one day she's pushing him along the street going toward Central Park and it's the end of March and rain was coming down with lots of wind and—wham! This car jumps the curb, hits the pram and it crumples right up, Seth inside it. People are screaming and running over, and Josefina, she's screaming and crying and trying to dig him out of this scrap heap. She said the pram reminded her of a fortune cookie, the way it was closed up. But there's a space where she can reach in and she manages to get him out and she's holding him and she's hysterical and then she realizes that he doesn't have a scratch on him. Nothing. He's just looking at her as if to say, *What the fuck just happened?* He didn't even cry.

"Anyway, that was why she called him *Suerte* instead of Seth. She always said that he must have been born when Jupiter was big and fat. And I think some part of him believes it, which is why he's such a nihilist. I think he imagines he's sort of invincible. And can never be satisfied. He survived something, and he wonders why. We both have the drinking gene, or the drinking habit, anyway. But I can stop and he can't. He's almost old-fashioned, you know? He does Vicodin the odd time, I think, or coke or whatever a friend might be doing, but he's largely just a drunk. An old-school drunk. And a bartender, at that. How do you stop drinking when that's your job? And he's good at it. He and some business partners had a bar of their own, until they edged him out. On account of him being unreliable. But he's so functional, right? Runs ten miles, kayaks, climbs, skis, all the shit that he lives for, except that—and here's the paradox—he's drinking while doing that shit, and how he can do that, I don't know. The people he's with—I don't know if they know. They must. But I think when he's out there, he's just drinking less and then he gets back to the city, and it starts all over again. And so you think, if you're a sensible person, why not move out of the city and stay where the forests and mountains and rivers are? Why go back and forth, why be so split between the two?

"When the partners kicked him out, it devastated him—that place was his idea. He named it, he talked up the crowds every night, and he was serious about his mixology. It was like science experiments to him, or an art. He told me once—we were at his place and he was making me his spin on a manhattan, and he'd made his own bitters, and I think these ones were chocolate—and anyway, he told me that making this simple thing, just a few ingredients in a glass, and having somebody drink it was like they were drinking him. I told him that sounded like he was Christ or something, but the truth is, I could sort of see what he meant. He said that people ended up ingesting—this is him talking—something that was meant to evoke a place or a time or a sensation or whatever. He said the idea had to have a kind of purity. Which sounds like bullshit, but anyway. At the bar, he had little burners set up so he could make syrups with herbs or whatever, and he infused vodkas and gin, too. He also kept a lot of bourbons—some of them were a thousand bucks for a bottle, and people actually paid to drink them. He's got charisma, and maybe even more so when he's drinking, and he was slinging drinks, schmoozing, and inventing concoctions that people would line up for, and somehow he was still . . . he was fucking up in slow motion. The purity he was talking about, well, it was like he was infested with something. With whatever makes him drink.

"I was staying at his place one night, and in the morning I sat on his bed to talk with him. I was telling him, actually, about Ellena, because we'd started to see each other, and he's sitting there, listening—first thing, right? Hasn't gotten out of bed to so much as pee, but I had brought him a cup of coffee, and he reaches over to the bourbon, which is cheap by the way, right beside his bed, and he pours some—a lot—into the coffee and it's, I don't know, not even seven in the morning. He wasn't trying to hide it, or maybe it was just automatic. And I'm a coward, so I didn't say a fucking thing. Not one thing. I didn't blink, I don't think. I just kept talking. Ellena Ellena Ellena. Cover it up. Don't notice a thing, or give the appearance not to, anyway. I do believe that makes me an enabler. And you know what? I think on some level I wanted him, or Ellena, or whoever, to enable me, so I didn't want to get in his face about it. Which is all very convenient when you think about it. Sort of quid pro quo."

Molly

When it's warmer out, there are people in the park who lie down. They sprawl at equal distances, and sleep so deeply that their weight can be felt with the eyes. A person lying on the ground to get some sun often does so with legs straight; a book may be open on the ground, but the person isn't reading. Someone lying on the ground because there's no other place to sleep will usually do so on their side or flat on their back with one leg bent out to the side, in the manner of a corpse.

This park sits over the remains of twenty thousand people, though there isn't a sign. Nothing that says that at one time this was a potter's field, a burial ground. Poor people and slaves were buried here, and those who had succumbed to an epidemic of yellow fever. It is a sacred place, but the pigeons fly into the sycamores and preen along the dark branches, saying nothing. The city vibrates so intensely with the totality of its souls that you can be in the park, right over the bodies and not know their presence at all. But the bones are stacked and jumbled, the skulls like chalices now filled with the soil that was poured over them. All the cloth eaten away, all the flesh transformed.

The sycamores and London plane trees have mottled bark, maps for regions that are hard to know or attain. Regions appear to shed other regions, other skins, other realities. The dogwoods hold out their branches almost quizzically, as if posing a question, or giving up.

Luna

That tree is a honey locust. One of the most common trees in this place. They used to have thorns, for protection, I imagine, which is a good idea, but nearly all the ones now are a thornless variety. *Forma inermis*. You open the seed pods and find sweet stuff inside, hence the name. But I don't personally care for it, so I suggest avoiding. People don't notice trees much here, even though there's five million of them. Well, you get the folks who do some looking after, and the ones who form protest groups when an old one is going to be cut down, but in general, I mean, they can vanish. That one is a silver linden. *Tilia tomentosa*. They provide good shade, which is not inconsequential. Temperature can be one hundred degrees, and all that cement and metal warming up creates ambient heat. I arrived here when it was just beginning to warm, so I had sort of a head start. You get acclimated to your ideas.

There's a liminal period when you decide to leave everything and pick up in a new place. You have to decide what to bring with you. Symbolic things, too, like a name. People hiking the Appalachian Trail, they pick a trail name, or it's supposed to be given to them, and they write it in a book. The name is a different version of yourself, maybe truer or not. Think of all the immigrants who would have a new name when they got here, maybe something supposedly easier for other people to say. But in this case it's not about other people's refusal to wrap their tongues around your foreignness. You become foreign to yourself, maybe, and so you find another sound, a new name to call yourself, which is easier for you to say.

I had a notebook, which I always hid. I wrote in code, but I'd still have to explain its existence. Maybe it took me five years to get up the courage to leave, once I got the idea. The problem with *things*, though, is that you get attached, much the same as people, and there's a moment where you stand at your door for the last time. You look at all the symbols in the box called your house. Maybe some people bolt out the door so they don't have to look back, but I looked. Your name stays in the house, too. If you leave right, you don't hear it again. But sometimes I do hear my old name, because it was common, and I get a jolt.

I picked the new name Luna, because she was a moon goddess— of Roman origin; also Artemis, in the Greek—when they had such a thing. The moon disappears in parts, and sometimes the whole is gone. I suppose you can find comfort in a lack of substance, but it depends on who you are. I got to talking with a person recently about the limbo after death. She said, "Do you think there's a bardo?" and I didn't say anything, so she asked me again. Then she asked me a third time, "Do you think there's a bardo, Luna?" and the third time is what does it.

"We're in it," I said, and she looked at me, gobsmacked. Then she ran her fingers over her arm and said, "You made my hair stand up." And I nodded and said, "That's good. You still have some of your faculties."

•   •   •

I did bring my watch, which does have heft, though you could argue that time doesn't. The tall, thin man who turned out to be my husband also turned out to have an invention or two up his sleeve. He came up with a better snow shovel—which is interesting because it barely snowed where we lived. He said he got the idea in a dream on a hot night, which was the beginning of being what they call well-off. He sold the patent for a lot of money, and he stopped by a jeweler on the way home to buy me a watch, an expensive one. He didn't understand my wrist size, but I never had the watch fixed, because I liked it swinging around. Liked it so much that I brought it with me. You can't have a nice thing for a minute here, but no one has stolen it from me because everyone assumes it's a knockoff. A man two blocks over sells them.

In Heidegger, guilt shows up in different forms. I wrote that down, too. I have a notebook that I keep in a pocket. They aren't hard to find, as there are a lot of unfinished notebooks in the world. When I fill one I pick a spot, a subway stop maybe, and leave it there. Lincoln Center, Kew Gardens, Ditmas, Kings, Castle Hill. Even Rockaway. But mostly in Midtown, and sometimes on a bench, or sometimes I actually bury them. Or take out a few pages at a time and distribute them. I've left them at the libraries, too, and sometimes I do research and get photocopies and sometimes there's a person who helps me. The library is a second home, though I don't have a first home anymore, unless it's possible to reside in places you don't understand, which I contend it is.

•   •   •

I hadn't been to this city before, but you can know a place before you get there. Maybe we have collective knowledge, and you know what you're supposed to do, even if they say you shouldn't be doing it. Not everything has a cause and effect that you can see.

The city has vastness, which I call a baroque emptiness—which is not the same as nothing. The most acute form of ownership, I think, is when you've lost all the things. If you can see the emptiness, then the place is yours in a way it won't be for other people. You can see what they don't and possess knowledge that isn't expected.

That tree by the red fence is what many consider to be a weed tree, a royal paulownia. They say it's invasive. Legend goes that the seeds were used to pack shipments coming from China and that they fell along the railroad tracks in this country and began to spread. This is how a story unfolds, or that's the inference, anyway. You land here or you land there, and really it's your own business if the roots form or not.

The Twins

When Stella thought of the missing man, she wondered what he looked like. If she should ask her mother for a picture. Or if she might find one in Molly's study, and so, while their parents were out, Augustin kept watch at the door and Stella stood in the middle of the floor, looking around. She and Augustin both knew better than to waltz in unannounced, and so they always rapped softly on the door if they wanted to say something, lurked on the fringes as if the room was cordoned off from their use, which it was. They understood the unspoken qualities of territory, this one in particular, the violation of which was unexpectedly thrilling. Stella stood up taller. Somewhere in there, she could feel it, was a remnant to do with the missing man: a photo, a name, an article clipped out, a file even.

She looked at the photographs on the walls, the framed ones of the various dance groups and productions over the years, examining the men's faces. She tried to imagine each one vanishing, leaving holes in the visual arrangement. She went to Molly's desk, opened drawers and rooted around. She ran her fingertips underneath the top, because that was what the spies in movies did, and then selected a few books that she shook in case something fell out. But nothing. She studied the masks on the wall, before deciding to lie down on the floor to see if that vantage gave her the answer. But she quickly jumped up.

"Gus!" she whispered. "Are they coming?"

"Nope," he said.

She went to the desk again and sat in Molly's swivel chair, spun it gently. When she came around to face the papers stacked up there, she decided to hunt through them. She sighed, folded her arms, and leaned back in the chair, putting her knees against the desk—which jarred it slightly, waking Molly's computer. The black screen vanished and was replaced by the face of a man.

"What is it?" said Augustin. "Why'd you gasp?" He stopped, and they both peered at the face. "Who the heck is that?"

Stella shrugged. She had never seen any face quite like it, because the one staring out had reddened skin, eyebrows and beard fringed in ice crystals, and the eyes were widened, as if in fright; the mouth was open slightly, though Stella could tell that it wasn't making any sound. Only the rasping of breath. The man's hood had been pulled back and his goggles pushed up on his forehead. His knitted hat was off to one side, ready to fall. She couldn't tell where the man was, but the place appeared to be very cold and windy. A clump of his hair went off in a strange direction.

"I like him," she said suddenly, and Augustin looked at her. He wanted to agree with her, because their likes and dislikes were often entwined, germinal, but Stella was sometimes fast to love in a way that mystified him. He narrowed his eyes at the man, but the man stayed the same, frozen in a fathomless existential crisis on his mother's computer. "I don't get it," he said. "Is he skiing? Is he lost? Is he on a mountain? Why does she have this—who is this guy?"

Stella touched his arm to stop his questions. She watched the face, and the familiar aspects gathering there, how the man seemed to know he was already gone—the exact dark shade in the expression she had been expecting to find, a telltale thing. She didn't say anything for a moment. The concept forming before her was too unwieldy and strange to speak aloud, so she kept it only in her mind, hoping that her brother would know. The thought was along the lines of, *He is us*.

Molly

You thought, I imagine, that you had miscalculated.

I have wondered if you encountered a bear with her cubs partially hidden by tall grasses as you crested a hill, or a mountain lion slithered up behind you, hugged you with teeth and claws. I have shut my eyes against the fur and felt my own body folded in. But the human brain can't configure the devouring, which we thought was ours to do.

I imagine another version of you; that you deliberately settled into a wild place, tucked yourself into your tent and sleeping bag like a good explorer, swallowed some pills and waited to be overtaken by a cold that no amount of gear could assuage. Perhaps you wrote in a notebook, intending to write some kind of message, or snapped a few photographs of the light coming through the nylon over your head, or intended to do those things but then decided, no, there is nothing to be done. The lists are nothing now. The stacked imperatives, the collated desires. The small wiggles and symbols representing such. All of them ideas, all of them air.

The world is full of messages now, they pelt our skins.

The Struggle to Breathe

Stella's face appears on the screen, and she pushes her face forward in the attitude of a kiss, draws back, and says, "You won't believe it!" She claps her hands once and begins to tell me something that starts with "Augustin—!" when he comes up behind her and clamps his hand over her mouth. She is half laughing, half struggling to breathe.

"She's got nothing to tell you except that she's a pain in the butt!"

Stella shrieks, "Yes!" through his fingers. "I do!"

Stella

Stella imagined the missing man to be in a place of lost things and people. He could be anywhere in there, though whether she thought it was wild or urban, she couldn't decide. She remembered when her mother had created a piece around the poems of Elizabeth Bishop, called *The Intent to Be Lost*. The people onstage moved in a world that was entirely their own and unreachable. Perhaps the man had placed himself inside a city no one else could see. He walked around in it not knowing who he was. Maybe he chatted with the other missing people and they remarked on their curious circumstances, or they wept with wanting to be home. She herself would want to be where her parents and brother were.

She had been lost once, when she had taken too long to follow her parents and Augustin off the subway car. She had been looking at the feet of passengers, as her mother often did, and when she looked up, the doors were gliding shut with uncharacteristic smoothness. Through the fingerprinted windows she saw her family swallowed by the crowd because they hadn't noticed yet that she was still on the train. She felt her stomach drop as the subway jolted and they were on their way. She glimpsed, just before the train disappeared into the tunnel, the face of her mother. It was registering both surprise and—could it be?—amusement. The space outside the train window turned black and reflective, and the sound of the wheels on the track filled her ears. She hadn't been so aware of being in a tunnel before, though she had been in this exact one many times. How the world was held overhead and how badly she wanted to be out in it with her family. A ghost version of her, a doppelganger, had peeled off from her body, was moving up onto the street in the way the rest of her was supposed to be doing.

She felt the hand of an older man tap her shoulder. He smiled down at her and asked if those were her parents who had just gone through the doors, and what could she do, she finally decided, but admit to him it was.

"I'll get you back to them," he said. "Don't worry."

She clung to the steel pole and watched the man carefully, the unsettling neatness of his fingers, which were nothing like the stained hands of her father. He peppered her with questions, before he said, "Oh, I'm sorry. I'm enquiring about too many things."

The train rocked, made the known world tilt. "We'll figure out what to do. We can go to the ticket agent at the next stop or I can put you on the train going back. Which do you think would be better? Maybe your parents are waiting for you on the platform . . ."

Stella continued to watch, saying nothing. The train rattled on, and the next station seemed like it was never going to come, and she would be endlessly inside the metal box, inside the tunnel, watching this man and feeling the sway of the car. Suddenly, light filled the windows, and when the train arrived and the doors opened, there was the station platform. On the other side was a waiting train in the opposite direction, though she couldn't know if it was the right one, if it would stop where her parents were possibly standing, waiting for her.

She bolted through the doors when they opened, shot across the platform banging into various people and going through the open doorway of the new train, the one that she hoped would take her back. She could hear the man calling to her, and the doors slid shut again, but this time they seemed like something vulnerable. She wanted the train to hurry up and move. She looked up and saw various passengers looking back at her. She sat down in an empty seat and put her hands under her thighs and tried to look like she knew what she was doing, and moreover that she belonged to someone. She scowled at the faces around her as if by doing so she could prevent the questions that were forming, the offers of help.

Leave me alone, she would say if they asked her. *I know what I'm doing*.

Though this didn't seem true, and they surely knew it. If the train went into the tunnel again and kept going, she would need one of them to help her, possibly the middle-aged woman who was sitting opposite, in a blue suit with a briefcase between her ankles.

But the train did halt, and the doors slid open, releasing Stella onto the platform where she saw her mother and Augustin waiting, though her father was missing. She ran a few steps and then stopped abruptly, because her mother and Augustin didn't seem worried at all, only amused and happy to see her, as if she were a visiting relative and *Hey, it's been a while!*

Fury boiled up in her as her arms hung straight at her sides and she balled her hands into fists. She held her place on the platform and watched them advance, how they were smiling with relief, and possibly even laughing at her. "Are you serious?" she shrieked, as she felt her mother embrace her, and she whacked her fists on Molly's sides.

Molly laughed, "You're fine, you see that? Just fine." But Stella was beginning to sob, which caused Augustin's own bottom lip to tremble, in the utter confusion of this reunion. Molly hugged both of them to her hips. Stella heard her whisper part of Bishop's poem, the one about losing two cities, two rivers. "These things, you know, Stella, they happen."

The Documentary

The girl has met a grisly end, the sister knows. They had had their bicycles midway on a long road, one with grasses and in the distance the draped, almost hooded form of a willow. The slow approach of the car, the muffled music that was abruptly cut and the window rolled down. *Hey, girls.* His arm moving then to the metal of the door, which was hot from the sun and caused him to recoil—the momentary rage as fast and gone as a snake's tongue. His smile again, *Hey, girls. Whatcha doing?* The neatness of his hair, combed carefully over, but a crowded arrangement of teeth. Blunt fingertips that did a strange little wave at them, the slow blades of a propeller. The girls stood holding their handlebars, their torsos pointed forward in the direction they wanted to go, on the gravel road where they had stopped to walk their bikes on account of a deflating tire. Their heads turned in the direction of the man. A rosary dangled from the rearview mirror, though it was partially obscured by the sky reflected in the windshield. A head of some kind jiggled on the dash, the car creeping forward until the man's face, his body, was closer to them. *Hey.*

When the sister is older she will wonder at this, how easily their plans in 1982—the forward movement along the dirt road—had been disrupted, simply because this man decided it. *Time's up, here's your ride.* The younger girl wordlessly, inexplicably, absorbed into the car as if she were liquid being drawn through a straw. But they had been trained to obey. Adults were not to be trusted, but they also held belts, loosely, lazily, so that the tip rested almost sensually on the floor, or a bit of wood, casually, as they spoke. *Hey. Get in.* The set of the teeth was somehow the same, the tight jaw, the spare order. She watched her sister, as if hypnotized, rest her bike on the ground and then stand with her arms at her sides. Again, *Get in*, this time uttered so near the parental tone that it did the trick. It removed particles of her sister right where she was, the girl was already gone.

People would say to the older sister, later on, when they thought it was safe to, *Why didn't you do something? How could you just stand there?* As if their questions made sense, as if the girls had agreed somehow to a fate other than the road they were on, and she to relinquish her sister. She noted the occurrence of the present tense, *stand*. She was still there, on the side of the road. The parents, too. They bought presents for the missing girl on each of her birthdays, and at Christmas. They left them in the original packaging, arranged around the carefully made-up bed in the room whose posters and books and records remained in their places, waiting, because, the mother said, *You don't know. She could be a good girl and come home.*

Molly

She looks so much like my mother. The woman glances over at me, at the dozen people who hunch, kneel, stand, block, are posed at various levels. I couldn't have arranged them better, if we're speaking from the viewpoint of aesthetics. The view from the ground is less appealing, with nostrils and double chins and the way that skin will pouch a little when a face points downward. But the faces are a comfort.

The woman takes in the sight of me and my grimace, and she turns her head again to look ahead. She keeps on striding, her legs as firm and straight as a fascist's. Knee-high boots in deep brown. And somehow, at the top end of that body I have put my mother's face, attaching it with my own sutures; nothing in the rest of this woman resembles her. Only this face, a mask, which in spite of its coolness and determination to look ahead, has uncannily the profile of my mother. A softness around the eyes, a prominent nose, a bone structure that will still be noble if the face lives to be eighty. My mother, walking by, seeing me, not seeing me.

The Cell Containing My Mother

Just her voice. I couldn't see her. I stood on a subway platform, waiting while it was hot and a pigeon that was lost underground flapped erratically into the tunnel, drunk on its fear, and there was her voice. I can't tell when she will show up.

Flashbulbs

Her migraines came in a way that was not unlike my seizures. This was my prototype. The weather affected her, certain foods, or a mysterious presence made her turn inward, away from the light that stung. Curtains were drawn, and the room took on the quality of a cave and the walls turned damp. I could stand in the doorway and feel her breathing as if the room itself were alive. Her body curled on the bed with her back to me, her hair over the pillow, the nodes of her spine visible if it was summer and she was wearing a halter top or a bathing suit. I would lie down with her when she allowed it, press myself along her back, but often she refused me, saying I was hurting her. Just the presence of me was another kind of knife, my voice, even if soft, was a biting thing. She flapped her hand behind her, waving me away in the darkened room. No choice but retreat.

My father retreated also. He is a phantom, slides through far-off doorways and windows almost ghoulishly. He vanishes. I call to him, but it doesn't make him properly live. The glimpse of him is like a scarf in a breeze, dark blue perhaps because of a shirt he once wore, or the veins of his arm where there was scarring along the crook, the marks of whatever drug could be shot through a needle. He had stopped using, however. They were a remnant of something gone, though he continued to smoke and drink.

My parents were believers in a certain directness, one that could obscure the things they did want to hide, and so my father spoke to me plainly, when I was just five or six, about what the marks were. They meant nothing to me, which was part of the point. He spoke to me as if I were an adult and could comprehend that kind of desire, but it was just another cloak.

The two of us sat on the front steps of the house on a cold day as he told me about that rapacious want and the head of a needle, and it was meaningless. The only treasure was the jewel aspect of the scars, their compact opalescence. I couldn't decide which they were: ugly or beautiful. When I was older it seemed to me that both could be true. It seemed to my childhood self to have something to do with an adult in the throes of telling one truth while hiding another. He was done, he said.

Ignition Switch

He stood in the night with a bottle that once contained gin and now contained lighter fluid, and a rag hung from the mouth. He didn't hold matches or a lighter, however, and had nothing in his other hand but the cold air of spring at night. I was the one lurking, vanishing, hiding in various places while watching him, moving quickly from one stack of boxes to another. I listened to his breathing, which was noisy, and I watched his back, his shadowy form in the dark with the light that was coming in from the full moon. The full moon, which my mother always took to be trouble, and the cause of whatever wildness, good or bad, that was moving through. The full moon was responsible for crime, for lovers' breakups, for bad decisions, or for lottery wins. She would have been one of the people, centuries before, convinced that the epileptic was affected by the moon. Maybe I had angered its goddess. Either way, when I told her what I had witnessed, her words played on the dream: *Could have been anything. Something strange in the moonlight.* Neither of us could pin down or define.

He is mostly gone, though this one part of him remains to the exclusion of the others. I have not understood this murkiness at all, where its edges are, where it begins. How he came to find himself in the living room this way. The grandfather clock says it is 1:17 in the morning. My feet are bare, digging in. I am the watcher for something that doesn't want one. The simmering inside him hasn't made him more electric or alive but instead obscures him. Erasure moves over him like a cloud of bees, and I watch as it eats him. The consuming form has an undulation of delight.

The Temporal Lobe Is a Witchy Thing

The seizures take memories and tear them up. Flick the pieces into a light that scorches. Déjà vu comes on, the assertion that I've created these dance moves before; I've met this person before; I've seen the ocean exactly this way from the ferry, with a man in a striped hat to my right and a tantruming child to my left.

Exactly that way, I've been here before, I know that I have. But I have not. Which is just one kind of knowingness followed by another. Lost in the dream, awakened, lost again. I have known that dripping tap, the drawing that Stella brings to me, Raf standing naked with a half erection near the end of the bed with an unlit cigar stub between his teeth, smacking the magazine he's holding up and laughing so hard at what someone wrote about his work that he can barely tell me the story.

I've seen this before.

I've done this before.

This is all exactly so.

I have seizures, and sometimes the seizures have me. They have me in the waiting, in the in-between, which is a distilling of life in general: we wait for death, not knowing the exact moment, only the inevitability of something we don't, at present, believe in. So we wait, and the waiting is resplendent, almost grand, in the way of cathedrals and views from mountaintops, because it is not only waiting, but a drama. Waiting is expansive and becomes, at some point and inexorably, the thing you're waiting for. Possession.

• • •

In the ancient writings about falling down, not much distinction is made between seizures and similar events induced by hysteria. The lines blur. The seizure was a result of spiting the moon goddess or wading into someone else's dark magic. It was assuaged by gulping the blood of a gladiator, or nibbling the gladiator's liver nine times, or the use (mysterious) of seal genitals, or hippopotamus testes or the blood of a sea tortoise, or by avoiding the following: onions, quail, red mullet, eel, goat, deer, and pig. An amulet containing coral, peony, and the root of Strychnos might be worn around the neck as the moon grew smaller. If you were not the one with epilepsy but the observer to the seizure and concerned about it leaping from the victim to you, then you would spit.

This is no small thing, the spitting. The custom of which becomes the burnishing of otherness, a shorthand for fear, disgust, abhorrence. Rejection, formed in the mouth, let go.

I have a theory, which has to do with faces, how we trust them or don't, love them or hate them. So much resides not only in the eyes, but the type of nose, the position of the lips, number of wrinkles, the teeth. The face of the person in full embrace of a seizure is a face found to be so primal in its urgency, its turned-inwardness, and its remoteness that the person is set further adrift by those watching. Death, we think, is right there with that voltage. We shove them away.

"She's not stopping. Where's the fucking cop?"

"My sister-in-law had this—she'll be okay. You just have to wait for them to stop."

"Were you fucking filming her?"

"Stop swearing. She can hear you. There's a kid, too."

"Hear us? Look at her!"

"I read they can still hear."

"Just, you know. Be quiet. Quiet."

"Quiet? This is New York, man. Go upstate you want quiet."

"Ma'am? We're here. You got lots of folks around you."

"You'll be okay. Ambulance is coming. Maybe you hear that siren. Be here real quick."

"Yeah, it's coming. You hold on there. It's coming."

"Ma'am, you hold on. You be okay."

"People around."

"You hold on now."

"Her breathing—"

"Better than not at all."

"Crazy, right?"

"Of course it is."

"Just another day in New York, man."

"Just another day."

"Ma'am?"

Molly

I watched him wait. This was different from the usual sort of observance. I sometimes watched the people, for instance, outside Penn, trawling for cabs. The expectation, the boredom, the checking of watches. The burden of luggage and unwieldiness of plans. The bobbing heads of pigeons ticking off the seconds. Everything becomes a clock. A clock in your breath. I watched people waiting and wondered where they were going, how they would spread out from this spot into the city, traverse the synaptic gaps between here and there, between desire and arrival. The movement tidal, surging, epileptic. This was 1999.

I stood outside the café, early by twenty minutes, maybe because the plan was forming in my mind without a full awareness of what I was doing, about to do. My body knew, however, as it does; it brought me here. I looked at my watch. A man pushed me aside on his way into the café, glared at me. I even had my hand on the door before I understood that I wasn't going in. I was drawn backward onto the sidewalk, where I nearly toppled an old woman. "I'm sorry—so sorry!" There, you see: remorse, little flecks that can be ground out like pepper. I made sure she was fine before she walked away and was taken up again by the stream.

I took another step away from the café, and another, pulled away. Litter blew between ankles. I felt the surliness of a baby in a passing stroller, gripping the edges of its knit hat as if to corral its brain. I took in that dark as easily as air. I crossed the street, ignoring the mail truck and bicycle. Crowds and traffic can be parted with the right gaze. I saw the doorway I wanted, with interior stairs for a Greek restaurant on the second floor, one with windows that looked onto the street and the café. It also happened to have an open table with exactly the right view.

A waitress took my order. Tea and lamb kabobs. Something about the lamb seemed apt, sacrificial. I spent a few minutes lining up the flatware and finding just the right placement for the bud vase and candle with a blackened wick. I felt a silkiness in my stomach, that softly rising wave, and I thought briefly about leaving, but the promised spectacle of waiting kept me in place. I felt hot and took off my sweater, hung it on the chair back. I shook the little sugar packets to dispel the tension gathering in my hands. Somewhere, I thought, a rat wiped its snout with its paws as a subway ground to a halt and released Seth. I folded my napkin into a fan and unfolded it. Instead of checking the time, I watched the street below, people's gaits, how they moved. I filled in the dialogue for a couple who appeared to be arguing. I guessed at the occupations of a dozen or so people.

Seth appeared, stage left. He dodged a little pug with a pink frill that darted toward him before it was reeled in like a trout by its owner. He stopped at the corner and dug into his pockets for money to place in the paper cup of someone slouched against a wall. He kept walking, but when he grew close to the café he seemed to slow. He looked around. I worried for a moment that he might see me in the window, but then he went inside the café and the shapes on the sidewalk changed, closed in. Someone locked up their bicycle and strolled away. I counted a few people talking on their phones before I stopped and took up hats instead. A striped awning over the café suddenly released on one side, right as I was looking at it, swooping downward and causing a scurry of people. Two café staff came out to ponder the fabric. I began to wonder if I had somehow caused it, the intensity of my stare had loosened fasteners or caused a wind gust to rush across the street. It actually gave me a better view. Seth remained inside, and I could just discern a shape inside the window, not far from the door, that I knew to be him. The right smudge of colour for his jacket, his slouchy posture with his elbows on the counter that stretched along the windows. He turned into a kind of painting. I watched him wait.

You think of all the waiting that leaks out around us. Our waiting set to music. *Your call is important to us*. It's a state of grace, a tension that can't resolve itself. He sat there, seemingly immobilized. Presumably he checked the time, drank his coffee. Got up briefly to order a bagel. Waiting sluiced out of him as if he were a rocking cup and worsened as the minutes went by. But he had nothing to do except stay in the place, watch the door, finally grab an abandoned newspaper and begin the performance of reading it.

Time is an idea that takes shape, becomes an insect lodged in the ear. It burrows in, creates a nest, generates hatchlings that invade the brain. Dementia soon follows. The person is stricken with the urge to end the suffering, and they begin to shift their body (the body contains the waiting), stretch their legs, check the watch again, wonder. The various scenarios play out, horrible and delicious. Perhaps I'd been hit by a car—though he, too, had long ago noticed my ability to cross against traffic and live—fallen ill, fallen, or maybe I was simply not coming. The wonder entertained and rejected, but then entertained again. And another minute snapped and gone. Time ransacked and decimated, ravaged by questions, interrogated to no avail. No answer. *Your call is important to us.*

Here is where the person waiting begins to career between logical explanations and illogical ones. They try to reason with absence in the field of others, strangers who are not waiting, not explicitly at least, but are deep in conversation with the special people who have bothered to show up, not be hit by a car or kidnapped. These others seem remarkably present; no waiting for them. Time morphs in one of my episodes, which is what happens to the person waiting. The scene is a pornography of time and waiting.

When he emerged from the café he looked like he'd been in a fight. Somehow, in the space of an hour and a half—which is how long he stayed there, and how long I stayed in the upstairs window watching—waiting had detonated inside him. His hair was messier than usual, his clothes askew. He walked slowly at first, stiff. Stopped and looked up the street and down it. I thought for a moment that he might look up and see me there in the window, and then it happened. I imagined that the white-blond of my hair telegraphed easily, that even at that distance I was recognizable. Perhaps I wasn't. Perhaps he thought to himself that the shape couldn't be me; perhaps he understood absolutely that it was. Whatever the case, after a few seconds, he turned and strode out of view.

The waitress brought a second dessert for me, baklava with a hundred honeyed layers. The first had been almost too glorious a thing to eat, but I had inhaled it. I could have eaten three more. I felt, watching from that perch on the second floor, like a god. Ravenous, terrible, and drunk. I felt rage or grief or something scabbish. Triumph. I ate, drank a full glass of water, drained the rest of the tea. A child with eyes dark as plums scuttled under the tables and was yelled at by her parents. I smiled at her, and stood, leaving bills under the edge of my cup.

Then the room was inside me, instead of me inside of it. The light from the windows, now deep in my solar plexus, broke apart. I tilted back, plunged. I was squeezed and pulled at the same time, for how long I don't know. A few moments may have passed; possibly a year. I felt the cool wooden floor on my cheek, a buzz in my fingertips. Someone spoke to me. For a moment my eyes were open and seeing. Or my brain believed the scene as it presented itself. A hard curl of bread was a foot away. Beyond the pant cuffs and the buckled boots and the crouching knee lay a dark sprinkle of mouse scat along the baseboards. I couldn't stop looking at it. It was a notation, like dashes, or stitches, this reality being a thing sewn together.

How About the Man?

The one the city tucked in, though no one noticed him anyway. He was already hidden, absorbed. He moved in the way of air streams or particles of dirt or the languorous sprawl of a stain. He was the pulse from the lights, a horn blast. Molly walked—and what a walk—the cat prowl (because she was once a dancer) alternating with something cumbersome, as if she was reminded every now and again of the body's burden—far ahead of him, vanishing and appearing. She crossed Ninth, headed north, snapped her taupe scarf over her shoulder. Snowflakes, just a few. He remembered that late autumn was her favourite time, the first appearance of crystals in the city, when snow was not yet invasive. She went inside the café and he stayed against the glass, saw that her husband was already seated inside, waiting. The husband looked through large black glasses at a newspaper, sleeves rolled up, grey hair messy; he may have been handsome once. Coming up behind him, she slid her hands over his shoulders, kissed his head, and, when he stood and turned, his mouth. Smiles, another kiss. They laughed about something before a woman appeared at their side, was brought into their embrace and released. He watched the three of them settle in at a round table, warm, conspiratorial. The window had a mercurial sheen because of the hour, and printed words across it mentioned the types of coffee, staff wanted, a relief effort for a distant country. He moved back across the sidewalk through two large women, little dog, hydrant, bicycles, until the subway vent and its deep breath, where he was drawn in.

Caterpillars

She handed me the cup of tea—not the other way around, even though it was my apartment we were sitting in.

"Let me," she said. She smiled when her fingers touched mine. Two of her teeth on either side overlapped with an almost unbearable symmetry. She let a hair strand cross her cheek as she bent, before sliding it behind her ear—her ear that had a chandelier earring with red stones and higher up two large studs in the cartilage. A tattoo crept up from under her collar along her neck, the tendrils of a vine. I should have been impressed, but she had nothing on me if she wanted to talk the endurance of pain. She was lovely, though, and in fact, she was just the sort I would have pursued myself not so long ago.

I snorted and she startled. "No, no milk," I said. "Thank you."

She was a shark. I had observed something of this in the journalists who had come by over the years to interview either Raf or me. In the case of this woman, Claire, she had interviewed him and now, months later, she wanted to talk with me. She seemed hungry, her face had a naked appetite while her smile was large and unbridled, as if she had just spotted the small animal she was going to consume. I wondered if this expression was a component of their sex, if she seemed similarly voracious when she took him in her mouth. She settled down into her chair and crossed her legs.

"I'm wondering," I said. "Does he know that you're here?"

She looked down, examining her tea. Then looked up again, smiling. "No, I don't think so."

She cleared her throat and put a notebook on her lap. "I'm curious about something. Can we just jump in? Yeah? Excellent. Your work is sometimes controversial. Does it bother you how people react, or does it make you more determined?" She actually grinned, dark as a great white. The dead eye, hot as a pin.

I watched her for a moment and decided to stir some sugar into my tea, which I rarely did. "I think you're asking about something in particular."

She smiled again. "I'm thinking of *The Trial of the Body*. I didn't get to see it, though."

"No, you would have been too young." I sipped my tea. "It was a long time ago."

She watched my face.

"A couple of people threw up in the aisles," I said. "Five, if I recall correctly, who actually passed out. Ambulances came to a few of the performances. There was a small fuss in front of the theatre—maybe it was after the fourth or fifth performance. We started with empty seats, and by the end, the house was packed every day."

"It turned into one of your most popular pieces, didn't it? Iconic."

"That's the thing about the grotesque. One of the people who passed out threatened to sue, and reviewers wrote on their blogs and in the papers about what they said were my atrocities. But the atrocities weren't mine. They belong to all of us. Rape and torture and lynching and betrayal. We used a lot of rope, a lot of binding. Think of dictatorships, covert operations, what people call third world countries. Think of this one. Your own neighbours. Domestic disturbances. Torture is a common language."

"So is blood, yes? You had that, too."

"Fake, naturally, in huge quantities on a specially made, recessed floor so the dancers could literally dance in it. And it became too much for some people, though their experience is what enlivened it. That's how blood turns from a bunch of food-grade chemicals whipped up in a bucket to the essence of human life. People said they could even smell it, but that was their imaginations, of course. People were brought face-to-face with their unconsciousness in forty-eight minutes, and they revolted. Some stormed out."

I paused here and stirred my tea again. "The point is, dance can do a lot of things, *be* a lot of things. It has enormous capacity, but time is needed to develop a shared language between the dancers and the audience. It's all, in the end, a collaboration."

She nodded, sagely, the tip of her pen between her lips. She took it out and said, "You had some dancers who lived on the streets, didn't you?"

"Five of the twelve dancers came to us through an outreach program. They were all young people; one had actually been a professional dancer, for a time, but the other four were novices. The company was kind of rocked by their presence—weeks went by before we started to see the work come together. There were a lot of divisions. But I look at people's bodies, the stories they hold in their structures—it's not always necessary to know dance. I mean, generally speaking, I use professionals, but this was an opportunity to see movement in another way. Their bodies showed the toll of being relentlessly vulnerable. They had a lot of input in terms of what they would do. It was poignantly perfect in some ways."

"And what happened after that?"

I shrugged. "In the end, everyone returned to their former lives. We lost touch, as people do, and it all felt rather useless. As if the whole experience hadn't happened. Somebody asked me who I thought I was. For a while I stopped believing in the power of art, and dance especially. I had wanted to see us all transcend something. The suffering." I picked a cat hair from the arm of the chair. "So there it is. This is the nature of our existence."

"What do you mean?"

I thought for a moment. "Someone said that poetry is the closest medium to our nature, but I disagree. I think dance is the closest, oldest, most essential expression we have. It comes before spoken language. But maybe the place I went to was too dark for us all. As a choreographer, you play, quite literally, with other people's psyches, both the audience's and the dancers'. Art is an alive process, and you don't ultimately get to control its course. I wanted connections and found them broken, and where I wanted meaning I didn't find any. But then the reverse also happened in ways I didn't expect. It's the piece people still want to hear about. And sometimes that's how it goes."

"You had regrets."

"No," I said. "I'm saying that maybe it's enough to spend time with other people, making something. And that's all we have."

She was silent, inspecting her notebook. She checked her phone, which she was using to record. I sensed the swirl of a small tempest. "Raf told me that during that period you started throwing things. Including an heirloom vase, I think he said."

What bothered me, apart from her face, was not just that I threw things—which I did, as I was entirely captivated by my own futility— it was that I picked a vase to pitch straight to the floor. I didn't expect so many miniscule white slivers, as if ten vases had exploded on the hardwood. A supernova of porcelain, almost beautiful. I wished I had chosen something else, something that was not a fragile vase once owned by Raf's equally fragile mother.

There was the matter, too, that he had told her this, and now her expression was changing, to one of feathery terror, because she had just realized what this receiving of information, this bit of pillow talk, from Raf implied. She was caught. She dangled, twirling, upside down in the middle of the room, almost elegantly. She spun like a caterpillar on an invisible thread. Honestly, she was really beautiful.

"As you get older, you will learn not to mind so much what happens," I said. I took a good gulp of tea because I needed to wash down the cold speck in my throat. "Everything except dangling in the open air with your twat on view."

Later on I did regret saying this. It was nothing like my usual thinking. I had been her, after all, or some aspect of her. And I had always wanted to be one of those people, as Henry James said, on whom nothing is lost, but I also wanted to be someone who gave no impression of it. I didn't mind appearing dim, in conversation, at least. I should have kept the last comment to myself. All I did was be a hypocrite and give a kind of testimony that she could take to Raf. He would know I knew. And she would dangle there between us, spinning charmingly, until one of us reached out and squished her with our fingers.

He said that he didn't understand me sometimes, the rages that he could see under the surface occasionally shooting out, that this had been happening lately, that I hadn't wanted to talk about it, that all I did was work.

"Where are you," Raf said. "Who are you?"

And then he said, "What are you?"

So it is true. My brain as a scintillating thing, all fibres and filaments and threads and strings and connections that lead to a certain backward tangle. My parents still alive. Going about their business, utterly naive, uncomprehending, and the dog, too, and the house still standing, still packed to the gills. It was glorious, that aliveness, though I didn't know. Everyone still there, and the sun late in the sky, and my mother on the lawn, dancing, and she may well have been high, she probably was, but she was gorgeous and she was mine. She picked me up and spun me around, held my feet so I dangled and calmly watched the world from this vantage, still as a dozing bat. She was the first to help me understand my body, though she could do nothing to help me with my brain.

Volkova, ever one to employ elements of the circus, has her dancers drop from the ceiling upside down on cables, one by one at a pace that is excruciatingly slow, until they are all dangling at differing heights from the floor and call to mind spiders or caterpillars. It is difficult to tell, however, if they are the victims of their suspension or the ones in control.

—review of *Efredra*, *Dance Magazine*

Arms!

Charlotte was exhausted.

We had been at this too long.

I wanted her heart to break on the uplift and come back together on the landing. The sequence was an athletic one, intended to be long and frenzied, filled with difficult jumps and landings. Slow, considered movement has a place, as does standing still, but this composition needed the frenzied energy of the maenads. The clean had to alternate with the filthy and undomesticated, and in order to do this, she had to leave behind the known, the effort of which was stalling the progress of the entire piece. I wanted to see abandon. I could smell her sweat, even the fear in the droplets, though I wasn't the only cause. What she feared was the apostate inside her, the emergence of her true nature. The body is a famous betrayer.

"Arms!" I called out again, and the body obeyed. She looked like she wanted to cry.

"Again!" I said, and a ferocity licked out from her and tried to sting me. I asked for a dip of her shoulders, I asked her to adjust that elbow, those fingers.

"That was better," I said. "Again, again!" We were getting closer to what was being excavated, which was shame—in order to be rid of it, be delivered from it. The defecating, urinating, itching, orgasming, perspiring, ejaculating system that carried her energy also left her deeply, and unknowingly, conflicted. It held her back.

She thought that she knew her body, that she had a kind of liberation and willingness that others didn't have. She would be the perfect conduit for whatever combinations of steps, jumps, falls, flights, and, moreover, the accompanying *ideas*. She had accepted, unflinchingly she thought, those ideas, as well as the gaze of others. Her art as vocation, if an impoverished one. She had done psychoanalysis, and meditation retreats, and mushrooms. She believed that she had learned years earlier to merge the mundanity of elbows, shoulders, ankles, knees with the fantastical: asshole, clitoris, nipples, tongue. To declare them equal and without shame.

She would have said that she was integrated and performing with abandon already, but she hadn't even been close. Until this day, when the others had been sent home three hours before and the world outside the studio obscured by our task. The branches of the trees swayed outside the windows, almost scratching the glass. People in the office across the street had sex on a desk and were as oblivious to the larger schematics as she was. Nothing existed for her but this floor, sweat-streaked, the space contained above it, her body and exhausted breath, my presence. There were no taxis and buildings and hustle. No eight million.

I knew she wanted to cry, to yell, *Fuck you, Molly!*, but she was entranced by the emergence of a monstrous shadow suffering from its exclusions. We were now too far gone and the energy couldn't be stopped.

I don't normally push this far, challenging the possessions of a murky subconscious with a veritable cattle prod. I worried that I was doing something irreparable, verging on the criminal. She was growing too tired, and though I worried about injury, I didn't feel I could stop her. The momentum was hers.

She sped through the sequence one more time. Her articulation was now erratic, her gestures and landings like an open tear as the other creature came through in one brutal thrust. She transformed so completely that she emerged toothed and clawed. The room smelled of colonizing animals. It was one of the best performances I had ever seen.

Finally, she ended by folding down and placing her forehead to the floor. I waited until her breathing slowed. When it did, I said quietly, "There it is," and she sat up, nodded, wiping her nose in the gesture of bloodied prizefighters, and got to her feet.

She said, "Again."

Not that I am defending myself. Most dancers would have left long before we reached that point, or even quit entirely. When I was still a dancer, I wouldn't have tolerated bullshit in a choreographer. I would have said, *Find another*. I would have said, *Stick it up your ass*.

Which is perhaps one of the reasons I became the person inventing the sequences. This dancer, however, made the allowance, she forgave me, and when the other performers gathered the following day they found someone entirely altered. She was palpably larger, more fluid. The light in the studio seemed to bend and reflect differently around her, and when the practice was over, the others were likewise affected—they *regarded* her. Which spawned ignitions of jealousy in one or two further down the line, but that, as they say, is another matter.

Hyenas

The young man to my left is laughing. Hand over mouth. "This is unbelievable!" in a loud whisper. The Joker sees a wrong creature, something dark and mangled. Forgotten or bereft. The primitive part of the brain fears the loss of the tribe, being left to die. His gut is in turmoil; toxic. He tastes something bitter, but he can't look away or stop the laugh that bursts out from his lips, almost like a hiccup.

The other people around him aren't sure they heard him right. But when he tries to suppress another laugh, the sound comes out almost like a fart or as if he's choking. His body shivers with the effort of controlling it. His shoulders shake, his chest and stomach, and he is both appalled and delighted. The mix careens inside him.

A large woman with a ring of keys, absurdly thick, attached to her waist—she is a keeper, apparently, of gates and doorways—glares at him.

He snorts again, and she says, "Fuck's the matter with you?"

The Gatekeeper rises to full height because she had been kneeling, and for a while her hand was holding mine. But she has let go of me and she appears about to shove the man. The stances, the dance between them—if there was still time, I would use it, I would create a new piece. At the same time, I want to say to her, *Hold on to me, don't let go*.

I say, "Don't." But none of them hear me.

I reach my hand up to clasp hers, but all it meets is air. The Gatekeeper is facing off with the Joker, about to shove him. Hands spread wide on chest and a push with massive force—in a performance the Joker could jettison across the stage, slam into others. One action begetting more action, karmic, comedic, and propulsive.

"No, don't," I say, or think that I do. The words are there, I'm sure.

Theory

Did he walk into a forest or a sea? All the people who have gone missing have fallen through the membrane that separates the living from the dead. They have a secret society that doesn't refute their individual isolation. Did he leap from a bridge in the city or climb up a mountain with the intention of not coming back? It makes a difference in some way, if the volition is his. It makes a difference, too, if he is alive and well and has erased one identity to assume another.

Perhaps he is like the *johatsu* in Japan who shed a miserable identity for the fresh start of a new one; maybe he's been aided by a professional *yonige-ya*. He has just walked into another life, turned in his name for another, one that conveys an image he had wanted all along to project. Someone gave him a new birth certificate, a new passport, with a name slipped from the ledgers of the deceased. He has shaved his beard, or his entire head, donned the clothes of a businessman or a construction worker. Maybe he's still in the city, absorbed into the streets, and maybe all his money is gone. Maybe he drives a taxi, deciding who is a worthwhile fare, or he is drunk beneath a bridge. He washes dishes in Chinatown, or he stands on a pier with the hood of a parka covering his face and a line cast into the water. Every shape of a certain size begins to resemble him, and he—his form—is replicated until he can appear simultaneously all around the city. He is not missing or lost at all, but has simply spread himself over a much larger surface area, like ashes that have been scattered.

I begin to think: What is alive, what does that mean exactly, and what is dead?

A Chimney

The house was gone, but not neatly. I stood on the property with other people, an adult's hands on my shoulders, the weight of them to hold me back or down. A miscalculation, as I was as still as the frozen air. The ground was a scab of resistance. Metal lay heaped on ashes that were black in places and mounded and shocked white in others. A few grey beams tapered up to the sky, like the dead trees in swamps.

Lines wouldn't stay. Whatever had been straight was swollen or deflated. My mind searched for the known and found muffin tins, springs, canisters, railings, the woodstove. An impossible book whose cover was still bright orange and lay on a pile of folds and shards. Worse, though, was the chimney, which still stood. I was exactly opposite and had a clear view of its lonesome tenacity, the slight curve to the left at its middle, as if it might lie down. I wanted to lie down.

Even though the air was cold and our breath came out in puffs, no one shivered. Snow and ice appeared in patches over the entire area. A balsam fir, just four feet high and intact, was close to the house and silver with long icicles where it had been sprayed with water. The town had only one hydrant, so the firefighters had had to draft water from the only nearby pond large enough not to be frozen solid. The ground was marked with a long trail of gashes. Ice poured from a dirty yellow firehose lying the full length of the driveway and which they wouldn't be able to pull up until spring. My mother's car and my father's truck were burned and gutted in the front half and mostly intact at the back. I wondered about the items in the glove compartments. The mind wants the small as much as anything.

I wanted there to be a smell, too, something doused and animal, but I found nothing. Whoever held my shoulders had my hate. We had arrived in a caravan of cars, and perhaps there were eight people, though I seemed to know no one, not even my grandfather. He stood a few feet away, staring into the debris. Neither of us belonged to the world. Evidence of the rift was right at my feet, fetid and terrible, and yet I couldn't get the scent of it no matter how hard I breathed in. The person holding me thought I was sobbing, but I clawed for remnants.

Others, too, wanted the traces. I felt the shadows of the carrion eaters. Somewhere above were the turkey vultures with their bare heads and the ravens as they circled, just to check. I turned my head to see my mother's favourite blue spruce, untouched, and the leafless maples. Beyond that, the forest stood all around, looking as it ever did, sunless and complete, saying nothing.

The Neuron Containing a School Desk

When we practiced the safety drills in elementary school, we curled ourselves underneath our desks, miming our defense in the case not of mass shootings but the less personal atomic obliteration or acts of nature. I wasn't frightened of this pantomime; it excited me, the orderliness of the teacher—nameless, frail-looking under a long blade of hair—how we dipped our heads into that strange space beneath the desks (look up and see three wads of gum and dried paper), folded our bodies so that our mouths touched our knees.

I saw the collective curve of our spines, our fingers around our shins, the remoteness of our salvation. Another girl, two desks over, had eyes drilled black with terror. I almost laughed at her, but stopped myself. I was already thinking like a choreographer and liked this coordination of the entire room, the way we used our bodies and desks in a way that we didn't normally. We were made synchronous by threat, by a symbolic enactment that couldn't save us, and yet the ritual was fascinating, even beautiful.

One of the first professional dances I created had a stage set consisting of a dozen oversized desks and chairs that dancers hid beneath at the start, everyone curled up in a posture that was either terror or readiness, depending on your interpretation.

All Structures Are Unstable

The buildings flow, too, though you can't see it. In this city of losses, the colossal twins shuddering straight down, showing that all along they were rope and smoke. Poured then into the streets, expanding, taking in. Billowing obscenely.

The size of the loss necessitates ignoring, or unconscious absorbing. Fill the void with people rushing and new buildings and fresh problems. The mind can't fathom so many names and turns its tricks, and the day is like any other, and we eat our bagels and see the rats blink on the subway stairs and carry our grocery sacks.

When the towers came down, the falling figures mesmerized us. The videos were played over and over, the dark dots tumbling, or falling eerily straight, as if controlled. Then the appearance of arms and legs, the understanding of clothing, a person. Resolute and falling. Too fast and too slow at the same time. The feeling you get in your gut watching such an image, witnessing the moment just before someone's demise—its terrible suspension.

I watched the videos because I was touring on the West Coast the day that it happened, which felt oddly like a betrayal. Just like the night when my parents had the fire, or rather the fire had them, just like that, I was away. And I didn't feel it, no notion or dream or echo, no sense of a cataclysm, no feeling at all. I didn't return to the city until weeks later, and while I was away, I watched the videos, and I studied the grainy photographs in newspapers and online. I absorbed the formation of falling, or I understood something about it, the recognition of forces so large that the body can do nothing but employ the currents. No action to take, nothing to be done. Which the brain doesn't grasp. The brain can't do *not doing*. It doesn't do death. And so we can't understand the images, the people falling. They are without computation or logic.

Seize

Take possession of. To cohere, as in machinery, the friction or excessive pressure on moving parts.

To lay hold forcibly.

Confiscate.

Afflict. Clutch or grasp.

An abnormal electrical discharge in the brain.

Physical manifestations of. Convulsions, sensory disturbances, loss of consciousness.

Take prisoner.

To understand fully, as in apprehend.

Permanently Aghast

I sat in his apartment. The gear had been dry for days, but he couldn't bring himself to put away the tangible reminders of his trip, of the ocean and seabirds and the backs of passing whales whose echoes he couldn't find in the city. He had been sea kayaking, along the Inside Passage. The trip seemed to scar him in some way, if only because it was over.

"Something about coming home that breaks me," he said. He put Ornette Coleman's *Lonely Woman* on the hi-fi.

"It shouldn't do that," I said.

"It can't help itself," he said.

His apartment was laid out with the paraphernalia, his sleeping bag, tent, safety gear, first aid kit, tow straps, and a sea of items that were shape-shifters, folded, doubled as other things, could survive salt water or float. The air smelled briny. A collapsible kayak, yellow as a taxi—I never mentioned to him this particular expression of his subconscious—and seventeen feet long, stretched on the floor of his living room.

"I wonder where I left it," he said, not elaborating. His face, when he turned to me, was a ghost I'd seen before. I had a photo-graph of him, taken a year earlier, when he'd barely survived a storm while climbing on Denali. The sparse oxygen supply had aggravated in him what was already a feverish need to plant himself on the sides of mountains like a parasite. I figured he wanted revenge for the ac-cident that had claimed his parents. In the photo from Denali, he had a beard, snow-covered, and his skin had the red lustre of the newly born. His gaze, however, showed that he was permanently aghast at something no one else could see.

His expression now, as he picked his way through the debris field, showed one difference, which was desire. He sat momentarily

on the sofa opposite the kayak and watched me, and filling the wall
above his head like thought balloons were no fewer than a half-dozen
maps. The colours and lines resembled the diagrams of the brain and
similarly indicated succinct divisions that didn't exist in the real.

He poured a coffee for me.

"Your hand," I said.

"My hand loves you," he said.

"No. What was that?"

He appeared confused.

I thought I saw a tremor, involuntary and sly. "Never mind.
Never you mind," I said. "Put on Mr. Coltrane, why don't you?" I
glanced away.

"Just the thing," he said. "Just the thing."

––––––––––––

Abandon: *to forsake utterly*. We drifted apart on the surface of the city
until we had sunk into the millions of others and become unfindable.
But we always found the fated or synchronized or dreamed. A rent
in the material substance of one reality so that another only we could
see appeared. We were locked in the magnetism of that haunting.
Abandon: *to yield without restraint or moderation. To give oneself over
to impulses*.

We tried to obliterate each other. I wanted, deep down, to annihilate him. If I could grind him to dust, my terrible orphan twin, I
could change something about the hunger I had. I could be satisfied.
Or such was the theory.

Our merger had a comprehension so dark it coloured everything.
When he and I looked at each other across the tumult of the bed,
what we saw was another person who had been left behind in the
strangeness of this place, by the very people who had brought us into

it. Whether or not our parents intended it, they had abandoned us by dying. The elders had long ago left the building.

———————

He arranged his gear until nothing was left untouched, but it all looked the same. Sex then with a kind of robotic tension; frenzy and distance. We watched other people in our heads, or perhaps were not in our bodies at all. Maybe I was working out the piece—I considered nothing so important as the Project, even sex—and he was back on the sea or dangling from ropes or standing in an airport trying to convince security of the blandness of his gear. I still had long hair and he grabbed a fistful of it (to seize), twisting it up and pulling my head back (to clutch or grasp). He placed his mouth at my jugular so I felt the bare pressure of teeth along the skin, a kind of precipice or blunt knife edge, and then the fullness of lips and tongue (to cohere). But this was only routine. I went along that edge as always and then off the cliff into that desultory space, the one littered with abandoned objects and people (to apprehend fully). We had to play out a scene that was instinct or expectation or the last item on a list. Abandon, then.

In the Dream

They are gone from the house, and I walk around the rooms taking in the quiet. The boxes absorb sound, much as a black hole takes in whatever gets too close, and are coated in a layer of dust. My parents have neatly filed their desires and fears, and are unbothered by a silt of skin cells and pollen and strands of the dog's hair. Regardless of the context of doom or preparation, the boxes are bland and sink beneath the seen; they don't seem to register.

But the sight of my father in the night has gone to work on me, and I understand that I am a child of mystery. I don't know them, my parents. The boxes are all around me, silent, labelled, waiting. The arrangement might murmur about displacement or plans, but a house whose structure appears to be upheld by its own contents is another animal entirely.

The boxes snake through rooms and sit under tables and line walls, they line up one side of the piano, muffling its sound. In the large living room, the boxes reach the window ledge and a vase of flowers sits on top. A blanket is folded on two boxes beside the sofa, creating a kind of end table; there is a smudged ashtray, some pulp fiction, and a book of Rumi poems. Boxes in front of the sofa create an ottoman on top of which my father has placed a large rectangle of local maple that will remain one of the most beautiful things I will ever see—its haunting gleam causes the eye to disregard the boxes underneath. Other boxes along the south wall proclaim in tidy, exact lettering, numerals spelled out:

Seven Collapsible Pots or
Two Dozen Instant Potato or
Twenty Cans Beef Dog Food.

Some of the listings are more whimsical:

Fifty Spools Silk Thread, Pink and Purple,
Nineteen Assorted Drawing Pads and Journals,
Fifteen Cases Ink Pens, HB Pencils, Nibs, Sharpeners,
Assorted Books: Children,
Assorted Magazines: Travel and Life.

There are also some odd pairings, revealing a lapse in the system, gaps in the organization, and you wonder how, like mismatched lovers, they came to be together:

Iodine and Tube Socks,
Dried Chilis and Ball-Peen Hammers,
Suction Cups and Jockey Underwear (female, small).

But I haven't looked inside any of the boxes; not one.

5

The Documentary

The professor of psychology is being interviewed. The scene is a deli, where he is having coffee and a pastrami sandwich, and sitting across from him at the table is the woman conducting the interview. A salad sits in front of her, untouched. She has waited to interview him, because he's been on a book tour for a tome about people who lose things. The professor has some ideas, too, about missing people, the cultural aspects; he thinks about how one bad decision leads to another, about subliminal expressions. He agreed to be interviewed on the condition that the filming take place in a deli and that they order food, because he is of the opinion that documentaries lack this sort of arrangement.

Also in his mind is his own colleague, a woman who taught metaphysics at the university, who went missing two years ago when she went for a hike and never returned. He was one of the members of the search party, though he declined to mention to anyone that he had, at one time, known her intimately. Or that he had been the one to tell her about his favourite hiking spot, which was less than an hour outside the city limits. That their original plan had been to hike together, but then their negotiations had soured and she ended up going alone, not returning.

He doesn't mention any of this to his interviewer, who stabs at some lettuce and puts down her fork again. She had been asking him about his idea of pain and what the missing person means to those left behind. He has seemed preoccupied or enjoying his pastrami too much. She says, "It's interesting, don't you think, how many people go missing? I mean, just vanish. Happens all the time." She gestures expansively, a little impatiently. She waits. He picks the crumbs off his plate with his fingertips, licks them thoughtfully in a way that reminds her of a cat.

"I think what's interesting is that we're surprised," he says, then takes a sip of his coffee.

"But why are we so captivated? Missing people, or even objects. You wrote a whole book about that." She leans forward, smiling, maybe a little too harshly. "What's behind that, Professor? Why are we so interested when something is gone?"

He signals the waitress for more coffee, which annoys the interviewer because it complicates the shot. "Two things. One is fear of death; what happens to us beyond this place. The missing person on the news becomes a surrogate experience, whether or not that person is actually alive. Being missing is in itself a kind of death—Thank you, that's perfect—instead of worrying about our own existential situation, we can work on someone else's."

"And the other?"

He rests his fingertips on the hot mug and settles in. "Say we have a bombless existence, that we have a life of relative ease—as in, we turn on the tap, and it works; we eat at restaurants with abundant food; our beds are warm at night, right? We still feel it. 'It' being a wrongness so acute, so alive that it can make us want to end it all and in some cases we actually do.

"When things are ticking along with the least resistance and the most peace we don't realize our luck. We don't think, *This is as good as it gets*. Our belief that there's more glitter, somewhere in the future, is that powerful. Or our belief in inadequacy, our own shortcomings or the inadequacy of the house or the car or the business we're in is that strong. Something is always missing, yeah? Or not quite right. We feel the misery in such colour and complexity that the torment itself transforms.

"By that I mean the torment actually lives and breathes, it becomes a creature. One entirely fed by our own thoughts. Nurtured, even. We put the creatures into the world, millions of them, and they run everything. All inspired—born!—by the idea of lack. Not actual lack, because, remember, that's just an idea. We conceive something because we've imagined nothing—which is, in some respect, impossible to do, imagine nothing.

"So maybe what we imagine is really an edge that runs along nothing, and we believe in its reality, because we can cling to it. The nothing is what we're afraid of. It's the emptiness made by the person or object we believe we're entitled to but isn't there anymore. Most of us feel entitled to possess a person or an object, along with our own existence, ad infinitum. It's all a story, though, a figment of our imagination."

He drinks his coffee, puts down the cup, and drums his fingers on the tabletop. Then he smiles and bops his index finger toward the interviewer like he's tapping her with a wand. "But you know what? The monster howling at that edge is real enough, for sure. And we invented him."

Molly

This place on the sidewalk, for instance. A microcosm of the larger wonder. I feel the warmth of the people around me, and wish that I could tell them what it means. The faces leaning in—the marvelous noses, the cracked lips, the eyeglasses and hats, the tired scarves—cause a terrible love to ripple through me. Even if I am perplexing to them. I can see their helplessness, the beauty and electricity of their panic is like the shower of sparks from a welding torch. In this moment we are being forged together, a single creature with many arms and legs and hearts.

"Please," someone says.
"Oh my god, please."

During a fall of this kind I have to rely on the goodness of the world that I'm leaving. The contortions of my own face and body, however, obscure the communication. The storm out at sea must feel the same. It would talk of vulnerability, it would say that it loves. How short its life is.

The boy with the lion in him has wandered back, and he bends with his chapped hands on his knees. In order to see me better, in order to understand what is taking place.

Place has everything to do with this, I want to tell him, and nothing. Lion Boy nods at me, a flicker of that comprehension passing through, a flame that catches. I can feel him breathing.

Rafael Was Morose

In spite of the text, he was lacking words. He had been doing a series of mostly white paintings, and so shades of it bloomed on his clothes, on the toes of his leather boots. His current obsession was, I think, an unconscious attempt to whitewash, to cover up the murkiness of his love life, the other thing that preoccupied him and which he couldn't mention. It hovered around him, forlorn and wanting expression. There was a splotch of paint on one side of his chest that resembled a bird. The top of one wing beat above his heart. He scrubbed his chin as he was thinking, which he didn't realize he was doing. From the outside it would appear as if we were having a conversation about the twins' school, about an upcoming performance in which Stella and Augustin were pirates, one good and one bad, which was causing a kind of identity crisis, but this was only a surreal film and we waited for the spider to finish its sentence. He scratched at his scalp and looked concerned.

"I don't," he said, and then he looked at me. We communicate sometimes in the manner of the twins—they have taught us. I know what he referred to, that he was giving me the depleted line: *I don't love her*. Encapsulated in his denial was an offering, but it was only air. I had already rejected it before the full stop. A white jellyfish on the thigh of his navy pants seemed to undulate. Tentacles traced down the leg and around the knee. He is clumsy.

He turned and walked into his studio down the hall and I followed him. He was talking about the twins again, laughing when he wondered if Stella and Augustin negate each other. Against the far wall, perhaps a dozen paintings leaned. Drawings were pinned to a wire that stretched across one side of the room. The wing on his heart tapped against him as he moved around the room, looking for something. The looking was a pretext, as he wanted something else. Desire is our greatest invention. He squared his back to me, his fingers flipping through a box of supplies on one of his tables, and cleared his throat.

The problem of his current work, these white paintings that were not really white—they were, if you looked close enough, containers of blues and yellows and violets. The more you looked, the more colourful they became. Which was a beautiful effect, but they weren't aligned with him yet, and I hadn't told him so, because I was waiting for the right moment.

"I wonder if," he said. "No, never mind." He pulled out one of his notebooks. It was stuffed with photos, and some of the pages were wrinkled because he used paint or graphite or glued in various bits of found images to create new collages, so that the whole thing swelled like it had fallen in water, and the spine creaked when he opened it.

"I have to . . . ," he said. He rummaged. "Stella said something to me the other day." A paper spilled to the floor, though he ignored it. He looked over the top of his glasses at me. "Who is this man who is missing? Are you planning on telling me?"

I watched him for a moment, the sudden poise of his old face and the irony drifting about unsure of where to land. I said, "Are *you* planning on telling *me?*" and a little smile escaped, because, really, I wanted to laugh.

He put the notebook back on the table and then walked toward me, taking off his glasses and putting them in his shirt pocket. When he reached me, I felt the wave of heat from him. The body is radical in its honesty. It admits to its ideas, regardless of intent. It has a thing for territories, for areas it wishes to surrender or to reclaim. It has a thing for symbolism. His expression was dark, confident.

"Let's fuck," he said. Sex was the exit, the way out of whatever loomed. I leaned back against a table, and with one hand behind me I shoved the drawings lying on top of it, letting them fall.

Vanishing

This had seemed so reasonable only moments ago.

Let me reduce sex to a theory. Drain the fun and guts of it.

Convey that I wanted to flee, where only a minute earlier I had been his completely. This is a trick of the body—it convinced me, again and again, that I would locate something long gone or out of reach or never there to begin with. Its mystery could be understood if I turned my body over to our bartering, which swung on the idea of wholeness, and that Seth was the completing force. These were not casual encounters, my much-preferred mode. Whatever we were about to do, whatever the degradation to either one of us or loss of self or negation, it hardly mattered as the acts themselves became the conduit we needed to locate that missing item: the other us.

And then, the aftermath, the collapse of the system.

I pulled the covers around me, as if I were a modest person, but I did this to keep my hands busy. I didn't want to show him how quickly I had cooled, that I could barely touch him. I knew if I spoke, my voice would contain none of the huskiness and warmth that it had only moments before. I was already constructing my to-do lists, already working on a piece, and realizing that Sosha's entrance was too early and that a duo would be better off deconstructed, perhaps done away with. I ticked off the seconds in my head, calculating when I could get up without alerting him to my sudden indifference or even aversion. We were a thing I had to leave, but I had to carefully stall the desire to bolt and vanish in increments.

I slid to the bathroom.

I came out with a towel around my waist.

I listened to him talking while I pulled on my shirt, my pants.

By the time he was finished speaking I was fully dressed, with my earrings and watch located and now in place and my jacket over my arm. He looked at me with a haze of astonishment, but he was so sleepy, he decided, and lay on the bed again while I headed for the door.

White Space

I went into Raf's studio when he wasn't there. Not to rummage for the traces or cast about. I'm not so petty. The question of *why*, for instance, rising electrically from the dark, was more interesting to me than the lover. She was only a condition that arises and fades. It was the *why* I wanted to keep. Its light was like an animal at the ocean floor learning to gleam with the silence. The way it appeared and sank back under, seeking its depth and pulling me with it.

I looked at the north wall of the studio where three paintings hung side by side, all in the mode of the white grids. The dark lines were sharp and thin and regimented, with the exception of a few places where the colour had bled into the white field. The lines were actually indigo. I realized suddenly as I stood there, my bare feet on the paint-stained floor, that envy shrouded my heart. I was jealous of the lines. Or rather, that he could make them. That his art allowed for the razor-like transmission of an idea. The line, untouched by other forces, could be a line, a straight cut. That whatever imprecision might be there at a smaller level wasn't noticed by the human eye.

Nothing I could do with my body or with the bodies of my dancers could approach the discreteness of the indigo lines. I have to rely on sets and backdrops, columns and polygons. Painted structures that are unsparing in their crispness and appear even sharper against the vulnerability of the bodies. The human form, born in entropy, defies the straight and tends toward bowing and folding. An unending expression of variance.

The lines of Raf's paintings were made by someone who is himself rumpled. He veers drunkenly when he walks, even when sober. He is held up by walls or the backs of chairs when he stands. His hair flops into his gaze, and his clothes and limbs are fluid. His abdomen swells a little over his belt. Clouds of smoke or scents or the density of his feelings drift around him. He appears tangible at the same time as dispersed, like a red wine stain on a white carpet, or a traffic accident. This is the man who, using whatever painstaking method, applied the lines to his canvases with the same insistence of the people who made the city's grids. A studied and careful violence over natural forms.

Soft light entered the west-facing windows. The particles bounced on the white paintings, reams of paper and canvas rolls, white walls. His knapsack was moody where it slouched on the floor, just underneath one of his worktables. I resisted the urge to touch it, but then gave in, and held it in my hands, before opening it. My fingers felt down one side of the interior and then another until they found a gauze fabric and I pulled out a rolled-up scarf. I let it unravel to the floor. Abstracted shapes of apricot and ochre and a few splotches of dark green. I rolled it again, placed it inside the knapsack, returned the knapsack to its place under the table.

Beside the knapsack, buckets were arranged, most of them empty. But one held the white paint that Raf was mixing for a large piece and which he planned to transport to Queens. Perhaps he had abandoned the attempt, as the paint was thickening in the bucket. He didn't care about waste.

I took a large flat brush, about four inches wide, from his worktable and stuck the tip tentatively into the paint. Stirred gently. I liked the thickness very much, how opaque and plaster-like it was, how viscous. I pulled the brush out, holding it over the bucket so the paint slowly oozed and dropped. Then I picked up the bucket's handle and carried it with the brush over to the three paintings on the wall, setting the bucket on the floor. The shade of white it contained could be called obliterating. I loaded the brush with paint and decided where to begin, settling on the painting on the far right. Moving from right to left seemed apt, like backspacing. I touched the brush to the surface and felt the bristles gently bend and curve as they deposited the paint. Then dipped the brush again, and again, continuing to paint until all three panels were well covered and those impossibly straight lines were gone.

Emptiness

It's possible I hated Seth with a purity so annihilating that I studied his face to practice restraint to not claw or slap it. I remember wanting to commit it to memory, but then I think this isn't true. I studied it to forget it, obliterate it. I looked closely enough that all of its details could blur and a void could form with one last hiss of dispersing energy.

On the other hand, this was the face that I had kissed innumerable times. I had seen every possible expression cross it, including this one of distance, as if we watched each other on crackling video monitors. But I saw the stain across his cheek, the wrinkles around his eyes, the grey hair that still surprised me. Impossible to render the details without the mundanity of exactly these things, but the commonplace is what strikes me now as memorable and even desirable. The face I see in my mind is a face I would like to touch again.

Once You Know the Name of a Place, You Are No Longer There

A brook, called the Minetta, used to flow past the park. Before it was buried. People still say that it lives, in some sense, underground, and that construction digs down to the appearance of clear water. But the ground where I am is not a permeable thing. It doesn't allow. I want to sink into it, however, if these people would let me go.

There is a silver-haired woman about ten feet away, with clip-on pearl earrings and a snakeskin clutch. She watches me, thinking how much younger I am than she is, that she should be the one disappearing, except that she has no intention of doing so. The city isn't done with her, she theorizes, or the winter day, which will turn bright eventually. The park will erupt, three months from now, into blooms and leaves—and the haunting, dark branches of the catalpas will be covered. She will be here to see spring, and she says this with her body, how she stands apart from the people touching me and watches. She thinks about the sight in front of her, this roiling mass, but she also pictures coming in her front door, a grocery bag in her arms.

Her eyes narrow at my body; she recognizes a circumstance that could belong to her—a stroke maybe or just a slip on the ice. "Such a pity." She begins to recognize me, and knows she's seen me either on the street, because she belongs to this neighbourhood, or elsewhere.

Elsewhere. A lovely word—ethereal, nebulous. I have misplaced you, and you are elsewhere. I have lost the thread, the trail. You vanish, or I do.

Clothing

Dr. Lucia Chen said, "Looking satisfied is another form of armour."

We were sitting in her Harlem office, and she was more forth-coming than usual. I had made the observation that the city had its effects on people; their souls, too, maybe. Polar ideologies showed up in the face. The yin-yang of this existence. But hustling was a form of armour, and the wearing of black clothes. So, too, looking satisfied, apparently.

"Not you, of course. I mean people generally," she said.

"That's a relief."

Whatever the effect of having countless patients pour their big and small tragedies into her ears, however, it didn't show up on her face. She was the glistening exception. She didn't have the purplish swatches under the eyes, the defiant glint in the irises, the set lips of the urbanite. Her back wasn't as straight, though, as you might imag-ine for someone practiced in meditation, as she had a tendency to slouch or curl herself into the large armchair, almost as if she would sleep if you'd only shut up. She wore clogs or sometimes sneakers in too-bright orange or pink; sometimes she kicked them off and tucked her feet under, and the sneakers lay askew on the floor.

"Are you going to explore that?" I said. I pointed to the white-board she kept close by, and which she used to write topics or aphorisms, or sometimes she made intricate diagrams of one's issues, balloons and squares and stick figures in mystifying combinations, which by the end of session possessed utter clarity. But all she had written on today's board was

ALL STRUCTURES ARE UNSTABLE.

"Self-evident," she said.

"Okay."

She said nothing, which was one of her tools. Eventually the space was big enough that you'd fall into it.

"You want me to continue where we left off," I said. "But I'm still recovering from last week's whiteboard."

"What did it say?"

"You don't keep a record?"

"No," she said. "Why would I do that?"

" 'The problem of absence is the supposition of error.' "

"That's a good one," she said, shutting her eyes. Then she opened them again. "Did it help?"

"I guess. You want me to get used to it. Accept."

She brightened. "Sooner or later. But better sooner."

I sighed and examined my hands.

"How about I say something not popular thinking here in the West?" she said. "Ready for it?"

"Sure."

"There is grace in looking at suffering. Really looking at it."

Neither of us spoke for several minutes. Finally, she said, "No, I'm going to say two things that are unpopular to the Western mind."

I waited.

"Look death in the face."

"Okay. Except you yourself said that death isn't a concrete thing. Only an idea. So, there's no face to look into."

"Nice try." She laughed. "Death is friendlier than you think! Face or no face. You know what the Dalai Lama says about death?"

"What?" I smiled. I couldn't stop myself.

"I'm paraphrasing but, *Change your clothes*. That's all it is. You change your clothes." She shrugged.

Sidewalk

But the boy startles. I have frightened him again. He had lost his fear; he was curious instead, and now—

Seven minutes will pass, is passing, have passed. Pull apart the word *minute* and you have the sixtieth part of an hour. Also something chopped small, of very small size. Something lessened, diminished. Think of a diminishing note on a piano, which won't be held or sustained or kept. The dissipation is essential and can't be helped. You can only play another note. Seven of them, maybe. Look up *seven* and it will say, absurdly, *six plus one*, but you won't be able to argue. The tautology won't end. The only way forward is forward.

And now. What minute are we in? The seconds contain multitudes. I am lost in them. The boy shivers.

The Cause Is Unknown

One of her favourite buildings is the ten-storey, neo-Renaissance one that sits close by. It shows only subtle signs of its history, and is now owned by the university. She favours it, not for its secrets but in spite of them; if she can find love for the tan and terra-cotta exterior, the smallish size of the building, perhaps she can also forgive that it holds somewhere in its framework the memory of a fire. Unknown by most people who pass on the sidewalk, the anniversary is marked each year with a memorial. The city absorbs its histories to such an extent that they can become invisible. She wonders what happens to the knowledge, how it is hoarded.

Molly

The papers read: *Cause Unknown*. Whether my father was the one to start the fire that night or whether the boxes simply became tinder for some other spark is unofficial. Either way, the bottle of his nameless rage, the problems he couldn't configure, and the expression of my parents' ideas, their desires and fears and sacrifices to the gods of worry, were compacted into ash with little left to distinguish the parts. Their stockpiling was a form of prayer. They provided fuel for the monster that turned up and confirmed himself to be a bad guest. They fed him, and then he ate them, too.

Cajal

No one notices the cane's print in the snow. Naturally enough, the people see the body having a seizure. Possession and a bad angle.

The Lover, who had felt repulsed and whose mistress is currently two blocks away making, perhaps, linguine with a white wine sauce and checking her lipstick in a spoon's reflection, moves from the left side of me to the right. He stops in his new position and places his hand, unconsciously, over his heart. He was an inelegant man who is suddenly elegant, the precision and gentleness in the placement of his fingers a single movement that would take some people many hours—or perhaps years—of practice to attain. The thought radiates from him, *I'm so sorry this is happening to you.* He will tell his lover about this, about what happened on his way to meet her, and he will hold her close, breathing into her hair.

The Blue Girl has been coughing and has had enough. She steps away. She is a regretful prince and exits backward, stage left, slowly, then faster, before turning to face the remainder of her day. We have lost her.

The boy crunches the snow underfoot and switches between looking at me and the other people, and examining his feet.

———

On the ground not far from my head is a mark in the snow. The sidewalks have been cleared, but along the edges snow remains, and the corners have blackened crusts, as if burned. But the area I'm talking about, maybe eighteen inches by fifteen inches, is pristine, with none of the ashy flecks that ride the air currents and settle. No yellow stains, no red (apparently a good number of people with nosebleeds or cuts or punctures trickle in this way, largely unseen, until the snow shows the leaks).

In the centre of this area, where the snow is only about two inches thick, lies a single print. The end of a cane. The cane is the metal kind (I've seen it and the old man who belongs to it) with a rubberized tip. The print, about an inch and a half in diameter, is a series of circles, one ring inside another, so that the snow is embossed like water after a pebble has been dropped in it.

The man usually has a large black hound with him on his walks, and the hound is docile but giant. Their movement along the sidewalks is always careful and patient, or rather the dog is careful and patient, and the man is brooding, wanting to be home. Despite being one of the least vulnerable of the sidewalk, thanks to his dog and his grumpiness, he feels the closeness of his end, which seems near but not near enough. He wants the depression of his armchair, the cane resting against it, and the light of the television that moves like a flame or a tongue; he can be licked by it, as the hound sometimes works the taste of sausage from his fingers, and therefore consoled. Not the sort of thing he can form into words. The idea rests at the edge of his mind. He has never noticed the bottom of the cane, or its prints in the snow, how he marks down infinity with each of his steps.

I have seen a seizure of mine only once, on a bit of video that captures a point when I was talking to a few of the dancers in the studio. I'm backlit by a glow from the windows. I seem to move through a shadowy space that takes my shape. Melanie, Jon, and Staale are watching me intently in the video, which is soundless. I'm gesturing, and they're watching, waiting to catch the movement I'm trying to show them, a twitch of the hand I want them to make, and suddenly I can see, when my face emerges from the shadow, what they can't, that my temporal lobe is gorging on a bad current. The video captures the gestural language of a complex partial seizure, almost elegant, and an opaqueness that draws across my face, another skin or mask. Otherworldly.

They watch me with the same expressions, thinking that my gaze and the way my hands reach for my side, so smoothly, is the exact thing I want them to do. Their gaze, so attentive, wanting to get it, their bodies miming what I'm beginning to unfold and taking on my absence so that it appears to spread out among them.

Moments pass. On the video, about twenty seconds (but I may have wandered lost inside that absence for weeks, in another realm been reported missing). Finally, I'm arriving, slamming doors behind me, making an entrance when I want them to think I've never left. My eyes meet theirs again as I shake my head and try to recall my last sentence and obscure the trip I've taken. I can't tell from their faces if I succeeded or not, or if they said to one another later that I had seemed so strange, and did that seem funny to you?

Others have described my seizures, but they miss the mark. My classmates said the unimaginative: a flopping fish. The movements I'm told I make are sometimes antithetical to what shows up inside my head. My body and the territory I inhabit often don't correspond. Sometimes I find a void, or hot or cold, sometimes a prickling terror in the stomach. I become enormous, without boundaries, a me without me, a will without a will. Language is a vanishing thing, and therefore thought also, leaving only a watcher, still and receptive. Sometimes I feel ecstatic.

The drawings of Cajal point to the source of what I experience. When Cajal depicts the olfactory bulb of a dog or the cerebellum of a rabbit, he also draws the ecstasy and terror and the spectrum in between. A retreating perception shows itself in the combination of lines and colour washes, the alphabet labels. The purple circle on many of the drawings, made by a rubber stamp and which reads *Museo-Cajal-Madrid*, sits like a moon in orbit. Sometimes the diagrams are kitten neurons, or lizard, chicken or rat; sometimes they are human. The lines are dendritic and sizzling, and form axons and synapses and glia. I have thought, *The other side of this is silence, and that is the language for it*. Our big eye pressed to the magnifying window. We see the particles, and the particles within particles, though we never get to the end of it all. A presence lies either darkly or brightly just beyond the veil of the drawing, and Cajal has made it seem that if we simply wait long enough, we'll see the veil pulled to the side.

The Point Is Not to Win

"You there," Seth said.

"And you there," I said. Another dropped thread of ours, several months long. I couldn't refute his assumption that I was alone and not meeting someone, because it was true. I had spent much of that day at a workshop in the south end of town for a piece I was trying to set, followed by missing an appointment with my doctor who had been dangling the prospect of a new medication. The lapse had also been a lapse in taking the pills that made me feel, more than ever, the misaligned layering of one reality over another. A diptych of me.

"You look well," he said.

"And you," I said. But we were ragged at the edges. "Sit." I wondered if he could see the shimmering of my brain, how it was gathering its constituents, beginning to murmur. Each time the café door opened I heard the traffic and the voices, and something beyond them. The flinty scrape of leaves—pin oaks and callery pear—as they tumbled on the concrete. The air being disturbed, a change in the weather. Something galactic being consumed.

I thought about leaving, but as the waitress took our order I could see her writing. She didn't join the tops of her *o*'s, instead leaving them open, like cups. Which pricked in my brain all manner of possibility, decisions and destiny, the movement of bodies. I felt Seth's knee against mine, but simultaneous with the urge to put my hands on him was an arterial hardening.

The waitress filled the coffee cups of two men playing chess and asked them who was winning. One looked at her through the hair that covered his eyes and said, "The point is not to win but to annihilate."

She asked if they wanted cream, but an answer didn't come. Questions rattled the air, important ones, but went unregarded. Seth looked at me and smiled, but I felt the tensions of the room. Inside the pattern of our comings and goings was the imprint of our parents, how they appeared and vanished.

I told him about a man I saw once. He was an expert in the data concerning missing people, giving a lecture at the library. I was there to view old dance films and had come across the room where he was speaking just as I was leaving. I ended up sitting in one of the chairs near the door in order to hear the last twenty minutes. The man, who was middle-aged and had carefully combed his hair to the left, made a lot of little jokes to which the listeners responded enthusiastically. He talked about the kinds of things a missing person tends to do, the behaviour they exhibit when they aren't yet missing but are about to be. The person faces a transformative moment when a course of action has to be decided. They become wrapped in a chrysalis of options, erroneous and otherwise, for long enough that they emerge, fully formed, as one who is now lost.

Seth studied my face. "You think you're making a bad decision."

I stirred a spoon in my cup of tea, listening to the sound of the metal against the ceramic. Desire rose into the high ceiling of the room, up past the cascading spider plants and vines on the walls and the false windows, and with nowhere to go came back down.

The mugs were replaced, the plates taken away, the chess game completed. We were there for two more hours, as people came and went, and leaves tumbled in the footpaths of oblivious people, the ones who knew where they were going.

Somehow the sea entered in. "This place will flood," he said. "If either of us has children, it will be in their lifetime."

"A flood that's just passing through, or one that stays awhile?"

"A permanent attraction. It won't be an island anymore.

Manhattan will turn into words, memories, film. It will be mythical."

"It's already those things. It's already mythical."

"It will disappear," he said, or perhaps he said that he would disappear. "And what we can't see anymore becomes something else. Something bigger."

"Hence, a mythic place."

He wasn't concerned, however; contemplating the demise didn't fill him with dread, it seemed. And when he talked about this, our thighs pressed together as we sat in the very centre of the place we were discussing. I found myself saying Okay. *Okay*.

We drove his car out of the city, not to flee the ocean but to head toward the eastern coast that pinned it back. I already had a change of clothes in my bag from the workshop, and he kept his gear in his trunk so he was always ready to leave the place he couldn't seem to escape permanently. We were prepared, we thought, and unbothered by our lack of a clear destination, by the presence—far away but pulling us toward it—of the roiling autumn sea. We drove for several hours and, just after dark, pulled into a hotel driveway. The surrounding buildings were squat and shuttered, and closed for the season. A huge moon hung in the sky. The hotel, grey in daylight, appeared warm and amber, and we grinned as we got out of the car. We were enveloped in a briny wind that rushed unimpeded over the sea and didn't yet contain the stops and starts of enormous buildings and their people, their breath, their sorrow.

"Did you know this was here?" I said, and he shook his head.

The hotel lobby was unevenly lit with some table lamps and pot lights, leaving the rest of the room mysteriously formed. A man in a brown suit gave us the key cards and we walked to the elevator through piped-in, incongruously driving dance music. The seismic oscillation of my brain made me enormous, too big for the elevator, and then too small; I would slip into the gap, vanish.

"Are you okay?" he said.

"More than," I said. But it was the floors that vanished, instead, and time, and the doors opened to the fifth storey. I looked at Seth, though nothing showed on his face except the terrible focus of the ravenous.

We turned the lights on in the room, put down our bags. What, then, to do with each other. I want to get this right, what happened.

We were hungry and ordered room service. I wanted oranges, and sacrifices. I saw the cruelty in even the most conciliatory forms of desire. He stood close to me and spoke into my skin. It was possible to think one thing and do another, to believe in a mode of symbolic carnage. To invite it. To filter the rage of this place through the interstices of two bodies. Dr. Chen had said, *Look death in the face*. She said this with the inflection of aliveness. Something or someone, it seemed to me, waited to be born.

Room service came. We stopped and retreated momentarily with the plates and metal domes, but they turned out not to contain our order and instead held the breakfast of someone jet-lagged and out of time perhaps. It no longer mattered. We abandoned their cold forms for the tangles of the arcane, leaving the trays out in the hallway so we could commiserate alone. His palms were hot, and his tongue. He smelled of the sea already. He spoke into my skin something guttural, and I felt the coherence to be my own. But sex is an obscuring thing. From inside its complications, we couldn't know the exact depth of pain and love. Outside the hotel there was the turmoil of the sea and the moon's wide-open eye.

• • •

I woke in the early morning and watched the room, how still it was. I knew that the sea was quiet and blue also, but a direction within me had already been set. He didn't stir as I stood up. I watched the arrangement in the morning light, the chairs and unshattered desk, the trackless plateau underneath. We hadn't destroyed civilization after all.

I decided on showering. I found an apple in my bag and ate it, while my heart began to race and a prescience grew in my brain, the opposite of a shadow. It was something white or a silver fish flashing. My stomach fluttered, rising, and I turned to look at him, wanting to tell him that something was wrong.

Something is wrong.

But he lay on his side like an arc of granite, his consciousness sealed inside. I went to the bathroom instead.

I stood inside the glass stall, and within moments of the water hitting my skin, I felt better. I turned the stream to its coldest setting, then hot, then cold again, and gasped as my body contracted. It was a favourite thing of mine to do, to rupture comfort in this way. Maybe I stayed there for ten minutes. Suddenly his face was Cheshire-like beside me, until he was real and touching me. He guided me from the shower, turned off the taps, and wrapped me in a towel, put his mouth on me.

"You're awake," I said, but he had nothing to say. He was still in the laconic setting of desire. We walked to the bed, and I had the feeling of cataclysm, but I wasn't afraid. We were still standing—it wasn't me who sought the ground, but a different version of me. He said something that was a denial, as though he had seen ahead and was trying to talk me out of it. The seizure came, as easily as a wave.

•   •   •

The point of departure, our realities bifurcating, peeling apart. He held his shock like a rifle. I fell instead. The diving down was clockless, a bright space.

There was something other than dread, my stomach scrambling for my throat, or being ground to dust.

A failure of language to fit an exploding star inside the banality of certain words: happiness, for instance, or ecstasy. Or wonder. How useless to say these things. A surge through my arms and out through my fingertips, an unrelenting supply of something nameless. I danced for him. I showed him everything I knew.

The oceanic depth of this. I didn't feel his revulsion any more than he could see into the portal. In that distance between us, something like snow was falling. The atmosphere shed itself in rips the size of quarters. How it went on for days.

Speaking in Tongues

Time stretched and buckled for him as well. Seth saw a woman on a rack. He heard an unsettling wail, followed about thirty seconds later by what seemed to him like outrageous, terrible snores. I urinated. He ran to the phone to call for help and tripped on the edge of the bedcover, which was pooled on the ground. He badly bit his tongue. My body pulled and contracted while he spoke into the phone. We were both relentless. Perhaps four minutes, maybe six. Seven.

The shine of belt buckles, the black bags, but no sound at first. I was arriving piece by piece. The EMTs wore practical black boots. The man tilting his head as he moved the stethoscope smelled of onions and rubbing alcohol. He listened to my chest, but the portal had closed and only my heart was there. A woman held my wrist gently, while Seth told her what he saw. Language came to me as branches, as roots. The room was too bright, so I closed my eyes.

When I opened them again, I felt confusion. The legs had another order; we had skipped ahead in the film. I said I was okay.

Okay. Okay. Okay.

He couldn't believe my words, what he said were my denials. The woman asked if I had a history, and I said yes, though I couldn't find it. I waved my hand and said I wouldn't go with them.

The woman leaned in close to me and said, "Are you sure?"

Then she turned to Seth and said, "We can't make her come with us."

He bled from the mouth and they shone a light in. I could see his anger, and I closed my eyes again, though I still felt it.

How long, I don't know. The EMTs had vapourized. I lay on the bed, and Seth was beside me, with a damp cloth at my face as if to fix or hide me.

He said, "I can't believe you never told me this."

I drank something, a type of juice that left a stain and made me thirsty. Eventually he helped to dress me, his fingers faint with pity, and then I felt it: a discharge of rage. No trace left of the joy that had been present in the diving-down space. I was exhausted—not post-coital, but postictal. This is what we don't understand, the transmissions. Soul latches soul. Then gone.

The time inside the world of things was 8:17 a.m. It was a Tuesday.

The Skull

Secrets are always under siege. Few people, not even the keepers, will defend the existence of them, the right of that energy to take shape. Secrets edge regret, or embarrassment, or the idea of exposure. Or exposure itself.

The bearer of the secret is said to be misaligned, malignant.

In the end, unprotected.

You might wonder where the secret's angels are, who the publicist is.

————————

We stood face-to-face for the last time. We had entered the hotel and been transformed, added to. Divided.

In the early days of our collisions, I had given him the bare skull of a baby bird. I had found it in the rooftop garden of the apartment building I was living in, nestled in the soil of a potted boxwood. I had thought it was a plump white mushroom. When I turned it in my fingers I found the exquisitely tiny beak and the holes for eyes. I was so taken with it that I eventually created a piece where dancers wore masks exactly like it. The skull was impossibly light, and after I gave it to him, he placed it on his desk where it was prone to taking off and blowing across the room in summer if he was running his fan. He said it was his most prized possession.

A few weeks after the hotel, I stood in the entry of my building beside the wall of brass mailboxes and opened the box he had sent to me. I found the bird skull, crisp and empty-eyed, along with a piece of paper. It was a letter in which I found his disappointment, how I had withheld from him the fact of my seizures. How, despite the years of coming and going, I hadn't trusted him. How he had been terrified.

Humidity

I have asked my dancers to show me ecstasy with their bodies, though I've realized other people don't have the foggiest. Their attempts to dig it up are painful to see, and their inevitable frustration when they can't grasp it. They try for the sexual, a bubble shaped with their arms that is the volume of an orgasm, a scrunching of the face, a pelvic thrust. I tell them that they misunderstand me, but, then, of course they do. Keep searching, I tell them. And their puzzled faces seem so young. So unecstatic. Keep searching.

The body is in time, it is time. It shows the passage of it. Which is why dance can be hard to translate, why filming it so often seems inadequate. The body reveals space, making us aware of what we take for granted. Conversely, the camera flattens space. Movement is something you have to be in the presence of, in order to fully see how a space is rendered in three dimensions. You have to be right in front of it. Bear witness to it.

I created a piece in which men and women removed each other's clothing only to find increasingly ragged, increasingly red layers, darker and darker shades, like a flaying of skins, set to Stravinsky. How to uncover the shadow with a balance of horror and grace, and thereby uncover its secrets.

We were good at this, the leaving and not-calling, the going on about our business as if the catastrophe of failed love hadn't happened. My parents wouldn't have understood us, our callous ways. Previously, I had written his name on grocery receipts and drowned them in the kitchen sink, hoping to flood out the tiny grains he had left under my skin.

I am sorry to employ the subcutaneous and the erasure of names. We were like everyone else who thinks their love is unique. And that was the problem, maybe; it was perfectly ordinary, a faint thing, and so we kept looking, waiting for the next entrance, the possibility of another *Other*.

Thinner

Rafael Massimo did know about my condition. He was thinner then. He was so enamoured of the body and its complications, its absence of regimentation, that he had been to see a show of mine five times. Finally he asked to see me. We had been tangling up for six months before the hotel and Seth and the white space. Neither of them knew about the other.

Raf had already seen—I had allowed him to see—a few of the subtler seizures, though none, yet, of the falling-down variety. Perhaps I recognized in him something that wasn't there on the surface, a deeper ability to contain. Perhaps I saw, too, a man who, in spite of his own wandering allegiances, was also waiting for a family. The idea of it. When I returned from the hotel, I told him I had had the mother of all seizures. I said nothing of witnesses, and he didn't ask.

I went to bed and stayed there for nine full days, getting up to stretch or eat, while Raf left messages or delivered takeout to my apartment door. When I let him in, he gave me the Sunday edition of the *Times* and told me filthy jokes. Inside my blankets, I kept my copy of *The Idiot*, which was soft as fabric. Dostoyevsky, fellow sufferer of epilepsy and ecstasy, wrote that the joy and rapture he sometimes experienced during his seizures was worth ten years—or more—of life. But he had had the repeated experience of that ecstasy, many times over, and I had only the hotel that day and my unwilling witness. I slept, curled around the book, with the pages of the paper layered around the bed and the paper boxes of rice, until Raf cleared everything away.

"You should know something," he said.

"Which is?"

He offered me chips of ice in a cup, as if I had had my tonsils out, and yet it was a purely perfect gesture. I held one in my mouth and savoured it.

"I'm not afraid of your seizures."

I said nothing for a moment. "Why should you be?"

He sat on the bed. "Listen to me." He put his face close to mine and looked into my eyes. "Your seizures don't scare me."

"Fine," I said.

"Molly."

"Yes." Barely audible.

"Your seizures don't scare me."

"No."

He inched even closer and stroked my face. "Not one bit."

"Not at all."

"No."

"You're an asshole," I said.

He smiled.

I put my hands to my face and began to sob, perhaps harder than I had ever sobbed. My body shook, seizure-esque. My breath in huge, staggering gulps. He held me as if my life depended on it.

I sensed, even as early as that, habitation. The water that Raf gave me tasted better than any other water. He hovered at the edges of this unfolding territory. He understood the presence that was gathering there, the one people call fate or destiny. He couldn't look away. Grief at my losses was dulled by the sense that as I lay on the bed, my body was surrendered to building and creating. An experience new to me, but recognizable. My body as cup, as transmogrifier. I was thirty-eight and Raf eleven years older. I knew what I wanted to do.

When he turned from me to open the blinds, I said, "I think I could be pregnant."

He turned back in slow astonishment, as if what surprised him was that he wasn't surprised, and then he frowned.

"Are you teasing me?" he said, and I answered, "I have no idea."

"You are testing me."

"I doubt it. But maybe."

The look that came over his face was a delight so profound that it annexed any talk of logistics, lightning of the brain, or permeable condoms. It radiated from him and was so singular that I began, unreservedly, to love him. I found it painful to do so, so malfunctioning was the equipment.

I had nothing to say for everything that I had left out. My omissions were suddenly reasonable in the force of what was being created. A state of grace made me lucid in one respect. I said softly, "I think there are two of them," but he didn't hear me.

A Slingshot

I hardly felt the cut when it happened. My brain was busy, clamped as it was on our bodies, our sex, and I no longer had the physical knowledge of the glass beneath my chest and raging heart, that I was strong and the table weak, that it would somehow, like a horse, fold its legs to the ground. That I would try to stop my fall with my palms slamming into the shards. A single arrowhead came alive and dug in, peeling up a triangle lined with fat and a lazy glug of blood. The healing left a tenacious scar, and so I carry him with me, embedded in the skin, in the shape of a wishbone. Or a slingshot.

This is what happens to the missing, they are dispersed as pieces, as glimpses, and scars. The voice up ahead sounds like his, but isn't. A figure ghosts through the crowds and subways and markets. The city is full of fragments, which might be sewn together to make another likeness. In this way the missing are transformed.

The Documentary

In the documentary, the woman sits on the bed, the one she once shared with her wife, and talks about the disappearance.

"We'd been watching TV. Normal-like. Nothing much out of the ordinary. A little fight earlier in the day, but I didn't think much of it. We watched TV, and she had a peanut butter sandwich. I remember that, because she didn't eat a lot of peanut butter. And the bread was white bread, and that was out of character, too. I said I was going to bed, and I got a glass of water and went up. Something seemed different while I was in the bathroom, brushing my teeth. The water was running, but you know how . . . you know how you feel something in the house? I shut off the tap and listened. It sounded like the front door and maybe she stepped outside for a minute. So I just finished brushing my teeth and got into bed. I read a few pages, fell asleep with the light on for maybe half an hour, or an hour, tops.

"When I opened my eyes, she wasn't in bed with me. I thought maybe she'd fallen asleep watching TV, but I got up to check. I had this feeling in my stomach. I guess you could call it foreboding, and I remember walking really quietly down the stairs. I thought at first she was on the couch, because of the way the blanket was balled up, but when I got down there, I could see she wasn't. So I looked outside and her car was gone, and then I really knew something was wrong. She wasn't one to just go out late at night. She liked pubs and stuff, but she was mostly a homebody and she was early to bed, you know? An early riser."

The woman smiles, then turns solemn again. "So she was gone, and her car was gone. But she had left her phone, which I thought at first was good—it meant she'd come back. Even if she just forgot it in her rush to go out, she'd come back for it. I decided to go back to bed, but that was a bad idea. I couldn't sleep at all. I called a friend of ours, but it was late and she didn't answer. I sent a couple of texts to my mother. But we don't know that many people. I don't have many relations, not around here. I didn't know when to call the police—how long did you have to wait? So I hung on and just kept wandering around the house. I wondered if, you know, somebody came to the door and took her. Forced her into the car. That was why the phone was left behind.

"Then finally morning came, and she still wasn't back. She didn't report for work, and that was helpful in terms of telling the police, because then it wasn't just me saying something was out of character . . . This was all a year ago. It will be a year next week. That's a big deal, the first anniversary. Life changes after that, I'm told, though I don't know how. I guess I'll know when I get there. I still put up posters—I tape them around telephone poles—and I give out fliers, and I try to keep her in people's minds, because they forget. They move on, but I'm still here. Though they tell me to move on. I get a lot of that. People say, 'Well, she left you is all. Don't you get it? We don't know her whereabouts, but that's not quite the same as missing, is it?' But, you know, I feel like she's out there in the world, and maybe she needs help. Maybe she, you know, needs help coming home."

6

A Word from Our Sponsor

The city doesn't always know what to do with itself, so it invents, it makes new. You can't step in the same city twice. It tends to covet and sometimes wants to have the tallest buildings and bridges, the land parceled and sold. The hills scraped off and placed in the lakes, with a grid on top. Or a park two and a half miles long, organized in scene after unfolding scene for the wanderers. Sometimes it wants an underworld, with gruesome murders or drug deals or forced weddings, or all three at once. It used to want crammed tenements and disease and one hundred languages and famine and wood construction that easily burned. It wanted stone mansions with society ladies and their vicious husbands careening inside, and cockroaches that polished their own pointed faces. It wanted the Dutch, the French, the English, the Chinese, the Italian, the Irish, the slaves, though none of them wanted each other. It wanted them tangled and sooty and preferably cholera stricken, at the same time that it wanted money and more people and lacquered fingernails. It couldn't leave out theatre and art and circuses and amusing food and the world's tallest woman and the smallest man. It wanted fires, lots of those, and riots and ticker-tape parades. Most of all it wanted jazz, its favourite thing. And the rising and setting sun to fill the aligned streets with precisely laid apricot light twice a year each. Then a little peace. But it considers peace to be a kind of sleep, which it is suspicious of, so now it wants riots again, and hurricanes, and hip-hop.

Luna

I saw a man scale up the side of a building on the Lower East Side, swing onto a balcony, way near the top, and disappear. In Koreatown, I saw a baby drop from the fourth floor and be caught by somebody on the second. I've seen people jump off the bridges, all of them, and one or two of them live. I once saw a woman on Fifth, nicely dressed, throw up into a paper coffee cup and place it carefully in a garbage can. Keep on walking. They all do that—not the coffee-cup part. They keep on walking, you know, regardless. Not that they're without compassion. They give the compassion, they keep on walking. Sometimes you see them give compassion in the proverbial cup, and sometimes they do the equivalent of throw up in it.

There was that man who saw me, who gave me the theatre ticket. Shiny head and suit jacket, which told me something was up, but he said he was an arts lover who couldn't use his ticket—had other plans or whatever—and gave it to me. *Go on in*, he said. *Enjoy*. I love the ballet, but he told me this was a different sort of dancing, modern. So I went in with my ticket and met some resistance. I told the girl, who was young and had great big eyes almost like something was wrong, that I was as legitimate as she was. I said, *I'm real, baby*. I told her about the inside and the outside and borders, and then I think she just got flummoxed and she let me in.

The seat was in the mezzanine, so that's where I sat. When the lights went up there was a small building like a cage, a skeleton of a building,

in fluorescent orange. When the shiny man said contemporary I figured he meant the people wouldn't be doing much, but these dancers were acrobatic. The show was inspired by the Triangle Shirtwaist
fire and the women who jumped—it said so right in the playbill. The
people fell, but then they got back up and jumped again. I'm still not
sure how they did it, it was a trick of the eyes. And something happened in me that was transcendental, like a blown fuse, and I loved it.
But how do you describe a dance in words? After that, though, there
was some mayhem and a woman passed out. The problem was the images, you know, the projections of people falling from the towers. Or so
it looked. You have to remember when this was, time being essential if
also nothing at all. Only two years after the towers. But I was told that
my presence was part of the problem. I decided to leave in case the cops
were called, which they were, so I slipped out, and the lobby was full
of people. I had to push my way through. When I got outside, rain was
pouring and the shiny man was there, just a little way down the block.
I thought maybe he saw me, but when I looked at him, he just looked
back. He didn't seem bothered at all by the rain or the siren. The ambulance was coming, and those things are always showing up in a way
that is also uncanny. Then he turned and walked on.

A day later I fished a Sunday edition out of a garbage—the whole
thing, pristine, too, with an apple pastry, like somebody had bought
breakfast for the can—and I read the arts section first. There was an
article about the show, about her, the one who made it. I didn't see
her at the theatre, but there was a picture of her. Real elegant woman.
Spiked-up hair like her finger was in an electrical socket. I figured
she was the sort who could take some criticism. The article talked
about a riot, but it was really a kerfuffle. I've seen actual riots and
that was just a few people getting upset. The wording suggested that

she had gone too far. So, gratuitous. And too close to 9/11 and those falling bodies. They used the word *callous*. They also said some parts were too beautiful. I don't know how something can be too beautiful, but there it is. You know, people and the sensitive membrane—it's like one of those meat-eating plants that shuts its mouth when the little hairs get bothered. They quoted her as saying she was *merely delivering the news*. I think she may have been what you call ironic.

The show was years ago, but I had that uncanny feeling that I might run into her sometime. You'd be surprised who you see here. The place generates meaningless connections like that's its purpose, and you can pluck one of those bits and try to fashion something from it. A potentiality. The dream you were in gets disturbed with another dream and suddenly you notice where you are and wonder how did somebody else get over there? And that's why the people were so mad, you know, because they preferred the dream they were in and not knowing they were in it.

I wondered if the shiny man knew something about me, because of his expression. Most days now I don't think about my family so much. Time has changed me, and changed my face, which it does for us all. The watch has all the secrets, every right action. And every wrong one. The fragility of another body, which resides forever in the hands that move around that watch's quiet quiet quiet face. You say it three times—very effective that way. The empirical evidence being that it keeps staying quiet. So you tend to it, in your way. And this is my tending, and what I do is move around the place and in so doing, come across. You come across the uncanny and the potentialities and the people at the end of the line, all the time.

Molly

Carl Jung wrote about a woman who ordered a blue frock and received a black one by mistake on the day a relative died. The function of the synchronous is inside the colour black at that moment and
means something to the receiver of it.

The twins themselves are a living sample of the synchronous, even if
their gender, habits, appearance are in opposition. In many ways they
could not be more different, but their fetal movement was a joint one.
Congruous, fluid, and set to heartbeats, sloshings, the visceral music,
each in their own balloon. They felt each other's presence, and their
separation was only a vague idea, belonging mostly to the future.

The day I found out I was pregnant with them, a lunar eclipse
happened. I hadn't been expecting to see it, and then when it appeared, it was sinister, a terrible hinge in the sky. The water creatures
inside me were sanguine, however, or that's how they seemed to me.
They breathed fluid, they floated and spun, pressing at the edges with
their feet and elbows. They had no use yet for the exterior world.

Sabine

Sabine stood looking into her brother's closet, and though she didn't trust her sense of smell, she thought she detected the warm scent of him, and also something acrid—perhaps the signature of whatever had swept through and claimed him; an impulse, a weariness, or worse: something malevolent. As she held the cuff of one of his bartending shirts, feeling the threads and the small plastic buttons, she listened to the sounds from an apartment above. They were comforting, because they said she wasn't really alone, and they said other people had problems, or drunken brawls. Or maybe the sound was something jovial like a party.

She couldn't configure this last one, as happiness and laughing were well out of reach. They had been removed from her when her brother disappeared, and she wanted them back. In their stead was the insatiable entity that wanted to know, to understand what had happened. *Where the fuck are you?* she whispered as if she might be overheard. Which indicated other people, watchers and listeners. Or a single watcher and listener. His clothes were right there in the closet before her. His hairs were in the corners of the bathroom, skin cells in the tub, fingerprints on the cabinet knobs. A T-shirt lay underneath the bed and it still had the energy that was his when she had picked it up. Now, too, she carried with her a fragment of Molly, whose startled, pained expression she couldn't get out of her head.

·   ·   ·

She shut the closet door, walked to the little kitchen and rummaged, feeling suddenly hungry. On her last visit, she had thrown out all the rotting food from the refrigerator and had even wiped down, haphazardly, the interior. When Ellena had called she told her to open a box of baking soda and put it inside the fridge, which she had dutifully done, and which caused her to think of states of decay and the decomposition not only of bodies but of all things. The little plant by the window would eventually, though she had given it some water, bend and dry and crumble. The oranges she bought from the market at the corner would develop white and greenish-blue mould. Her own hands seemed more wrinkled here, in the yellowy light of his kitchen, as if she, too, were shrinking and disappearing.

"It pisses me off," she said. She opened and slammed the fridge door, and opened it again, took out the six-pack of eggs, some butter, and the ketchup bottle. She removed a skillet from the cupboard by the sink, whose stacked-up, crusting dishes she had been ignoring, and put it on the stove to heat up. "Because either you're out there, which is a GD problem, or you're dead, which is also one. I would like to know which it is, because I can't go on like this." She attempted to knock a cockroach from the edge of a plate in the sink but it vanished before she even got close. "And you made me see the one person I didn't want to see. Or who I did want to see, which is my own GD business, frankly—" She covered her face with her hands. "Want to cry."

She uncovered her face and yelled "I would fucking love it!" so loudly that she then stood frozen with her arms out like she was holding an enormous ball. The silence was palpable, startling. She slowly brought her arms to her sides. Then clapped her palms together. "Well, that was fun. Let's make some incredibly fucking excellent eggs, shall we, with a side of cigarette ash. And don't tell me not to smoke in your apartment." She stabbed the air with her finger.

Once the eggs were made, and eaten standing up and straight from the pan, she poured a bit of bourbon into a plastic measuring cup and drank it, then poured more, sat down at the small table and lit a cigarette. She imagined Seth sitting across from her.

"What do you really know about another person? When it comes down to it. Maybe I should read some of your self-help books. Maybe they would help me get a grip. Maybe there's one in there about disappearing . . . How to vacate the premises so nobody, not the cops, your friends, your enemies, or even your sister have one freaking, solid inkling of what happened to you. That's some pretty good shit, I have to tell you. I need to read that."

She heard a quiet knock at the door and stared in that direction for a few moments, not quite believing it, but then it happened again. "Like I've never heard a knock before." She dumped her cigarette in a glass of water and went to the door. She stared at it without looking through the spyhole. What did it matter who was on the other side, and then it occurred to her that maybe it was Seth, and he had decided to knock, which made her laugh. "I'm such a dumb fuck." She opened the door to see one of his neighbours, Ira.

"You're too hard on yourself," he said.

"I'm really not," she said. "Nice to see you. He still ain't here. Well, not in the actual, corporeal sense. If you want to hang out with his belongings, you're welcome to come in."

"I think I will, if you don't mind. Thought I'd get an update."

"*Entrez*. I'll pour you some bourbon."

Ira was already holding a coffee mug. "I'll save you a glass. Just dump it in here."

"Good choice. Hey, you want something to eat? Eggs? I make decent eggs. Not much else. I have some bread, though, too, and some cheese—"

"Naw. I'm good." He looked around as Sabine watched him,

noting that the hand that held the coffee had yellowing rippled fingernails. He wore a blue cardigan with a subtle sheen to it, and something stuffed into the pockets. She thought that he seemed smaller
than the last time she saw him, but he didn't have the cane. When he
turned to her again, his eyes glittered. "He's a good guy, you know,
your brother. I miss him. I do. Sometimes, neighbours . . . not so much
exchange, if you know what I mean. Sometimes too much, on the
other hand, but usually the thinness of the walls and floor makes
for enough communion. People don't say much, or they grunt." He
smiled.

"These are thin walls."

Ira sipped at his drink. "Now that's an improvement. Well, this
place was built in the thirties, you have to remember, sparse materials.
Lean times."

"Oh, is that why—"

"No, I'm kidding you. I have no idea why they made this place
as thin as an old man's—never mind." He waved his hand. "Tell me
something. No, thanks, I don't need to sit—it's the up and down that
can be convoluted. Tell me something—did he mention the window?"

Sabine frowned. "No, but the landlord did." With Ira following
her, she walked through the living room to the windows, which faced
north, and examined them, leaning in. "They did a good job. You can
hardly tell." She straightened and turned to Ira. "Do you know what
happened?"

Ira shrugged. "I heard a commotion, maybe a day or two before
he went missing. Can't tell you much else about it, though. It sounded
like a man yelling, but you know, I've never heard your brother yell
before, so . . . Like I told you, he looked a little, how would you say,
disheveled last time I saw him. I don't know what it means, if anything, and I figured, well, I figured he'd be back by now."

"Huh." Sabine looked back at the window and then at Ira again.

Her face softened. "I don't know what it means, either." She put her hands in her pockets. "He was a drunk, you know."

"I know."

"*Is* a drunk."

He turned briefly and she thought he might be leaving, but then he stopped and said, "Ever thought about going to a psychic?"

She burst out laughing. "Why the fuck would I do that?"

He smiled. "Just an idea."

"It just popped into your head?"

"That being the nature of ideas."

"I would feel exploited, I guess. Right? I don't believe in that kind of thing."

"I know what you mean. I don't believe in it, either."

"Then why'd you suggest it?" She lightly punched his arm.

Ira shrugged. "Because your brother is missing, and that seems like special circumstances."

Neither of them spoke for a moment. "I do have someone in mind, should you change yours." He dug into his cardigan pocket, removed a business card and handed it to her. "I met her at a card game. Tried to get a date, but she said she wasn't my type."

"She would know, I guess."

"Maybe she doesn't like old men. Real nice, though. Pretty lady. Just a couple blocks from here. Name is Miriam."

"You want me to see her."

"Up to you."

"Did she read your palm or something?"

"She does cards. And nope. Said I didn't want to know. She said it was just as well." He laughed and sipped his coffee, looking at Sabine merrily over the edge of the cup. "Sometimes you have to think outside the box, so they tell me. You and me both. Thanks for the touch up. That was better than the swill your brother drinks. I'll leave you to it. You need me, you know where to find me."

After he left, she put the card on the refrigerator door with the one magnet, a small black dot, that had been floating there and looked at it. Then she pulled the card off and ripped it into small pieces, and then smaller ones, and put them in the garbage.

Molly

The floorboards of the house—somewhere on the edge of a forest—are oak, not just worn, but scarred, and possibly he is not who he says he is, but an animal instead, with claws that drag and cut. All possibilities are alive in the house. A curtain flutters in the kitchen window in the way of all kitchen curtains—nothing that says he is the breeze moving it, and nothing that vibrates with the past touch of his hands as he reached to close the window against a sudden downpour. He came here in winter, likely stomped his feet across the threshold, banging off snow and ice. But the thing of his disappearance is how precisely gone he really is. I can hardly feel him here inside this house, and the only evidence I have of him are the claw marks on the floor. So deep they form channels, like a subway grate or the ridges of sand on a hard beach, and I feel them with my feet, which are bare. I look down at my toes, how strange they feel, and I see a set of claws, and then I know it's true, that I have been here before.

Pleased to Meet You

I had met Sabine only an hour before.

"That's who?" I said. "Your brother?" I was shouting a little, to be heard over the noise.

Sabine smiled at me and said something. The windows of the loft were open, letting in at the edges of the party a steady influx of wind and water, but the room was filled with people who didn't notice. Whoever was standing near the windows was drunk and wet and oblivious. The inner circles churned slowly and clung to their drinks and tried to be heard over the music. The head of the man I had come with bobbed on the far side of the room like a ball on a sea.

A bar stood to one side where Seth was directing someone who had brought in cases of beer and wine. I didn't know it at the time, but he was the good friend of the couple hosting, who later on would be investors in the bar he wanted to open. For the time being, he was helping them out at the party.

"Yeah. Brother. Don't we look alike?" She laughed, almost uncontrollably and wine sloshed from her glass. "Shit." Then she laughed again. She got behind me and pushed me in his direction, her hand on the small of my back. I allowed her to nudge me to the bar. When I turned to look at her I saw how blurred her expression was, how she wobbled. She gestured and the movement was uncontrolled. "That's him. That's my brother! You two need to know each other."

I smiled. "Is that so? Now why would that be?"

Her hair was an enormous, unwieldy creature that she scooped up in her hands as if she were going to pull it up, but then she let it fall back down and into her face. She grinned, bending forward a little. No makeup except for a dark stain on her lips that was a bit crooked. She was beautiful and unkempt and interesting. "A surrogate meeting. A surrogate. Sublimation."

"What?" I said. "What are you saying? I don't think I'm hearing you right."

She shut her eyes and swayed, thinking. "Surrogate. Good word. Fucking right."

"I don't—"

"He can get to know you like I'd like to know you." She opened her eyes and looked at me, and then seemed surprised. "Oh, I said that out loud. I'm sorry. I'm fucked up." She looked serious, but then burst out laughing. "Never you mind, Miss Molly."

Before I could say anything, she grabbed my arm, and I liked this, I liked the force behind it, and turned me toward Seth, who was walking over. "That's him. The big brother. Seth, Miss Molly Volkova. And vice versa." And then she was gone.

Forgive me. I have to tell you about a bear. I know you won't like the sentimentality of this, or perhaps it's me that is the curmudgeon.

When I was young, when my life was still my life as someone with parents, and the packed house still existed, and the city in another country was far beyond me, well ahead, I sat on a hill of grasses in the rain. I didn't have to be home yet, and during the day I roamed where I wanted to. It was late summer and getting cooler, but I didn't mind and I didn't mind the rain coming down, in part because I was watching a black bear. He sat on another hill, close to the trees' edge, and I had been surprised to see him, both because a sighting didn't happen often and also because I had never seen a bear in the rain before. But he didn't seem to mind it and sat heavily, with his arms slumped by his rounded belly, seeming like he had been there for a long time. He was distant enough that I felt safe to watch him, and found myself unable to stop, wondering if he was wounded or ill, or simply enjoying the view. Even with the space between us, he resonated across the grasses and slopes of the two hills and reached me, so that I felt his size was far bigger than his physical parameters. I could be enveloped in his bearness so that he was no longer something other but the same as me, just a much more curious and powerful object, and the possibility was there that he could turn to see me. Time erased time by breathing itself out, like the huffing of a bear. I felt the air in my chest escape and then fill me again, a bearness, a beingness that I wouldn't have the words to describe to anyone and so would keep to myself. I carried it off the hill with me when it was time to go home.

At the party, all of this, which I hadn't thought of for so long, came back to me in a rush as Seth walked toward me, hand extended. A ferocious sound filled my ears, the noise of the party turning in on itself and becoming a whoosh as my temporal lobe processed the scene and clearly went mad. He shook my hand, but too firmly and the large ring I wore was squeezed against my fingers so hard that I winced. All sound stopped, except for him saying hello and then apologizing profusely when he realized he had gripped my hand too tightly. His expression became so tender, his dark eyes full suddenly of recognition and love, that I felt that the bear had turned to look at me. And he was indeed wounded, but completely present. We were both exactly thirty years old, the age of my parents when they died. And I was overtaken with a history, forward and backward, of what we had been and would be in the future. We were feral and misplaced, and I could see how our lives would play out, the back and forth and start and stop. I was overwhelmed with a love whose internal organs were shot through with what seemed to be an everlasting hate, but was really only the flawed structure of this place, these bodies. And the fact that I kept people from the furnace of my heart—the place where they could so easily burn.

All of that—ridiculous, I know—in a single handshake.

"Hello," he said. "Molly." He held my hand with both of his, gently, to ease the pain.

I left the party immediately after that, saying goodbye to no one, not even the man I'd come with. I landed in puddles that were forming around the curbs as I went along Houston, then turned up Eighth, and continued going in the opposite direction of my own apartment, which at the time was in Park Slope. An impossible cab appeared, in spite of the rain, the party hour, the night, and I took it to the Upper West Side where Daniel was still alive and well and twelve years away from dying. By the time I got there, it was after midnight. But they were night owls, and Emmitt buzzed me in because I didn't have my key. I ran up to the apartment, the door to which was already open. I stopped on the rug in the foyer, and dripped there while he and Daniel came to stand a few feet away with curious expressions. My chest heaved as I tried to catch my breath, and I thought how juvenile I was, how puerile, how *fucking idiotic*. They were both holding books in their hands and had glasses perched up on their heads as they looked at me. All of a sudden I started laughing and couldn't stop.

"Do you think we should get her a towel?" Emmitt said, turning to Daniel.

Daniel gestured toward the door. "She's gone mad, you know. Maybe we should put her back out on the street. She's making a mess." Then he gave me a funny expression that turned him into something like an old bird, and the two of them hugged me gingerly, trying not to get wet.

Sabine

She looked out the living room window, saw that it had begun to snow outside, and made the decision to delay packing her bag. She ran her fingertip along the frame where the glass had been replaced, then turned to look at the apartment from that vantage, as if it might tell her something, but it revealed little except that she had left clothes on the sofa and mugs on the coffee table.

This time, she thought, she would clean before leaving, she would right things, and dust and wipe surfaces, she would make the small gestures of erasure she had previously resisted. She would, she thought, be like other people, perform the habits of others and therefore be more commonplace. This was the way to manage time, which had begun to do strange things the moment that she understood her brother was gone.

Time at the beginning had moved so slowly that she thought she might go mad—the first few days seemed to occupy an entire month as she waited for phone calls and messages and walked her body along the edge of an invisible circle—but now the accelerations left her breathless and wanting to be home with Ellena and the dogs and the mountains. She no longer wanted to be in the portal that was Seth's apartment; she had had enough of sitting in the posture of waiting, feeling a key being turned tighter and tighter in her back and which only made her want to smoke and drink twice as much. She folded the sweater she had left on the floor and then opened her suitcase on the edge of the bed.

She didn't pack, however, or clean. She put on her big black coat and her boots and left the apartment. When she reached the sidewalk, she felt the sleet fall to her hair and burn her cheeks. She walked north and then west. Having memorized the address before tearing the card up, she strode along, past the butcher, the vinyl record store, the wine shops. On the corner, she saw the tailor that had been in that spot for five decades, with a window display of two headless torsos in dust-covered checkered vests that had been unchanged for as long as she could remember. People walked past her, tucking their chins into the tops of their coats or else pretended to be unmoved by the stinging crystals, and they were different people, a panoply of size and shape and colour, and yet they were the same people, the ones she was sure had always been striding along the sidewalk or darting away to cross the street or dipping into the markets. A few glanced at her, most did not, and all avoided touching her, and she them, no one closing the gap no matter how close the bodies came. The sun was nearly down and replaced by the light coming from the stores and signs and cars, simply a different kind of light, but the same, and the same dark, un-seeable lid laid over the whole works, impenetrable and vast.

She realized she must have walked past Miriam's doorway, so she backtracked and then saw the discreet sign, whose subtlety amazed her, in the basement window of an old walkup, between a violin- and bowmaker and a taxidermist, and beneath an accountant. She stood for a moment, glancing up and down the street, then went down the steps, which were damp with a skiff of snow on top. When she reached the black door, she stood looking at it, wondering if she really wanted to press the buzzer. The door seemed secretive, reticent, and the sign in the middle of it so small and strangely elegant, almost as if it wished to go unnoticed. *Miriam*, in a plain script. She half expected to need a password. She wondered, too, how Ira and Miriam had truly crossed paths, and she now doubted his story.

"Hullo there. We don't have an appointment, do we?"

Sabine startled and looked up to see a woman standing at the top of the steps and then moving down them, her gloved hand sliding along the railing as she descended. She wore a large purple faux fur coat, tall black boots, and an enormous grey scarf that hid her chin and made her dark eyes seem to peer over a wall. Her long hair, almost the same colour as Sabine's but well-kept, was piled up on her head and adorned with snow. She came to stand beside Sabine in the confined space in front of the door. "Well?" she said, clasping her hands together, and Sabine was intimidated, despite seeing that Miriam carried over one wrist an absurdly small purse in lime green that seemed to suggest a sense of humour.

Miriam smiled, and Sabine thought she looked older than she had just a moment ago. Also, her expensive earrings didn't match. The voice was deep and resonant. "I usually go by referrals and appointments."

Sabine didn't say anything.

"Who do you know that I know?" Miriam smiled patiently, or perhaps impatiently with a veneer of patience.

Sabine couldn't tell; finally she managed to say, "Ira." She suddenly realized she didn't know his last name.

"Ira," she said again.

"Who? That's okay, never mind. I'm Miriam. Just Miriam." She extended her gloved hand and Sabine shook it. "You have a name? And a question? Or a quest?"

Sabine couldn't seem to form the sentence from the emotions that welled up in her. She could smell Miriam's perfume. Someone bellowed from the end of the block. A drunk, probably, but Miriam didn't turn her gaze away. She waited, raising her eyebrows that had been neatly drawn a touch higher, Sabine could see, than her natural ones.

"Yeah. I got a question or two. I'd like a session. Is that what you call it? Like a therapist?"

Miriam gave a low laugh. "Sure." She removed her key from her purse, opened the door, and walked in. Sabine followed her into the vestibule and spoke into the space between them, looking at Miriam's back.

"First question I have," she said softly. "Did she ever love me?"

Bait and Switch

Molly crossed her long legs, and she realized they were aching. The teacup that had been offered to her, and which contained chamomile and honey, steamed on a side table under the concentrated light of a tasseled lamp. The room was otherwise dim, but she could see that the walls were crisply white, as were the bookshelves and door and window frames. In contrast, the sofas and chairs were upholstered in shades of deep red with velvet cushions. Paperback novels from the fifties, along with some self-help books, were stacked up on the midcentury coffee and side tables, and close to her teacup there was a large purple ashtray, as gleaming and amorphous as an organ, perfectly unused. Miriam sat down in an armchair across from her and folded one leg under, resting her index finger along her chin. She had been explaining something of her method to Molly while she prepared the tea.

"The typical methods were no good. Tarot cards are not my jam, as the kids say—they have limitations, so I decided to make my own cards. Why not, right? Then I got them professionally made. I use a system of shapes, letters, numbers, and colours." She picked up a pair of glasses from a side table and put them on. "I'm a synesthete. Know what that is?"

Molly smiled. "Sure. Like some people hear colours or see music. Different senses get mixed together. Someone hears a sound and they taste cinnamon or whatever. I have a little bit of it myself—the letter *A* is always red for me. Threes are yellow. Like that. Since I was a kid."

"Well now, you win a prize! So, what people want to know turns up as colours, shapes, numbers. People's auras say something. Their words. I shuffle the cards, very similar to using tarot, and I lay them out in a pattern. At first, just a few, then I add more as we go deeper. If a triangle turns up, it could mean a romantic triangle, or it could mean that a situation is a big deal spiritually. Because of the number three being king. Right? A square might be a person's home life, a half circle might be their birth, a black solid circle might be someone's death or near-death experience. Hexagons are usually secrets—I love those. Numbers come into it, too. And I rely a lot on what the person says. Just because I'm a psychic—or at least that's what people call me—doesn't mean I know everything. I rely on you, actually, to do the knowing."

"You don't consider yourself a psychic?"

"I'm Miriam." She smiled. "Like medium, isn't it? Empathic. An empathic transgendered synesthete. Just a little tagline for this life. A loaner. It don't mean a thing if it ain't got that swing. And all that." She put her fingertips together. "You ready?"

Molly held her teacup close. "I suppose I'm a little nervous. What do I do first?"

Miriam retrieved the cards from a wooden box on a side table and sat down again. "I start with a few questions and then shuffle. But I already got a sense of something from you, the moment you called me. It was a good connection. I saw some things. First one, I think, is an early loss. Big one. Your mother or father, or both?"

Molly nodded and held up two fingers.

"My condolences." Miriam shuffled the cards and shut her eyes for a moment. "You have a condition. Can't tell if it's connected or not. Something inherited?"

"Seizures. Not inherited, as far as I know."

Miriam laid out three cards in a triangle. "Neither of those things is why, exactly, you're here. There's a space. Someone else missing.

Absent, gone . . ." She flicked her long fingers in the air. "There's a complication—it's not a new thing?"

"No, not really." Molly felt distinctly ill and took a sip of her tea. Her head was aching and before she'd stepped into Miriam's apartment, a light had flashed in her peripheral vision. She uncrossed her legs and shifted in her chair. "I just want to know where he is. If he's alive or not." She felt sweat appear along her forehead. "I'm a little embarrassed, I think. I haven't seen him for a long time. A decade, actually." She gave a small laugh. "I don't know why I'm so concerned now."

Miriam had laid out other cards while Molly was talking. She examined them, moved one, then looked at the arrangement. A slight smile appeared on her lips. "My, my."

Molly cleared her throat. Miriam handed her the remaining cards and said, "Shuffle those well. Then hand them back to me." Molly took the cards and felt the weight of them. The backs were deep blue with a single gold dot in the centre. She shuffled and pictured Seth, Raf, Stella, and Augustin, and a wave of love passed through her. She thought of Sabine standing in her living room, with her black coat and bedraggled hair and her news. The fragility of certain connections, and their tenacity. She handed the cards back.

Miriam removed another three cards from the top and placed them within her arrangement. Molly had been trying to prevent herself from looking too long at the array, but she looked now. "Lot of hexagons," she said suddenly.

Miriam looked up at her and nodded. "Doesn't mean I can see all your insides, don't worry. Only what you show me. And I don't dig. No reason to. I like to protect people's business, if you know what I mean. You mentioned being embarrassed . . ."

Molly rubbed her forehead. "He's, you know, long past. And it was always wobbly, anyway."

Miriam watched the cards. "I see a lot of people, all with the same condition. Sexual love with a little putrefaction in it. Just my observation. No offense. And something I like to call *stickiness*. Maybe somebody else would call it karma. You get your karma tangled up with somebody else's, and it's not so easy to undo."

"No. It's not really rational, is it?"

Miriam made a sound. "Oh, honey, I don't think you're all that enamoured of the rational, but either way we are long past that." She arranged the cards in three rows of seven, a neat rectangle. She held the deck out to Molly and instructed her to take one and give it to her. She looked at the card without showing it to Molly and put it face-down on the table.

"Uh-oh. Why'd you do that?"

Miriam chuckled. "No need to worry. But I have some bad news, which is I can't answer your main question. Others are crowding it out. So the thing is, I don't know where he is or his, um, present condition." She looked over the top of her glasses. "So the question then is: Why are you really here?"

"What do you mean?"

Miriam waited.

Molly sighed. Her head felt so strange, and familiar. "I've been feeling a seizure coming on for days. . . . The piece I'm working on. Is it my last? I'm looking for solid ground and not finding it. My husband has been seeing someone else. . . . Not really new to either one of us, which maybe you already know. And my children don't know who their father is. . . . I lied." She stopped a moment. "I've never said that out loud. I've worked so hard, and then, I wonder . . . This man, he had a sister. I've missed her, too. Another thing I've never said. . . . My parents. My dear parents. . . . Grandfather, who I dearly loved." Tears formed in her eyes and she put her hands to her face. "My god, my children. My brain is gathering its forces. That's what I call it. *I feel in some strange place.* And yet I don't want to let go." She caught her breath and spoke through her fingers.

"Miriam," she whispered, "I'm so grateful. The beauty of this place. I don't want to go."

Miriam sat back in her chair, crossed her legs again and leaned her head into her hand. She regarded Molly with a gaze that seemed tender but regal. "But you must, my dear. In the end, it's what we all do. Everything's a loaner. And unless you can step out of what the clock says, you know"—she folded her hands in her lap—"I think your time is up."

Questionnaire

What if falling is beautiful, what if falling is useful?

What if the place I land in is as good as the place I was in before?

What if there is no real falling and no real death, what if we go on forever?

And by "we" I mean the underlying energy, not the thinker. What if the thinker dissolves but something else remains?

And the missing. What do we do with them?

Posters in the grocery stores. Once upon a time, the sides of milk cartons. Now websites. Collated reams of them, attempts to organize the dispersal. The ones who got away, the ones taken.

Last seen here.

Last seen wearing.

Call this number if you have information.

Information, that's the thing. You wonder who has it. Desire for.

The Window

Which was broken for a reason he couldn't imagine. Seth woke on the rug of his living room floor beside clusters of cereal and other unidentifiable crumbs, some hairs. A blanket was wrapped partially around him, with a cushion from the sofa under his head. From this vantage, cracks revealed themselves. Along the ceiling one appeared in the shape of a question mark. In the corner of the living room a vertical line ran from floor to ceiling as if the two perpendicular walls had come apart, and which he had seen so many times it was no longer noticeable.

But the window was another matter, with cold air rushing in from a hole toward the bottom left corner with slats that ran jaggedly from its outline. The hole was the size of what? His mind searched for the image of the projectile and could only come up with a baseball. But he was not an owner of baseballs. Had the object come from inside his apartment, for instance, or outside? Unlikely outside as he was five floors up and the adjacent building had been torn down and was just beginning to be rebuilt. Or could it? Nothing lay on his floor, except for him, the blanket, and, neatly lined up in a row beneath the coffee table, two empty wine bottles, a plastic tumbler and his phone. He shoved off the blanket and checked his body, which was naked, and sore in the diffuse manner of his worst hangovers, his stomach uneasy.

It was possible that another body lay on his bed, so he got up unsteadily and stood looking around the room for coats, boots, scarves. Glasses or plates or an ashtray. He heard something, but maybe he imagined it. He listened like an animal, suddenly alert and still. Then decided, reflexively, to check his phone where there were three texts but nothing illuminating. A sound from the bedroom made him put his phone down and walk to the bedroom doorway. Relief flooded him as he saw the rumpled, empty bed, the noise having come from another apartment.

He felt consternation, however, when he registered himself in the mirror that hung on the closet door. He stared at the man, at the haggard posture, how old he looked in spite of being muscular. Tattoos adorned the arms and chest: mandalas, a bear, complicated serpents, and Sanskrit for a peace he had never possessed. Then, on the right hand, across the knuckles and fingers, bloodied cuts that he also hadn't felt. He looked down, not quite believing what he saw or that he felt little pain until he touched his hand. He opened the closet, found the first aid kit and the gauze bandages inside it. After wrapping the wounds on his hand, he got dressed and went to stand again in the living room, looking at the hole in the window and relishing the cold that came through it.

A Knock

When he opened the door, he found the old man standing there. "How are you, Ira?"

Ira had a cane, though it was mostly for effect, to underscore his often amused expression or sometimes he gestured with it. "Good, good. But the question I have is . . . how are *you*?"

Seth rubbed his hair. "I'm all right."

Ira nodded, looking quickly past Seth's shoulder into the apartment. "I'm asking because of the ruckus." His head stood out from his neck a little more than usual. His sweater was large and loose on his frame, his pants were thin at the knees, but he wore a button-down shirt in soft blue with a sharp, spotless collar.

"Ruckus. Uh, I'm sorry about that." He rubbed his face again, his chin. "Funny question, but was someone here?"

Ira raised his eyebrows. "You're asking me? I'm an old man. I don't know anything. I just heard something last night and you know, it got me wondering. Thought I might see if you're okay." His eyes darted over Seth's shoulder again.

"Want to come in? I can make coffee."

"Oh, no, no." Ira stood up taller and put both hands on his cane. "I'm on my way to a breakfast date. Deirdre. She has a pension, if you can believe it, and more than that, her own teeth! This is no small thing, Mr. Stein. Once you've seen someone remove their teeth and put them in a glass, it's a miracle—a death miracle. It's all over after that."

Seth smiled. "Right." He didn't have the energy for the usual back and forth, and Ira studied him for a moment.

"I exaggerate. But you know that." He turned to leave. "You're okay, so that's good. You look like shit, but you're okay. Now I know. I can go eat my breakfast."

Seth gave a small wave as the old man walked down the hallway.

Ira didn't turn, but gestured behind him. "And take care of that hand."

Seth closed the door. He surveyed the apartment, which told him nothing. Nothing was out of place, off kilter, or new, apart from the smashed window, which he decided he would have to cover with some cardboard and duct tape. He checked his phone again. Nothing.

He picked up one of the empty wine bottles and examined it as if it were foreign to him. He was normally a bourbon drinker when he was trying to sustain a particular dullness, though his work as a bartender often put him in a position of drinking across a spectrum. Wine tended to make him hurt more, and he couldn't think what made him choose this one, an Argentinian Syrah, except that it was the sort of thing he would drink with someone else. He rarely lost consciousness, which made him wonder if he had taken something else. There was an inch of wine still in the bottle, so he drank it.

Sabine

The snow had stopped. Sabine walked back to Seth's apartment building and climbed the grey staircase with its humble black railing that she always liked because it was oily looking. She unlocked his door and went inside feeling not much of anything, until she saw the living room arrangement again, without her brother in it, and sighed. After taking off her coat and boots, she pushed up the heavy sleeves of her sweater and decided to begin the cleaning that she felt would enable her to leave. There was a rhythm and a way to it, Ellena had said to her, that was transcendent and would bring new energy. Perhaps this was why she had resisted. The inertia of the space in which Seth had stood was magnetic and self-perpetuating when she was inside it, so much so that it seemed like an unpleasant bender, one that she should simply wait out. Perhaps, Ellena had said, a good cleaning would break the spell. Sabine had felt rebuked in some way, and also misunderstood, as if some spray and washcloths could eradicate the state she was in, the state Seth was in, and the apartment, and for all she knew, the whole world.

She would begin in the kitchen, with its crusts and grease and flashing roaches. She identified part of her resistance here, not so much because of the insects, but because of the general conditions. The cupboards were old, and two of the doors swung too loosely on their hinges, which threatened to come right out. Additionally, a bit of grout was missing on the tile backsplash that ran along the counter, and some of the grime in the corners and around the feet of the small oven had an ancient quality. She didn't know how to clean what was already disintegrating and would crumble apart the moment she added some water. This possibility, she felt, infused the entire place. Yet the mottled, granular aspects of the apartment were contrasted with the outdoor gear that he had carefully organized in the living room and closets. It was not the cockroaches that would survive a nuclear holocaust but the plastic gear that shone with its hard, indelible brightness and self-conscious efficiency. Perhaps, she thought, she would begin in the bedroom.

She began with stripping the sheets from the bed; Seth had a compact washer-dryer stacked up in his bathroom, so she could clean the linens before leaving. As she worked, she became aware of the idea of Seth, the phantom shape, that slept in the bed, rose to have a drink, got back in bed. During sleep he was in that other existence, the one she felt was unreachable from here, and this seemed to pair well with the place he had come to reside. Molly, too, had been in this exact location countless times, over the course of years. Sabine felt a ripple of jealousy, and, bundling the sheets in her arms, tossed them into a corner. The gesture seemed to help.

His bedroom had two small closets, one with clothes and gear, the other with towels, sheets, and blankets, and a few boxes. She went to the second closet to pull out fresh bedding and stood, once again, peering into her brother's belongings. Objects gained power and didn't seem to know their place. Everything was haunted. The sheets and blankets were stacked up on shelves with surprising neatness. But neatness was one thing, disorder another. Tidiness struck her as the more problematic tone—he had been trying to keep himself together maybe, and had folded into the tight creases of the sheets, which were nearly perfect rectangles of similar dimensions—almost as if he had measured—whatever problem he had been grappling with.

To one side of the closet, she saw the shelf of his journals. When she had first discovered them, she assumed that he had separated them out from his other books because they contained deeply personal material. But she had pored through them, especially the last entries, and found nothing; they were merely logs of his climbs and runs, whatever workouts he had been doing, what he had been eating, how much protein, what the climate had been and its effects. Page after page of numbers and measures, to a degree she found stultifying to look at. No tally of his drinking, she had noted. A few mentions of injury, including tendonitis in one wrist and some joint pain in his left index finger, and another later mention of IT band syndrome; otherwise a mostly steady progression of workouts with only minor interruptions.

She reached for the most recent log and held it in her hands. She turned to the last page and flipped backward from there, landing somewhere in the middle at an entry about three months old. He had run a ten-mile circuit that included Central Park, on October 15 at 2:00 p.m. when the temperature was 50 degrees Fahrenheit, the humidity 93 percent, with an east wind. He wrote the times for each mile, noting that the whole run had been a personal record. He listed the shoes he had run in, the clothing, and that he had overdressed, anticipating a cooler day. Then there, on the last line of the entry, written in the same, unvarying hand:

Despair.

She stared at the entry. Then she flipped through the pages, repeatedly, trying to find something similar. She eventually brought the journal to the living room, where she poured herself a drink, lit a cigarette, and sat down on the sofa so she could carefully go from page to page. It was true that despair emanated, though she couldn't locate whether it was contained within her or the mind-numbing array of details in the log. After a half hour of searching, she closed the journal and sat back on the sofa. As ever, she had turned up nothing. She realized that whatever he had meant by despair, it was nothing new; underneath his broad smiles and relaxed demeanor—the very things that had made him a magnetic and sought-after bartender—was a darker creature, subterranean and blind. Even if he fooled others, and sometimes her, she had to concede that it had been there all along.

She got up and brought the journal into the bedroom, then put it in her suitcase. After making the bed with new sheets, and doing a half-hearted job of tidying the apartment, she saw that it was almost midnight. She folded her clothes more carefully than usual and laid them on top of the journal. She decided to sleep on the sofa, wrapped up in her coat, with the plan to get the first train back to her car in the morning. In three weeks she knew she would return to repeat the process, pay more bills, move around a few of his objects. Perhaps she would try to see Molly again, as she had something to say, possibly about the children. What that was exactly she didn't yet know, but in the meantime she would imagine herself curled around Ellena and the dogs in her own bed and wait to understand.

Molly

We have all the time in the world, as they say. Rushing is only for the other people, the ones who don't know. Stop and look, see how beautiful. The buildings are moving, though you can't see it. If you can't see the river, then feel it. We've neglected the dead, who pile up in a way that we misunderstand and think lacks charm, lacks ease. We say the bodies shouldn't be there. We've taken the whole endeavour too seriously, though we haven't seen it.

A sadist once told me that he was more fully himself with a whip in his hand or some rope, but I told him he was never further away from himself. And talking during sex is a waste of energy. The narrative should fall away. The implement is just a projection or a stand-in. It doesn't represent truth, only the point at which we try to wedge ourselves into another existence. Wear a skin that isn't ours. Later discard it.

You practice a dance for months, maybe in certain instances you stay with it for a year, or years. Your body takes the shape of the practice, and what has been required of the body changes the musculature, changes the body. Form follows function. I have an idea, and my idea shapes bodies, makes them different than they were before. I watch the bodies altering in subtle ways, but I can see it. And I watch the relationships develop, familiarity taking root as the bodies and minds learn the others' weight and touch and smell. They size each other up, surreptitiously, lots of nodding when they meet, fingers colliding in handshakes. Shortly after, they will be in such close proximity that a hair from someone's head will tangle in the weave of another's shirt. Intimacy is just part of the work, part of the currency, and the current.

And the body is shaped by the mind. The irony is that Stella and Augustin do resemble Rafael in some way. They are nine years old, almost ten, but perhaps they are much older. It's hard to say. He sees his lineage in them. His parenting, his presence with them, has worked on their bodies, reshaping them so the tilt of their eyes, the soft cups of their ears, are uncannily like his. He has helped to grow them in the belief that the material in their containers has come from his own cells. Their substance, however, even at the atomic level, is the concrete expression of a secret. Which is itself an echo of mystery.

The Documentary

The psychic sits with a cockatiel on his shoulder occasionally nudging his ear.

"I only have the one. I thought about getting him a paramour, but I don't have one, so why should he? So that's the sitch there. We're single together."

He opens a pistachio and offers the bird the nut, which is gingerly accepted. "The people up on the wall there, they're the ones I'm working on. It's too many. I normally don't work on more than three or four at a time, but I got a lot of requests at once. Plus, I needed the money. The ones that are solved, I put those pictures away in my binder system, so I have a record I can look at, but it doesn't occupy my visual field too much, if you know what I mean. The faces carry a lot of energy and can be hard to live with.

"I try to keep things more or less tidy here, so I can focus on those people. You get to know the faces over the days and weeks that they're up there, waiting. Sometimes I get deep into the details, and I do background research—I want to know if the families are on the up and up, especially if I'm dealing with a husband—and other times I want to know as few facts as possible because in some cases the facts are too . . . well, they can be noisy and get in the way—Stop that, bad bird. He really likes to chew on that, but he should stop—An example would be if the case has gotten a lot of media and the person has been gone for a while—that energy can get too big for me. I need to quiet myself and zero in on my intuition.

"I helped locate a Russian national recently—I was excited about that—I thought she was almost exotic, you know? She was visiting here and stopped communicating with her parents back home, or that was the story, and I didn't want to do too much digging. I didn't even look at social media—you'd be amazed how many people are 'missing' but still posting on their feeds. Especially the young ones. It's usually the first thing I'll look into, but the feeling around this woman was strong. She had eyebrows for days, and sort of reminded me of my mother, and I got strong images right out of the gate. They're like postcards from far-off places. What I mean is, the images can have a feeling like they've been through the laundry. That's when I know I'm dealing with someone who's lonely or isolated. If I get a ton of postcards in a short period, that usually means the person is in a busy place, usually urban, and I have to figure out which images are relevant and which are just garbage.

"With the Russian lady there were two that stood out for me. One showed a hand with a ring tattoo, which I figured was her hand. The other was a pair of bright red gloves. The red seemed urgent to me and a little wild, and the gloves could hide or protect, right? And I felt like she was still alive. That excited me—a much better result than otherwise, yeah? Assuming we want people to be found alive. The gloves also suggested shopping. She was from a loaded family, that much I did get from talking to her folks.

"And I had a hunch. I work sometimes with law enforcement, and so I contacted them to see if anyone was coming through the system that resembled her and bingo. Turns out she'd been having a manic spree at Bergdorf's that she couldn't pay for. She was arrested and gave a false name—insisting she was called Cassandra—and you know, sometimes you just want to be somebody else. With some new Prada. Anyway, they were just finding out who she was, but I do feel I hastened things along. I followed up with the parents in Saint Petersburg after that—I like to see the end of the story, you know?

But this Cassandra woman—I won't tell you her real name—she was back home, she'd been extradited tout de suite, if you know what I mean, but she was just pissed. I mean royally. She did not want to be found or found out. So I was happy for the parents, you know, they were pretty old, and they were worried. But I did wonder if I helped ruin things for her. Maybe there were reasons other than mania that made her want to be gone for a while. She just wanted a break, I don't know."

The cockatiel wandered back up the length of the psychic's arm, stopped on his shoulder and nuzzled his ear.

"Not long after that I did get another mental postcard: it was a red-gloved hand again. The fingers were folded down, except the middle one, which was standing straight up."

The psychic laughed. "But you know, she was home. And that's good. Home has some meaning, doesn't it?"

Luna

Death does happen on the subway, actually, sometimes at the end. One person dead as a doorpost, right there on the seat. Not that I like to witness, I just accept this particular employment. You know what some people do? Steal the copper cable out of the train tracks and sell it. I've watched them. You can't tell it has copper inside because there's a rubber casing, but they know how to pull it up and lug it to a scrapyard that'll pretend not to see the NYCTA written on it. And I wait for the electrocution, but I've only seen it once, because the copper just gets the stray currents. And the two people who were with him, working this copper mine, ran off and left him, which made me think these are people who hold the polarities, you know. Courage and weakness. But I can't rightly judge a potentiality as I might have been one of them.

So that's somebody's work. What they have to do. And that building there, which is just ten storeys high, has a lot to say. Belongs to the university now, but at one time, up on the eighth and ninth floors, there was a garment factory. The people made shirtwaists, which was a kind of blouse—think of the Gibson girl and you have the idea. Anyway, mostly women in there, hundreds of them, immigrants, and young. Teenagers a lot of them. Sketchy mitigations in case of fire, and locked doors because the foreman would seal the women in while they worked at their machines. It used to be called the Asch Building, and that wording is like a Freudian maneuver, a slip of a fiery homonym. Completed in 1901 with an incomplete fire escape, and some wood construction thrown in with the iron frame and the bricks and the terra-cotta decorations, because it was considered a small enough building. No sprinklers, and empty fire buckets. Maybe you know where I'm going with this. The fire the Volkova woman was on about, the dance she made. This is the spot.

The windows have been replaced, but I tend to think the frames and sills hold filaments of the women's skirts, you know. As they waited to jump. Little microscopic threads from March 25, 1911, when the fire was going from place to place. It started in a pile of rags, they say, somebody's cigarette or a match or happenstance. Happenstance being an altogether flammable substance. Tissue-paper patterns hanging from lines caught fire and started sashaying all over the place. Potentialities. Dropping themselves wherever, catching on more fabrics, until the eighth floor was engulfed and then the ninth. Panic, you see? Imagine them scattering for the doors and finding them locked, and then trying for the elevator and the fire escape. Imagine fire hoses coming apart in hands, and a fire escape that isn't one, until overwhelmed with people it plunges down to the street. That's some ride.

Fire trucks came but their ladders wouldn't reach and the water from their hoses wasn't enough. Many of the women jumped, either into the elevator shaft or out the windows, some with their skirts on fire. Flaming birds aiming for nets held out by men down below. But you know what? The nets broke because they weren't designed for people falling from that height. Bodies and more bodies, hitting the cement. A terrible sound, they say. One hundred and forty-six people dead, almost all of them women, but probably there were more. Hard to keep an account of a population not much cared for in the first place, and then turned to ash in the second.

So that's the trick of linear time, you know. You can't tell by looking at the building, even though it has a small plaque. If you just walk along the street in your thoughts, you can't see them. The ones waiting to jump, or lying sprawled out for an eternal nap on the sidewalk, all of it over in the space of half an hour. The end of the workday, and they were close to quitting time. Quitting time being the operative. Leave your life standing invisibly on the windowsill. *Alight* means *descend from the air and settle*. How about settle so hard into the concrete that I bet their molecules are still there, embedded? Atomic-level stuff. The delineation of such. *Indicating the exact position of a border or a boundary*. Here and then there. *Plop*. You are here, and then you're not. Or you're still there and nobody knows.

But I know. That's my employment, my personal project, to tend to the vestiges. The buildings have the secrets. The people just walk on by, not knowing.

Maybe they look for me, maybe they don't. You make a mistake and it's undoable. Her name was Giddy. Not her real name, of course, but what she was called by my two older children. She was small, and not a talker, barely a word, and always smiling. I hadn't counted on her presence. You can tell a child is different when they have a particular grace that stops folks in their tracks. People were always commenting on her look, how her face seemed to hold an old expression and a young one in the same spot. Her grandmother said she might end up being a preacher, if she should become a talker, and that was the sort of power she had, in her small body, her eyes. She was a collisional animal, something you would find in a forest, or a meadow, and carry home. She was maybe not intended for this world. She was light as a feather and slipped through. I was reading, entangled in an idea, I think, and I couldn't drop the page or what it was saying. I didn't know where she was. I had set my watch for a certain amount of time and didn't want the children prominent in my thought process at that particular moment.

So I said, *Wait. Wait.* I should have said it three times, as that's where the energy is. After my husband had sold the patent, and then another one, we moved into a house that was three storeys high. We called it the Big House, and it did have a quality of a prison, or at least that's what I thought. But I kept it to myself and marked out my reading time not to be bothered. The space of the house and its solidity were at odds and she was on the third floor, perched in the window. Behind glass, like a specimen, and wanting to explore that outside air, the potentiality called descent. That invisible border again, you see? The window was easy to open and it didn't have a screen. Was a fast fall, I'm told, a blink. And that's how one crosses over in the end, I've seen it.

You don't know a thing until you know it. Visage yourself in the mirror and wonder who you might be, underneath there. Subdural. And out there. Out in the world, authentic. If you take comfort in words, wear them in your clothes, I figure. But be careful of the turning ones. *Hew*—that's one right there. It talks of cleaving or cutting or chopping, but it also means *adhere*. You have to watch for those things, the potentialities. Even as he—and by he I mean Heidegger—even as he had some true ideas, it turns out he had nefarious thinking, too. So you wonder who is good and who is bad. He could chop and cleave and adhere all at once. You think he's on to something and then . . .

You have to hew lightly the monstrous. What you yourself might have done.

Molly

Daniel's last known location: a chair beside the living room window of the apartment. His hair was mostly gone and what remained was fine and luminous, showing the majesty of the skull, the curve at the back down toward the neck. Occipital lobe, cerebellum. His skin translucent and dry. He was ninety-five.

Not long before he died, he watched the umbrellas on the street below. "You always think the buildings will protect you," he said. "Doesn't matter how many years, decades even, you still think the illogical thought that somehow they'll stop the rain. But there it is. You get soaked anyway." No bitterness in his voice, but wonder.

I wasn't there for his exit, either. Another convenient placing of the body in some other, more tenable location.

Emmitt called me at 3:00 a.m. two days after I last saw them both. "I was going to wait until morning to call you, but I knew that you'd want to know." The sacred cracking of the voice.

I sat in my bed with Raf beside me; he woke to my hushed voice and placed his hand on my back. The phone glowed in the dark. I had imagined when I practiced Daniel's death, when I imagined him gone in order to puzzle it out, be ready in some sense, that my earlier experiences would make me eloquent, that I would know what to say to Stella and Augustin, only three at the time, to Emmitt, to myself. After all, I held the fragments of my parents' cataclysm like shrapnel underneath my skin, there was a roar embedded in my viscera. There was nothing in my mouth, though, except some quiet words responding to times and a call for an ambulance that had been too late and that he had died, Emmitt said, "magnificently."

Daniel had been sitting up in his chair by the window where he had insisted on staying. Emmitt had slept on the sofa to be near him and opened his eyes, for a reason he didn't understand at first, to see the outline of Daniel's shape in moonlight, recognizable and not.

"It was the silence," Emmitt finally said. "I've never known anything like it."

The Family

"Do you feel that?" Stella said.

Augustin walked a few steps behind her. They had been playing a spy game as they followed Molly and Raf along the sidewalk. It was a clear Sunday morning in the middle of January, and the four were going to get pastries at the twins' favourite coffee shop, Mack's. Stella had been watching her parents walking with linked arms, Molly seeming more relaxed than usual and leaning into Raf's shoulder as they laughed about something. Raf had on a hat and scarf, but only a rumpled linen blazer for a jacket and, because they were merely a few blocks from home, he still wore his slippers, which had made Stella giggle. Molly pointed out something in the distance, and they leaned into each other again. Perhaps they were even joking about the twins, as Molly at one point glanced over her shoulder at them, smiling, before saying something into Raf's ear. More chortling. Which had been fine with Stella, as she felt the happiest and most settled when her parents employed their own secret codes and conspiracies, and their laughter took on the lower, huskier tone that said that they were getting along.

"Do you feel that?" she said again, and Augustin nodded.

Except that what he felt was only regret that he hadn't worn his favourite sneakers, Molly having talked him into a pair of boots. Lately, he had found that his powerful connection to Stella had been loosened and she was prone to picking up on things that were mysterious enough to him to be almost nonexistent. Then she had been entirely keen on the idea of the missing man, before suddenly not wanting to discuss it. So he nodded, longing for the old Stella whose thoughts had been so seemingly one with his, and tried to make himself feel the pulse of whatever she was sensing.

"A sound?" he offered.

"No, dummy." She stopped and put her hands briefly on her hips. He noticed that she had her goggles around her neck, hidden partly underneath her scarf. "That follow-y feeling. Don't you feel it?" She placed her fingers on her stomach, as if to say the sensation resided there.

"Oh, that," he said, and continued walking.

She followed behind him darkly, and he hoped she would cheer up by the time they reached Mack's. It had always been their favourite spot in part because of its absurd size. Perhaps it was the same width as their small bedrooms, and not much longer. It appealed deeply to their love of the miniature, and the shiny black paint of the facade made the light within seem particularly golden. There was only room inside for four tiny tables, arranged closely together, and a tiny bar went along one wall, so that if you sat on a stool, you were practically at the tables. The place for getting the coffee and pastries fit somehow just beyond the seats, with a sliver of space in which to stand and wait for an order, during which time the twins always looked at the pictures that covered the walls, right up to the high ceiling. The size, however, meant that they likely wouldn't be able to sit, the trick being entirely in the timing which had to coincide exactly with people rising up from their coveted spots like kings and slouching on their jackets. When this fortunate event did happen, Stella and Augustin would end up sitting partly on Molly's and Raf's laps, even though they were really much too big, but which arrangement and its chance to seem small again delighted Augustin. The whole process never got old.

Before they reached the corner of the block where the shop was, however, they saw a stout, bald man suddenly bolt across the street and into the path of Molly and Raf. He was shrieking and hitting out in all directions. The twins could see Raf step between Molly and the man while shouting back and preventing him from reaching her. Molly turned and headed for the children with her arms out to corral them and move them back down the sidewalk.

Suddenly the screaming stopped and the man ran in the opposite direction, disappeared. Three people had emerged from the café to see what was happening, and others had stopped along the street, before everything slowly settled and returned to normal. The twins put their arms around Molly's waist and peered around her to see that Raf was fine. He was brushing off the sleeves of his jacket and muttering, but seemed otherwise okay.

"What was that?" Stella said, breathing into Molly's side.

"That was just something that happens," Molly said, stroking both of the heads that were pressed against her. "It's okay now. He went away." She straightened and turned, attempting to move them with her, but they were rooted to the sidewalk.

Augustin said, "Aren't we going home?"

"Of course not," Molly said, and laughed. "Why would we do that?" She still had her arms around their shoulders and she nudged them again. "C'mon, you two. Don't let it get to you. We have breakfast cookies to get. And, wow, I'm getting an enormous coffee."

"Exactly," said Raf, who was still seeming to shake something off, but he smiled. "Exactly."

The four of them entered the café and stood in line to place their order, and the room was crowded and warm and buzzing, and it was a relief to be held in that space.

Stella put her arms around Augustin and hugged him.

"See? I told you so," she hissed.

Aftermath

Raf lay on the bed with his shirt open, exposing his soft stomach and furred chest, upon which Molly had placed her head. After returning from the café, Stella and Augustin had decided to watch a movie, while Molly and Raf gravitated back to bed with the paper, but then didn't look at it. They lay down together instead, Molly practically wanting to crawl inside of Raf as she breathed in his smell.

"I'm amazed you didn't let me know this was going on," he said. He kissed the top of her head and pressed his arm more firmly around her. "We can let the police know about the threats. In fact, we have to. And I'll call Stefan tomorrow," he said, referring to their friend who was an attorney. "Who knows what the hell that will do, but it does sound good, doesn't it?" He laughed.

Molly didn't say anything, or mention the symptoms that had been dogging her, how ink stains and flashes in her vision and a fluttering in her stomach came and went. How she feared the electrical cataclysm of a seizure more than any human attack, and at the same time she wished for the portal of ecstasy that had once opened and been hers, if only briefly. She felt a rush of love and gratitude for Raf that caused her to bury her face in his chest. He thought for just a moment that perhaps she was weeping or about to, and it relieved him. When he kissed her, he found her cheeks were dry, but no matter—the effect was there, the discernible softness and receptivity that had been lately absent. He turned, pushed her legs apart with his thigh and kissed her deeply, smoothing the hair from her forehead.

She loved nothing better than talk of work, so he said, "Did you name your new piece yet?"

She smiled. "Indeed. *The Erotics of Departure*."

He stroked her cheek. "How goes the progress?"

She kissed him.

"Set design next week. We've been going back and forth—lots still to do. I'll go into the studio later." She smiled. "And I was thinking . . ."

"Of? You have a mischievous look."

"It's time, don't you think, for us to collaborate. We've talked about it for years. Maybe this is the piece."

"At last!" He laughed. "I thought you might be gearing up to ask me."

"And?"

"Shall I come to the studio with you, then?"

"Indeed!" She kissed him again.

"We are the lucky ones, yes?" he said. "Such problems to work on." She wasn't certain if he was being ironic or not, given the incident of the morning, but he was always one to have a short memory for the negative, a quality she often saw as one of his finest. She nodded.

They kissed again, and this time he felt that her face was damp. He pulled back to see better, almost wishing he had his glasses, and saw tears sliding away from her eyes. She stroked his cheek with her fingertips. "You're always running away from me," he said, chuckling. "But I have you now."

"You have me now," she said, and wrapped her legs around him.

Spine

Stella had been building a mobile with various moving parts held in a careful balance and which her father had helped suspend from her bedroom ceiling. It was large enough to nearly reach the floor, with space for her and Augustin to lie down underneath it. Pieces of metal and wire that she had formed into spirals and other shapes, along with paper cranes in bright colours, hung from threads and rotated via a small motor from one of her robot kits. The entire works spun lazily over her head as she lay on the floor. She felt it needed a light show of some kind. She got up to look for her mother and found her in her bedroom, rooting in the bottom drawer of a dresser.

"Mama," she said, and Molly turned her head and smiled.

"Hey, beautiful peanut. Nice goggles."

Stella had the goggles pushed back on her forehead like a mad scientist, or an explorer. She wore purple tights and an old red dress of Molly's, cut along the bottom and belted twice at the waist.

"How's your project? Did you get the cranes to balance?"

"Yeah, they're good now." Stella was sidetracked from her search for lights. She squinted at Molly. "What are you looking for?"

Molly sat back on her heels with her hands on her thighs, staring into the drawer. "Oh, just . . . I'll find it eventually."

Stella watched her root in the drawer again and become more absorbed until her mother seemed to forget that her daughter was behind her. Molly's body, hunched at her task, shifted in some way, an arriving transmission. Stella frowned, suddenly worried, as she felt that something was about to happen, but moments went by and nothing did. She finally walked up behind Molly and bent a little to rest her body along her mother's back in a manner she had seen the dancers do many times, one body bearing the weight of another. She felt the spine, the ribs, and muscles holding her up, and a presence she couldn't know with her thoughts. The content was possibly beautiful, possibly monstrous. "Are you there, Mama?" she said.

Molly said, "I don't rightly know."

In the Dream

Sabine and I are driving to the house by the sea. The house is suddenly there, weathered and grey with peeling yellow trim, and sits across an area of beach grasses and scrub roses. She and Seth were from a family with not just one home, the one in Lenox Hill, but two others besides. I wonder how they keep up the properties but then the question vanishes. Beyond the house lies a wide bar of sand and the ocean, deep blue and choppy. I open the car door and stand on the gravel. Sabine is already approaching the house along a stone pathway, to the front door, which stands open. She dissolves into the dark of the foyer, vanishes. I can see straight through to windows on the other side of the house where a piece of the white-capped sea shows against the dark interior.

Inside the house, sunbeams full of dust shoot through shadows and grey shapes, and I find her again, in the living room. She pulls large sheets from the furniture, balling them and tossing them in a corner. The old furniture's fuchsia-and-peach upholstery is suddenly there and still bright. Then she is in the kitchen, slamming white cupboard doors and scraping back metal-legged chairs that are incongruous and maybe Eames, and I can feel the house waking. It is discovering itself occupied, and I feel a chill.

When I go to stand near the corner where Sabine tossed the sheets, I can see it on the wall: a large black-and-white photograph of the mother and father on the beach, circa late seventies. The mother has her arm draped over her husband's shoulder. A thin scarf snaps out from her neck in the breeze, and makes me think of Isadora

Duncan, who was killed by her own scarf. Both the mother and the father are grinning so authentically, so without reservation, that I can see they are in love. Also completely blind to their end. Their unguarded expressions are marked with their ignorance. I have the thought, *If you want to know what haunts me, Doctor, it is that blindness.* They were people who went with their whims, to their peril. I picture them sailing, skiing, flying in small planes from one day to another, before slamming one into the side of a mountain. I imagine the father conducting business on various hotel telephones while taking a cocktail from the offered drink tray or tipping his cigarette ash into a planter. The mother painting her toenails on the edge of a settee, a hibiscus tucked behind her ear. She would have smelled like suntan oil and rum, maybe. She would have laughed heartily and placed her manicured foot on her husband's shoulder as he crawled up her body with his hands sliding up under her shorts.

Sabine stands beside me, watching me. She's holding two babies in her arms, but they become a bottle of wine and two glasses. I turn back to her parents and observe them, how their merriment stays here, which isn't a solace at all, but another indicator of the lack of deferments.

"Are you okay?" she says, then squints. "Are you crying?"

Her face is appalled, like a moon. "Molly," she says. "What's up? Why are you crying?"

I stare at the photo. I say something but it's gone.

There is a skip in time, the sideways motion of a boat, or a plane beginning to bank. She is concentrating on filling a wine glass. I'm saying more words, but the sounds are another language, part whale. I want, badly, to have some of the wine, which she doesn't know I can't have. The desire is fiery, almost unbearable.

She shakes her head and replies in her smoke-filled voice. "That's just crazy. Where'd you get that? They're fine! The divorce is pretty fucking acrimonious, but . . . why would you think they were *dead*?" She laughs darkly. "Where are my cigarettes? That was a fucking grim thought, Miss Molly. Did he tell you that? Did he say they were dead?"

Dead People

"But you don't believe in ghosts," Stella said. She stood with Molly offstage watching five dancers who appeared to her to be barely there, as if floating in the way of ghosts, seeming to call up something from another world, a life form maybe, if not exactly the sort she considered herself to be.

Molly was concentrating on the light, trying to decide what she thought of it. Members of a small band were on the other side of the stage, playing a composition created for this piece, full of drums, the opposite of ethereal, and this was the dress rehearsal for the beginning of twelve performances. "No, not really," she said. "You can't trust them." She laughed.

"Then why did you make a dance about dead people?" Stella was wearing her loose clothes, the ones she loved to move in. She wanted more than anything to be in one of her mother's productions. The dancers did astonishing things, and even though Molly was always talking about the naked essence and stripping down and revealing the true person, it seemed to Stella that they were never themselves, they were always transforming and shifting and slipping away. They were clearly changelings.

Molly

I had had a desire to hear his voice. Desire being an acute condition, and pitiless. While Raf was out, I called Seth's phone and listened to his outgoing message.

You've reached Seth Stein. . . . I will return your call.

Imagined emphasis on *will*. The words were jarring.

The message itself was a lie, openly stating his absence while claiming that he had been reached. I heard a slight crackle toward the end of it, proof of a wrong dimension.

After listening to it three times, I tried to hear the mutability of a living person, but each time the voice and the glitch were the same. I wanted the presence behind the absence, the place where he was really living. The evidence that was supposed to be held in the voice as it made its promises, *I will return your call*. Perfectly sincere.

I knew she was gone from his apartment, that she was heading back to Maine. I knew, also, that in my own apartment I still had the key to his. I had looked in the closets, tossing clothes and boxes onto the floor before putting everything back and beginning again. I tried to remember myself keeping it, even when I hated him most, and where I might have put it with the thought that I'd never forget its location. Nothing came. The one advantage to keeping so few things throughout my life, however, is the ability to find an object that I did still possess; I searched through the bottom drawer of a bedroom dresser and found it. I felt its small hard teeth, its chilliness. Stella came up behind me while I looked and put her arms around me. She had been building an enormous mobile that was going to be a surprise for Augustin, and so I left the key where it was and we went to look at her creation. We laid on the floor together, peering up into the system she had made.

"Stella," I said, astonished by its incredible beauty, the way she had connected the colourful threads and lines and lights, so that lying underneath, I could see a constellation that was both vigorous and ethereal. "It's so remarkable. And it reminds me of something."

"What?" she said, smiling.

"There was a man named Cajal who made wondrous drawings of cells and connections in the brain. Sounds boring, but he found the aliveness," I said. "And this is even better—three dimensions." I hugged her close and kissed her head. "Of course, your brother doesn't deserve it . . ." Which made her giggle.

Eventually, Augustin banged on the door and demanded to know what we were doing. He bellowed to Stella, "Stop being so lazy!" as they had a card to make for their teacher. He was laughing when she opened the door.

Hours later I returned to the dresser, already wearing my coat, and got the key, putting it in the pocket. I didn't bother to change my sandals for boots. A roar in my brain made me invincible. I took the train to Ninety-Sixth Street, went to his apartment building, and let myself in. I heard people yelling on the floor above. Once I stepped inside, I had a feeling of being welcomed in, though it was only temporary. Misplaced. He was alive and not. In another time and place I might have felt his energy coming over the hill, through the trees. He might show up at the door.

• • •

The apartment was tidier than I remembered it. His furniture was mostly the same—the sofa unchanged, but there were two armchairs I hadn't seen before. One had a compacted pillow that showed the invisible body pressing down on it. A mask I had given him was still on the wall. I touched its mouth. The coffee table was empty except for some file folders, filled with what I imagined were Sabine's desperate thoughts. I left them where they were and stood looking at his bookshelves. They had grown to accommodate what seemed like every running, climbing, kayaking, adventure diary and memoir in existence. How to survive the elements; how to be self-sufficient; how to walk out of a forest, jungle, glacier, sea, or desert alive. How to turn your windburned face to the camera and explain the void you have just seen. A few volumes of poetry. Also: how to be happy; how to be not depressed; how to be less anxious; how to stop thinking. How to be.

I stepped into the bedroom. More books. A different bed. I turned away from it. Another mask on the wall; a face in midsentence. I opened the closet quickly, then shut it. Opened it again and saw the amount of gear he'd managed to fit into a small space: helmets, first aid kits, water filtration systems, and a cardboard box marked *GPS*. Two life vests.

These items were stacked from the floor and above them hung his clothes. The shapes held the contour of him, but an altered one. I stroked his shirts in the way of widows and orphans. They were skins he had shed as he shapeshifted to become a new creature. The wool of the sweaters still smelled of him.

Over by the bed, a pair of his boots sat on the floor, still partially laced—I wasn't sure how he had gotten them off his feet—still with dirt on them. I tried not to look at the bed, but noticed anyway the phantoms at the edge of the mattress, too engrossed to see me. I walked out of the bedroom, leaving the door as it was.

In his kitchenette, I opened the cupboards. A faint layer of grease had formed around the silver knobs. Cans were stacked beside boxes in the way of a small city, neatly aligned, with cockroaches for citizens, most of which scattered while the others stayed in place and waved their antennae. I closed the doors on them, and stood by the counter for a moment, remembering him making me coffee. I didn't know how sublime I would find the memory, how the gentlest thing would be the one to stick. I saw, lined up against the tiles, the seven mostly empty bottles of bourbon, rum, and vodka, alongside three containers of chocolate vegan protein powder and a box of energy bars.

His telephone was the same, a landline that was large and black with a rotary dial and a notepad beside it. Exactly how I remembered it and emblematic of the kind of old objects he sometimes loved. He liked new devices and gadgets, but also explorers and machines and old ways of sending and receiving messages. *Imagine*, he had said to me once, *imagine those first sounds, coming from a box or something held in the hand. What it must have been to hear another voice*. On the note-pad were blue scribbles, which I recognized as Sabine's. I thought of the childhood game of telephone and the garbledness of messages. I wanted to hear from him, anything at all, even words in pencil on a notepad. A few scratches, an attempt, anything.

After a while, I picked up the phone receiver and held it to my ear. The dial tone was an open mouth. You wonder who thinks up a sound like that, how it comes to be. It was forlorn, disconsolate. I stayed there and listened.

——————

You come to a point of decision and look around, wondering, really, how arrival happened, what were the steps? You turn to see the path behind you, but the tracks are gone. If this were another kind of place, you might feel compelled to continue in the same direction, up a mountain for instance, to get a signal, any sound within the static. You could hold high your instruments, whatever they are, so they crackled with energy and noise. Maybe the beeps would be satisfying, the sounds as incessant as a hungry cat at your feet. You might hear the muffled distortion of far-off, peopled locations. The tangibility of where you used to be, and then you would know exactly how to get back.

Luna

The people in the van, for instance, who give her the sandwich, which she refuses because she has one already salvaged, wonder about her, notice how she is unlike other people. Is it possible to be human and more than? Her sandwich, she knows, is a perfectly good salami on rye, still with its fresh brown wrapper—a keeper, both the lunch and the paper. She accepts the bottle of water. They don't know exactly how old she is, what her real name might be. They try to find out where she's been sleeping lately, but she waves them away. She heads down the street, which appears damp from melting snow and ice. The afternoon is slightly warmer than usual. When her watch says 1:11 she eats her sandwich and when it says 2:22, she can cross Seventh Avenue, but not before.

She thinks as she walks along that people resent a secret. They dislike in others what is a function of autonomy. If she exists, it is almost entirely in public, and yet there is a privacy that resides in what she knows that others don't. You die, she has told them, and what happens to your thoughts but dissolution? They don't know what to make of this.

Thoughts, she says, are entirely between material substance and emptiness. They are part substance, part not, and so act as a bridge between the two worlds, she adds. Blank stares. That's okay. They didn't appreciate her theory on secrets, either, so she wrote it down weeks ago and carries it in a pocket:

Secrets have density and volume.

The region of the secret can be spacious, inside which the person (the secreter) may experience relative freedom.

A region (a secret) by its nature creates an inside and an outside. (Outsiders can be dangerous.)

A person with secrets may recognize the secretions of others.

The content (density) of secret usually opposes society that surrounds it.

Tension along border of region can be experienced as resistance to discovery.

Discovery is bad, even where secret is inconsequential.

Most secrets are inconsequential.

What matters to people is not content of secret, but hidden knowledge. Equals betrayal!

Overlooked: secrets are usually like secrets of everyone else.

Discovery is a concussion of mass and energy.

Followed by stillness. Silence.

Seth

He sat in his living room with his laptop open on the coffee table. After finishing the wine, he got his bottle of bourbon and drank straight from its mouth. Then decided that if he was going to make any gesture at all toward clear-headedness, he should at least drink from a glass, so he washed one and settled back on the sofa. His hand had begun to ache, which justified the bourbon, and he flexed his fingers, the mystery of the cuts coming to mind again and causing him to glance at the cardboard and duct tape that now adorned his window. His phone was momentarily lit with a text from his friend Jason, wondering if he wanted to go for a climb later. He answered simply: *No*. He didn't ask Jason for information, if something had gone on the night before because he knew Jason would know nothing about it, and the truth was that he never asked other people to fill in the details of a blackout.

He leaned forward to his laptop and clicked the start button of the video he had queued up. He drained his glass and sat back to watch Molly on the screen. She was being interviewed and he had the sound muted, just so he could watch her without distraction; her face, her gestures. The video was recent, she was now forty-eight, but she seemed ostensibly the same, only with more pronounced wrinkles around the eyes. He had watched the video numerous times in the last week, and various others like it, or ones that were recordings of her choreography, and even footage of her when she was in her twenties and still dancing. But this particular interview captivated him because of the closeups of her expressions and the sound of her voice. And the presence, halfway through, at exactly 15:12, of her two children, a boy and a girl. The interviewer, a man in dark slacks and a close-fitting T-shirt and who seemed to be a dancer himself, asks them about their design participation in one of their mother's projects. They both answer with such composure that the interviewer laughs, and the boy and the girl simply watch him with their dark eyes, hands in their laps and slight smiles. The camera comes up close to the girl first, and then the boy, and then backs up once again, and this maneuver is what Seth played, over and over. Girl, boy, the faces, dark eyes with thick lashes, cue the vaguely amused smiles, back up, again. Girl, boy, Stella, Augustin. The interviewer says their names numerous times: Stella and Augustin.

He left the apartment wearing his jacket open despite the cold. He was without his phone so he could escape prods and reminders and the dark sea of its face when asleep. He decided against the Ninety-Sixth Street station, wanting to walk instead, heading south and stopping for bourbon at a pub and then stopping for more at another, winding his way over the course of four hours down to Christopher, weaving then over to the bookstore on Broadway, where he lingered in the self-help section but purchased nothing, before making his way further south to West Houston and then up Sullivan. By this point, much of the day was gone. He found a bench on the edge of the park and sat down.

The haunted sycamores were especially dark against the sky, which was blue and sun-filled, and he judged it to be an uncomfortable contrast. It made his eyes ache. People with strollers and dogs passed by, and some students in sweatpants and wool hats, and not too far away from him was an older woman, bundled in layers. He had seen her before, various times over the years, as he had wandered the city, and she as well, so that their paths had crossed enough to cause recognition. He rubbed his nose, which was extremely cold, and wondered how she did it. How she survived. She stood at the corner, gesturing as she spoke, sometimes to the ground, or to the tree, a squirrel or a bench, depending on exactly where she was situated. She would talk for a while, and then walk a few paces, stop and begin again. She gestured at things he couldn't make out, nor could he understand her words. No one listened to what she was saying, however. If the people walked while looking at their phones, they deftly stepped around her without looking up, but otherwise she appeared to go unregistered. She spoke, effectively, to the air, to people only she could see. She spoke at the ground, then looked up at the sky and pointed. It lay over them all, so blue and unfeelingly.

She knew the man was there. Sometimes she had seen him run, and in all sorts of weather, which she approved of, since she herself faced every kind of climate, and often he wore very different clothing and seemed to weave or walk loosely in a way that was unlike the tautness of his limbs when he ran. He careened between being two people, another thing with which she had familiarity. She spoke to her unseen listeners about the history of the English elm on the other side of the park, and glanced at her watch, which told her about the time, three forty-five, and its potentiality. She noticed the man shift on the bench, looking weary, as if he might lie down, and she was sure he would, but then he straightened and she was surprised as he stood up. For a moment he looked right at her, unflinchingly, seeing her fully, and she regarded him in return. Then he walked by her, giving her a nod, and she turned slowly to watch him go. He crossed the street and moved along the opposite sidewalk, past an old man in a wheelchair and a child on a bike. He became smaller, then smaller still, and she squinted so that he was merely a black shape, a shadow. A bit of ink. Her vision wasn't so good these days and then she couldn't see him anymore at all.

Another Questionnaire

Do you believe that someone waits for you?

What about the things you made—do you imagine that they also live and that those things wait for you on the other side?

The other side of the ground I'm lying on is an arrangement of compacted ground and bones and pipes and the networks of tree roots. Cables and tunnels and sewers and stones and insects. The remnants of that tenacious river. My body knocks at the door, and begs to be let in.

———————

"No! Don't do this! Don't you fucking give up!"

"Please—"

"Is she—"

"Please stay."

———————

The man who searches for his wife years after the tsunami says he feels closer to her when he is in the ocean.

The couple whose young son disappeared into the forest go to the same forest, even though five, eight, twelve years have passed. Who do they expect to find? The boy they're waiting for is no longer the same at all. Will they know him when he emerges, rearranged, from the trees, from the edge of what had been previously dark? Will he look at his parents' faces and then turn to look back at the woods as if that is now his true home?

Perhaps the woman will rise from the silver sea and tell her husband, *Go away. I was never satisfied in the tellurian world. I wanted the fin, the wet lung. Leave me alone.* The new form of her will turn in the other direction, breach on the surface, then vanish.

The Documentary

"Oh, people want closure," says the man who searched for his brother. "That's what they say they want. People have to have an answer, but the one that they want isn't always the one that they need. This closure principle gets to be a problem. You have people who wait years for it, decades. They say they can't move forward, but if you look at them, look at their lives, time has moved them forward without their permission. They look older, because they are older. The person they're looking for is preserved at this particular age, right? Frozen in time. A relic, or object in a museum. Time keeps going and the evidence is all around. Until you see the images of the preserved person—the photo or video or whatever.

"So imagine it's two centuries ago and your sibling or your child or your wife vanishes. All you have is what's in your mind. Right up here, that's it. Now a person disappears and you not only have hundreds of photos, but you can watch them moving around, blowing out birthday candles or walking out of the ocean. Maybe they're talking and laughing, and so you have their voice, even. Everything there, right inside the screen. The family says maybe the person is still alive, they have to believe that. And they won't believe anything else until they have the body and this enigma called closure.

"I think closure is a mystical idea, you know? Esoteric, secret knowledge. And the people left behind, they become seekers for it. They have a question they want answered, and the body has the knowledge.

"But that's not the only thing going on here—there's also time.

The older the seekers get and the further away in time from those photos and videos, the more they try to find the way back. The body won't resemble, in any way, the images or the memories. The seekers say they want the body, but they also want to deny time. They already have the question, but, you know, people are unsatisfied with questions.

"The real answer is that we have to decide questions are okay. . . . How? Well, that's another question, isn't it? Go back to the body. We think it's the answer for a problem we can't solve. . . . Sorry, what's that—the problem? Well, I don't know, I guess it depends on the person. I can only speak for myself, but I think the problem is the basic one. Why the hell are we here? And if you really want to make your hair stand up, the other question is:

"How did we arrive?"

Molly

Leaving. Many of the trees are bare, but close by me are three deodar cedars with sloping, deep green branches. They stand out in this season, and their dark forms make them appear knowledgeable somehow, as if they are conferring. Conifers conferring.

You will notice that the sidewalk is comprised of hexagons. Pavers in the shape of hexagons. They run through the walkways of the park, too. Secrets, lots of them. With a coating of salted white sand on top to confound whatever ice had had the temerity to form.

Benches line the walkways inside the park and are laced together from behind with heavy black chains that keep them from leaving.

The Musketeers have nothing left to say. The Joker, too, is quiet. The Gatekeeper stands close enough to him that their shoulders touch. The Crones clasp their hands and bow their heads. Revenge checks the time. The Lover weeps.

Luna

It wasn't easy for her to get here. She had to take the long way around because for some reason so many people out today. There are more than twice as many births in this place as there are deaths, and so she supposes this means the expansion of the crowds. But she has arrived, and people are hustling along, except the ones who have stopped to circle the woman on the ground. She approaches slowly, casually, the tableau of onlookers and gradually works herself in. There is a natural parting, a space around her as she gets closer to the woman. No one touches her or pushes her away. She leans down and watches the woman, her grimace, the electricity coursing through. The ferocious beauty of a grand exit.

She notes, though, that the woman is underdressed and had the audacity to wear sandals. She herself wouldn't do it, even on a hot day. Not here. She pats the woman's arm and touches the face. A fabulous secreter, if ever there was one, and perhaps long gone. She locates the outer breast pocket of the grey coat and deftly sticks her fingers in without arousing suspicion. They would think she was trying to steal the woman's wallet or phone when all she wants is the folded-up paper. What belongs to her anyway, and the woman will not be needing it. This was never about falling, but rising.

She straightens up and walks away, clutching the paper, and then putting it in her own pocket. She consults her watch, and feels some satisfaction. It has taken her seven minutes to walk from the location of her brandy to here. A storm is coming. As ever, she has been right on time.

Molly

I see the woman shaking on the ground and hear what the others gathered don't seem to detect, the rumbling of passage to another place. Only a particular, hard-won knowledge can come from this sort of relinquishment. Being so taken over. She appears powerless but this isn't the truth of it, or the only truth. She has an immense energy, gold-spiked and full of terror, the kind reported in the presence of angels, ones that blind.

I watch her and note that her face is exactly like mine, her torso, her limbs. She seizes right to the tips of her hair. Today we've picked the same outfit, same scarf, same regrettable sandals. Same jacket in dark grey to mask grit and stains, the marks of travel to the underground. The people of the sidewalk, the ones who were blasting through only moments ago, have stopped and gathered. A common assumption about city dwellers, and these ones in particular, is that they'll step over a body if they must to get where they're going, but it isn't true. Not here, at least, where the people have worried expressions. An older woman leans over to touch the shaking woman's shoulder. Other people hover and jostle and murmur about emergency vehicles and a nearby police officer. There is a boy, too, and his mother. No one in this crowd yells or panics anymore. They listen to the woman's long, deep gasps. No one hears the horns blaring. Hands touch down here and there light as insects. The bodies stop the cold wind from reaching the shaking woman. They ring around her, ancient and tribal. It is possible that the people know a holy experience when they see one.

Acknowledgments

Many people and things have to align for books to be written. Sometimes the support is directly literary, and sometimes it is simple, loving friendship, or guidance, or an extra set of hands. Sometimes the gift is wildly astute editorial advice or the sharing of knowledge, and other times it is the prompting of a huge belly laugh (you know who you are). Sometimes I am rescued or uplifted or inspired by people in my immediate circle, and other times it is a complete stranger who renders what is needed. To everyone who has helped in ways big and small with the creation of Molly and her world, thank you.

There is a form of metta meditation that goes:

> *May you be safe and protected.*
> *May you be happy.*
> *May you be healthy.*
> *May you live with ease.*

I wish this for you, and all beings.

Thank you, especially,

Laurie Grassi
Nathaniel Jacks

Marjan Kamali

Patti Hall

Patricia Magosse

Ron MacLean

Ilan Mochari

Sarah Gerkensmeyer

Cliff Thompson

Georgia Silvera Seamans

Robin, Gabriel, and Samuel (to you, the most gratitude of all)

About the Author

PHOTOGRAPH BY ROBIN WILSON

MARIA MUTCH's memoir, *Know the Night*, was a finalist for both the Governor General's Literary Awards and the Kobo Emerging Writer Prize, and was listed in *The Globe and Mail*'s Top 100 and *Maclean's* Best Reads. Her debut short story collection, *When We Were Birds*, received stellar reviews. Her writing has appeared in *Guernica, The Malahat Review,* and *Poets & Writers Magazine*. She lives in Rhode Island with her husband and two sons. Visit her online at **www.mariamutch.com** or follow her on Twitter **@maria_mutch**.